8'6 I 2 . c n

PENGUIN B(
YOU ARE F

C000174487

Meenakshi Reddy Madhavan is the creator and writer of the popular blog The Compulsive Confessor. She wrote *You Are Here*, her debut novel, at twenty-five and is also the author of *Confessions of a Listmaniac: The Life and Times of Layla the Ordinary* and *Cold Feet*. She has been a contributor to several short story and essay anthologies. At present, she lives in New Delhi with her ginger tabby, TC.

PRAISE FOR THE BOOK

You Are Here is a good read, easy and mellow, and explores the power dynamics of both love and friendship without losing its innocence—*Time Out* Delhi

You Are Here is a honest, explicit, well-written and highly readable—Khushwant Singh

Saucy, wise and audaciously candid, *You Are Here* introduces a bold and irresistible new voice—*The Sunday Tribune*

Reddy Madhavan's protagonist is endearing, candid, witty and capable of seeing right into the heart of the matter—*The Statesman*

You are here

meenakshi reddy madhavan

PENGUIN BOOKS

PENGUIN BOOKS
Published by the Penguin Group
Penguin Books India Pvt Ltd, 11 Community Centre, Panchsheel Park,
New Delhi 110 017, India
Penguin Group (USA) Inc., 375 Hudson Street, New York, New York 10014, USA
Penguin Group (Canada), 90 Eglinton Avenue East, Suite 700, Toronto,
Ontario, M4P 2Y3, Canada (a division of Pearson Penguin Canada Inc.)
Penguin Books Ltd, 80 Strand, London WC2R 0RL, England
Penguin Ireland, 25 St Stephen's Green, Dublin 2, Ireland (a division of Penguin Books Ltd)
Penguin Group (Australia), 707 Collins Street, Melbourne, Victoria 3008, Australia
(a division of Pearson Australia Group Pty Ltd)
Penguin Group (NZ), 67 Apollo Drive, Rosedale, Auckland 0632,
New Zealand (a division of Pearson New Zealand Ltd)
Penguin Books (South Africa) (Pty) Ltd, Block D, Rosebank Office Park, 181 Jan Smuts
Avenue, Parktown North, Johannesburg 2193, South Africa

Penguin Books Ltd, Registered Offices: 80 Strand, London WC2R 0RL, England

First published by Penguin Books India 2008

Copyright © Meenakshi Reddy Madhavan 2008

10 9 8 7

This is a work of fiction. Names, characters, places and incidents are either the product
of the author's imagination or are used fictiously and any resemblance to any actual
person, living or dead, events or locales is entirely coincidental.

ISBN 9780143064343

Typeset in Calisto MT by SÜRYA, New Delhi
Printed at Sanat Printers, Kundli, Haryana

ALWAYS LEARNING   **PEARSON**

For my parents,
with thanks for love, genes and moral support

They say that men suffer,
As badly, as long.
I worry, I worry,
In case they are wrong.

—*Wendy Cope*

1. in which i introduce myself and the state of my life

NO ONE SHOULD TELL their story unless they're absolutely certain they have something to say.

I'm actually not absolutely certain that my story is life-changing or earth-shattering, but I know that the words are collecting at the tips of my fingers and that if I don't shake them out over the keyboard they could go backwards and form word clots around my heart. Word clots are worse than blood clots—because blood clots more or less kill you as soon as they reach a vital area in your body, but word clots just stay, occasionally giving you heartburn with all the things you could have said but didn't.

The problem, I believe, the essential *issue* with humankind, the reason we are all always at some level or another pissed off, is Reality Sucks.

No, no, really, hear me out. Animals don't have the same problem because, hey, face it, no matter how much your dog chases balls in his sleep, he's not dreaming about how great life would be if something were a little different. He's okay, really, with his schedule—scratch, eat, sleep. How wrong could you go with that? He's not in line for a promotion and there isn't this list of things he wants to get done before he's twenty-five, because he'll be a lucky dog if he lives to see sixteen.

Now people, since we evolved from cavemen and all, have issues. We tend to think that if so-and-so (or such-and-such) were totally different, our lives would be perfect. How many times have so many of us said 'It's not fair!' or 'Why (not) me?' Sometimes, if you're *really* lucky, you get a chance to make that change, live your fantasy as it were. And still, nine times out of ten, it's not enough. It's never bloody enough. We're greedy as a species, and at the same time a little pathetic because, well, we're always searching for something or the other outside of our everyday lives. And, really, who are the people we admire? We admire movie stars. People who *seem* to have their shit together. And who makes the most money? Plastic surgeons, for one, and therapists. And, again, people in the entertainment industry. Anyone who makes reality look a little less real. True story. You can Google it if you like.

The trouble with my life is that it's like a bra strap when you put your bra on wrong. So there's one part of the strap that's all twisted and sticking out under your T-shirt and you fix that, and then the part near the hook becomes tangled. Then, after you've struggled with it for a while, because you can't see so far down your back, and straightened it out, the bit near your boob is all funny. So if I've got my career sorted, my love life magically vanishes without so much as a goodbye. Then I've got my love life all perfect and I'm seeing us making fat, happy babies, and *boom!* my family is fighting, and so on. You get the picture.

My name is Arshi, and I'm twenty-five years old. I turned twenty-five about a year ago—I'll be twenty-six in a month—and I was totally depressed and all because, hello, here I was with a quarter century of a lifetime behind me and I had zero to show for it. My boyfriend, Chetan Saxena, aka Cheeto, aka Lying-Cheating-Bastard had just told me of his infidelity. We had been seeing each other for exactly a year and a week when he zoomed off to Manali with some colleagues, one of whom happened to be a pretty young thing who was also his work buddy, as in she went to the balcony to smoke with him and she was the one he looked at and rolled his eyes with every time his editor said something stupid and so, yeah, I guess they were pretty bonded. Evidently they got even more 'bonded' in Manali. I refuse to use delicate terms like 'made love' when it was so clearly fucking. He on the other hand insisted on saying they 'made love'. I hate that about Cheeto. He's always so forthright about things. I mean, would it have hurt him to *lie* a little?

That wasn't the only reason my life seemed so screwed up. I had this shit job as well, with a random PR company. Only it wasn't so random in the larger scheme of things, because it was one of the top agencies in Delhi, at least when it came to being classy. We always drew the most glamorous P3P for our dos, and handed out the best press kits—all fancy-schmancy and ribboned and with little tokens in them. One time, my boss, Shruti the Horrible, sent me to Janpath to pop in and out of the little silver jewellery shops they have there with the list of journos who were invited to some pub inauguration to, get this, buy *fifty-four* one-of-a-kind silver earrings for the women and *thirty-three* one-of-a-kind silver cufflinks for the men. Yes, ladies and gentlemen, this, this jewellery choosing, was my job description. My grandmother should've been working there. She might not have multiple college degrees but she still rules at picking out baubles. Besides, Dadi has No Patience for women who aren't nice to other women. A diehard feminist from another era, I bet she'd be only too happy to give Shruti an ass-kicking. 'Be nice to my granddaughter!' she'd growl. 'Women have to support each other; god knows men won't!' My grandfather was a sweetheart, though, willingly giving in to all her fussing. I think in the end she managed to bully him to death.

'What do you really want to do, Arshi?' asked Topsy around this period when I spent most of my nights weeping and most of my evenings in my PJs, refusing to step out of our little flat in Jangpura. Topsy is my flatmate and best friend. One of those friends who know everything, even the very minor details of my life, things even my mother isn't aware of. Like how I like to drink Coke with my meals, especially if we've ordered in, or how when I'm confused or can't think immediately of a response to something someone's said I play with my lower lip. She's also the sweetest person I know. I mean, sure, we get on each other's nerves every now and then but it's mostly either because I'm being grumpy or she's being super-organized. She has a very annoying habit of either being right or *sounding* like she's right or refusing to believe she's *not* right, which I tend to indulge but sometimes completely detest. But I love her, because she will Take No Shit when it comes to the people she loves, who include: (a) (and at the top of the list) her boyfriend, Fardeen, all-round good guy whom I adore; (b) Daman, her 'baby' brother and certified hottie whom I have gazed longingly at on many occasions; and (c) me.

Anyway, in answer to her question, and being in the dumps as I was, I sighed out a doleful, 'Oh, I just want to be happy . . .' and Topsy turned to me and said scornfully, 'Happy? You can't just *want* to be happy, you have to *do* the things that make you happy.'

'Then I want to be a TV chef,' I told her, sufficiently chastened. 'I can see no greater fun than neatly chopping up tomatoes and avocados on a perfect chopping board. And arranging the spices in pretty glass jars. And sautéing onions beautifully in a shiny black frying pan.' I scooped up my hair on top of my head while I was talking and made an Angelina Jolie fish-lips face. 'If Arshi can cook, so can you!' I said, looking into the pretend camera to my right and faking a Chinese accent like that Yan guy from the cookery show.

'That would be okay,' she said, the corners of her mouth twitching because she was dying to laugh and trying to look disapproving at the same time, 'but you can't cook, sweetie.'

'Um, hello?' I was most indignant. 'What about my Potato Pickle Surprise?'

'The only surprise was that we survived after we ate it!' she hooted.

Here for posterity is my recipe for Potato Pickle Surprise, guaranteed to win your admiration and leave you hungry an hour after you eat it:

Take four small potatoes. Boil, peel and chop into medium-size pieces. Melt three generous chunks of butter (yellow works, but I once tried it with white butter and it turned out rather well) in a frying pan. Add the potatoes. When they get all brown and crispy-looking (poke with a fork to see if they're cooked, otherwise they tend to remain tough), sprinkle some salt over them, and chaat masala—as much as you like (I use loads). When that's all soaked up by the goodness of the potatoes and the butter, take some pickle—anything will do, though I like the green chilli pickle, which I even put in my instant noodles—and add a liberal garnish. Let it sizzle for exactly fifteen seconds. Pull out the plates, or pour yourself a glass of Coke, before removing and serving hot.

We had buns to go with it because we couldn't make rotis, but you could also chop up some garlic and make toasted garlic bread (although I wouldn't recommend it if you're planning on getting any action that day, because the smell of garlic stays on your fingers and in your mouth for the longest time).

Anyway, my break-up with Cheeto had gravely affected my life. For one thing, I had a lot more free time and very little to do with it. I had exactly two good friends at this point—Topsy, of course, and Michael, who didn't count because I think he had a crush on me. I had sort of lost touch with everybody else and my best friend since school, Deeksha, had already moved abroad. So I was at a loose end, with no boy, no friends to distract me from my gloom and a crap job that had only the money going for it.

Boy, don't I sound like the typical spoiled, rich kid, so unhappy with frivolous little things when clearly there is much more unhappiness out there? I hate it, though, when people use that point to argue with me. 'Why are you complaining when there are so many people starving on the streets?' they'll say, like comparing my misery to the misery of poor people on the streets is going to make me feel better. Happiness is a finite quantity, you get a set quota in your lifetime, no more, no less, and I guess if you're sad and grouchy all the time you're wasting whatever little you have. But the truth is Misery is Not Relative. Many other things are. Like beauty, or age, though that totally depends on who you're hanging out with. But my sadness is my sadness alone, and even if you're stone-blind and were orphaned as a baby and brought up by a wicked uncle I'm not going to feel happier. Worse, I'll probably feel bad for you on top of feeling awful for myself.

But it's true that I've had no calamitous upsets in my life, unless you count my parents splitting up, which I'm now cool with. I hardly know anyone whose parents are still together, and most of the others whose parents haven't split up have weird things going on like the parents sleeping in separate bedrooms, etcetera. I mean, why remain married if you can't bear to stay in the same room? One thing I will say about my parents: it's thanks to their strange, dysfunctional relationship that I'm all sorted out about how I want my love life to turn out. Well, at least there's a plan: To get married by the time I'm thirty, perhaps live with the guy for about a year before that. Then have three wonderful children, whom I'm going to adopt from all over the country. One boy and twin girls, or perhaps three girls. I haven't decided that. And we're going to have a *Reader's Digest*-type relationship—dinner together every night, bathing our kids together, taking decisions together and being one combined very-together unit. We'll never fight about little stuff like who paid the electricity bill last month, or whose turn it is to walk the dog, or who put petrol in the car last. And, ooh, we'll read in bed. So perfect.

My parents started off pretty okay. My father's Goan Catholic; my mother's from all over the place but originally from Kashmir and mostly brought up in Delhi.

Now, my dad lives in Nashua, New Hampshire, in the United States of America, with his second wife, Barbara, a blonde American woman. She's sweet but equally annoying at times with her typical questions: 'Do you guys, like, have elephants?' and 'So what does that li'l dot your mom wears between her eyes mean?' and 'Oh I love Innians, they're so spiritual and stuff.' When Barbara met my dad she promptly decided to adopt all sorts of Hindu customs, despite his mild protest: 'Um . . . I'm Catholic, like you are . . .' She used to be his boss's secretary at the software company he works in, but ever since they hooked up she's been teaching yoga at the local community centre—which in Nashua means she teaches groups of old ladies with blue hair, or dolled-up American princesses looking to go to Boston or New York to expand their horizons. When I think of their house I think instantly of the smell of incense that lingers in their hallway. Every time I've visited their place, Barbara has appeared (in a sari sometimes, if she could contrive it) with a puja thali to do an aarti before I enter. Once I bought Barbara some of that novelty hippy incense you get at Paharganj, with names like 'Cannabis' or 'Opium', and she was awestruck: 'You guys worship this stuff, right? It's like an offering to Lord Shiva?' And she followed it up with a whispered 'Don't tell your dad but I smoked a bit of pot in school.' I was instantly confronted with that familiar feeling I have around her, a mixture of contempt and irritation and profound pity. I didn't tell her about being six and peeking into my parents' parties and inhaling the unfamiliar sweet smoke of hashish. There was no point. She'd never understand.

Ma indulges her by packing multiple bottles of pickle and more incense and statues of gods for her whenever someone we know goes to visit them. They're good friends, my mother and my stepmother, though I suspect my mom only cultivates the friendship in order to have something to laugh about with her friends. And my grandmother, my dad's mom—Dadi—who lives with them through some part of the year, attempts to be liberal to the best of her abilities but if I visit when she's around she strokes my head and tells me how pretty I am and asks after Ma, whom she loves.

Actually, most people love Ma. When my parents split up, way back when I was twelve, Ma decided to take up teaching once again. She already had all the degrees; she used to teach before I was born and then, for a very little while, she worked at the nursery school I went to. After that she just gave tuitions at home. As a child I would return home after playing in the evening to find a bunch of older kids sitting around and trying to learn English or history or whatever as Ma peered sternly at them over her rimless specs. I had to take steady maths tuitions from the time I was ten, but since Ma sucked at it more than I did I didn't have to learn from her. Good thing too, because she tried for a while in the beginning and got so frustrated that she wasn't getting it and I wasn't either that she'd yell at me and I'd start crying and run into my room and slam the door shut. After a bit, she'd follow me in and say, 'It's okay, darling. You know this stuff, really, don't you?' And even if I didn't, I'd nod sulkily so we wouldn't have to go through it all over again. Then we'd go for a walk and get ice cream and I'd promptly flunk my test the next day. If my dad was home during all this yelling and crying, he'd start shouting at Ma about how she sucked as a teacher and she'd yell back saying he didn't even try so he could just go to hell. I think she would have told him to go fuck himself but they were rather careful about not using abusive words around me. I picked them up at school anyway, but at least they didn't have to blame themselves. I'd be too scared to bawl noisily so I'd creep off to my room, knots forming in my stomach, and try to finish a set of problems so they'd stop yelling—and flunk my test the next day all the same.

Anyway, when Ma decided to restart her career, she joined my school. It wasn't easy at all, being my mother's daughter. Oh, not for the usual 'we can't bitch about the teacher when Arshi's around because she's her mother' thing. Nope. Actually, it was the opposite. She was *too* popular and the kids she taught (Class 9 and up) adored her. She was the first choice when they were looking for someone who'd stay back after school with the drama club, or when the astronomy club did their annual night-spend at school. She wasn't the kind of teacher who'd hover around if you wanted to escape somewhere with your best friend and talk for a couple of hours, or even if you wanted a moment alone with your boyfriend. But she'd set time limits: 'Be back in fifteen minutes, guys, I'm going to get some coffee.'

The few close friends I had at school, needless to say, also loved my mom. They'd come over to our place all the time, and when I'd hint politely that I'd like to see their places too, they'd say, 'But *our* parents aren't as cool as *your* mom.'

When I got to the ninth standard I made a specific request not to be put in her class. I can't explain why I did it. It was probably a teenage rebellion thing. I was being described as 'Abha's daughter' far too often and it had got to the point where I really wanted to be alone, have some space, be without her and not have to love her as my teacher. She didn't understand that and my decision really pissed her off, even though she was too much of a let-your-kids-do-their-own-thing person to ever admit it. And it made me wind up with the most boring teacher in the world, in the entire universe, in fact, for three years. So, while other kids crossed their fingers and begged and pleaded to be allowed to switch sections, I stuck steadfastly on in Nina-ma'am's class. She became quite fond of me too by the end of it, Nina-ma'am, and hugged me unnecessarily hard on the last day of school. When I finished school, Ma sort of graduated too. As in she quit her job and moved to this big-ass farmhouse right outside Gurgaon, a little away from Manesar, where she started a small school to teach a bunch of children from the nearby village. She's the saving-the-world type, my mom, and she has fun doing it.

That's my parents for you. One trying to live a normal suburban life, which has become *too* normal and *too* suburban, and the other going to another extreme and becoming hippy-like. Actually, when you think about it you'll be surprised that I'm not more screwed up than I am.

2. in which i revisit my first crush and you learn how bad my job is

THE THING IS, I guess—and this is what Topsy tells me as well— that I don't really know who I am. Well, I know that I'm essentially a good person and that I love the people I love and all of that. But a lot of who I am and where I'm going and all the rest of that is drawn from other people. By 'people' I mean those who are close enough to tell me intimate things like 'Oh, Arsh, you talk faster when you're trying to get out of something' and 'Being in a dirty room makes you depressed'. (This is a recent epiphany, though—not something I knew at the point in my life I'm talking about.)

At a very basic level, I suppose, I'm just insecure and, because of this, it just screws me over when a relationship ends and I'm supposed to stop feeling a certain way about someone. I mean, to return to Cheeto and me, if you don't mind, I loved him. And it was no use anyone telling me that it was over between us and that I should just get over him. I couldn't stop feeling the way I did simply because he'd decided differently. I *knew* it was over, but there were still the memories of his chocolate eyes and his sweet lips and his smile that stretched across his whole face and his voice that made me long for him each time I heard it. That was not going to change, because it was all real, and I couldn't just erase it from my head. Even after it had been long enough for me to want other boys, Cheeto remained in my mind as an indelible happy thought, a 'Kodak moment'. Smile frozen on his lips, arm around my waist, head almost touching mine. Perfect. He was a perfect kinda guy.

Cheeto's real name, like you already know, is Chetan, but everyone calls him Cheeto. That's how he introduced himself to me. We met at a fashion show. He was covering it, I was handling it, and we wound up arm-touching all night. It wasn't planned; I was even sort of seeing someone else at this point but we seemed to connect at some level. Normally there's this divide between journalism and public relations that professionals on both sides are very conscious of, but it didn't seem to matter at all where Cheeto and I figured on the hierarchy scale of the media. We were rolling our eyes at the same things and sniggering at the same things and generally speaking each other's language. Soon I heard him asking for my number and found myself giving it to him, easily and fluently, like I did it all the time (usually I don't even remember it because, come on, I don't dial my own number). Then I checked my phone every five seconds to see if he had called, till he finally messaged five days later while I was in a meeting. It had taken all of my will power not to message him first, I can tell you that.

He said something along the lines of 'Let's meet up for coffee' and we did, and I discovered we had more in common than I'd imagined. The coffee led to a drink, which led to him kissing me sloppily in my car. He was always a messy kisser, seeming to swallow my entire mouth or throat, whichever he focussed on. But oh, he made my panties flutter like no one ever had before, even with his sloppy kissing.

I slept with Cheeto a few times before we were 'official'. I loved his curly hair underneath my fingers; I adored his pointy, elfin ears and worshipped his upturned nose. I was moulded to be with Cheeto, for the uphills of my body to match the downhills of his. Or at least so I thought at the time. Now? Now I don't know whether anyone is made for anyone else. At one point I used to believe in the one perfect soulmate, the one person you would be with all your life, the one who made your heart suddenly pirouette and fall gently, gently on one ankle, for the smashing finale because you finally realized that no one but this person could make your heart do all that. Yeah, well, not so any more. There's no such thing as the perfect person, only idiosyncrasies that cancel out other idiosyncrasies and that too for a brief, magical time that's bound to end.

When our sleeping together got too intense for me to handle I begged Cheeto for a 'label', anything, to keep me grounded. 'Cheeto, please tell me,' I said one day, just after we finished loving, and I was in one sock and desperately scrabbling beneath his bed for my bra, 'what *are* we? A fling? We couldn't be a fling, it's not as meaningless as that. A one-night stand? No, it's been more than one night. I mean, is this going anywhere?' He looked across at me, took my face in his slightly rough, warm hands and said, 'I think it's going to a very good place.' Then he kissed me and I forgot about labels for a while. After we'd straightened the bed and Chhotu, the guy who worked at his house, got us coffee and looked at me, hair rumpled, mouth pink, curiously, he (Cheeto, that is, not Chhotu) asked me whether I'd like to date him, whether I'd be his 'girlfriend'. I blushed and smiled and nodded, and that was that. We were official. This was before I realized that sometimes labels don't really mean anything. I mean, you could be someone's girlfriend and still have to vie for his attention all the time; you could see your boyfriend's name flashing on your cellphone and press the Silent button so you didn't have to talk to him. And just because you're having sex with someone, just because his eyes are looking into yours and later you're spooning, butt to crotch, his hands wandering up your arms, it doesn't mean that you're connected in any way except physically. Because, before you know it, he will sit up and say something that will have you looking at him with your head cocked to one side, wondering what exactly you're doing together.

But screw it, enough about Cheeto. At this point in my life he was no longer in it. To be honest, though, his presence was in his absence. I saw him everywhere, in every place we had ever been to together. Like the McDonald's in Vasant Vihar where we landed up playing hooky from work and ate five plates of French fries, or the bar across the road from his old school where we both got very drunk and snuck into the grounds and tried to get into the bio lab. Delhi was a sea of Cheeto images for me, and as hard as I tried I couldn't erase them. Worse than that, I was drowning in them, being pulled under by a current, and I couldn't figure out where the *other* Arshi was, the Arshi who hadn't met Cheeto, the Arshi who was perfectly capable of living her own life, thankyouverymuch.

Fact is the objects of my affection have always been my idols. They can do no wrong. In school, whenever the boys I used to have crushes on got into trouble, I'd writhe for them. It happened often, because I always picked the boys who were most likely to get into trouble. I'd feel really embarrassed when the teacher ticked them off, so embarrassed that I wouldn't be able to talk to anyone for a while, even as the boys themselves grinned around at the class trying to show how cool and insouciant they were. Among the students, these boys were gods. The popular girls flicked their hair around when they were in the vicinity and allowed themselves to be teased; the other boys—the 'good' ones—shared their homework with them; and, like the gods they were, the boys I loved would bestow benefactor-like affection on everyone and lap up the adulation. I watched it all happen and yet my fascination for them refused to die down.

It had always been that way, even way back with the first boy I ever had a crush on. I think I was about eleven. Kon was eight years older than me, a friend of my then best friend's brother, and he was beautiful. I mean *really* beautiful, with high cheekbones and curly hair that almost reached his shoulders, and he was really fair, thanks to his Kashmiri blood, so in winter his cheeks would turn pink. Possibly the only flaw in his face was his smile—he had fallen from a ledge as a child and one side of his mouth was slightly crooked. But this only served to emphasize the rest of his symmetry and it worked, that crooked smile, on whoever he chose to use it on. He played the guitar, too—really well. Sometimes he'd play and sing in the park for all of us and the girls his age would draw closer and closer to him, almost hypnotized, till they could rub their cheeks against his rough denim jeans.

I loved Kon. When he spoke to me, I swooned. I took to hanging around my friend's place a lot more just to see if I could get a glimpse of him. She knew how I felt about him, and she sympathized, even pulled out old pictures of her brother and Kon together as kids, grinning with gap-toothed smiles at the camera, pulling at each other's school ties. For Kon I was probably just another one of those annoying children who hung around the colony. But he was a gentleman; he never failed to smile sweetly at me and say 'Hi'. If I close my eyes I can recall his voice, low-pitched and husky, which was perhaps that way because he smoked so much, but I believed it was like that because he was a musician and musicians had husky voices.

The summer I turned twelve was the summer Kon started dating Diya. Diya was someone we all admired. She was seventeen or eighteen, I think, when she and Kon started 'going around', which is what we used to call it then (now, of course, it's 'a relationship', to be said in a bored, blasé tone). She wasn't beautiful, though, Diya, at least not in a conventional way. She always wore loose, low-cut tops, so that when she bent over you could see she wasn't wearing a bra. Her hair was very long and slightly wavy, and her sharp pointed chin had a cleft in it.

I don't know why I never felt jealous of her. Perhaps it was because I never regarded Kon as someone I could get for myself. He was a god, to be set up on a pedestal and admired from afar, a gorgeous entity who should only rightly be dating a goddess. Meanwhile, I lived on the scattered largesse of their love, because they were both brilliant around young people. Luckily for me, my best friend's brother and Kon were really good friends and it was because of him that my best friend and I gradually came to enjoy a special status with Kon and Diya. We were not just neighbourhood children any more, but people they actively sought out for company or amusement. They treated us like family, tweaked our noses and told us how hot we were going to grow up to be, took us on long drives to India Gate and never failed to buy the ten-rupee ice cream sticks for us. I remember one of those drives. The air conditioner in the car was on max, while the sun shone outside and The Beatles sang their message: all we needed was love. I was just so damn happy I couldn't get the grin off my face. I might have been smiling too hard, though, because my friend's brother and Diya exchanged the kind of smile you get on your face when you grin about people you could have been eight years ago.

Pretty soon, just conjuring up Kon's face in my mind before I fell asleep wasn't enough for me. I needed a picture, something to kiss and slip under my pillow at night. I sought help from a slightly older friend of mine whose claim to fame was that she'd had fourteen boyfriends in school, all madly in love with her and ready to answer to her every command. As the rest of us went to different schools, this information was never refuted, although I did find out later that she had spent the most part of her school life being disliked. Still, back then she was in the same school as Kon and we sat together one afternoon pulling out seven years' worth of her school yearbooks, one of which she had told me contained a snap of Kon's graduating class. We waded through scores of photos, of boys and girls smiling hopefully, with the sun in their eyes, and of teachers who remarkably held the same dour expression through all those years. Finally she said, 'Found it!'—and there it was. Kaul, Kon, sandwiched between Kakkar, Swapna and John, Mary. I peered at the photograph, with his tiny face barely visible, and then I cut it out of the magazine and took it home. For a long time after that it held pride of place in my secret drawer, where I also kept a single cigarette with a lighter from a heady, scary day when we—my best friend and I—had bought three smokes and choked as we inhaled; a pressed flower which I had long forgotten the origins of; and my journal, a beat-up old notebook with 'TOP SECRET DIARY' written on it. I slipped the picture into an empty cassette cover for a frame. Kon had been out of town for a week, with a play as I recall, and every night I wrote to him on notebook paper. I spritzed the letters with perfume as soon as I wrote them, causing the alphabet to blur. Then I gathered them all up, tied them with a ribbon and let them lie next to the picture. I never sent them to him.

Kon and Diya had a lot of fights towards the end of their relationship. One of the last times I saw them together was at a dance party, which was the thing we did in those days. My best friend's brother threw one such party, to which she got to invite her friends as well. As we walked towards the brightly lit house, my heart beating faster as the blasts of music drew closer and closer, we saw Kon sitting with Diya under the statue in the park in front of the house. It had a circular paved path around it with some benches and in the evenings ayahs wheeled their charges there and sat around and gossiped. They seemed to be having a serious discussion and Diya turned her face away when she saw us. Kon, however, watched us walk towards the house and called out my name. 'Yes?' I answered, my heart pounding, my sweat pores suddenly active. 'Save me a dance, okay?' he said, smiling his lopsided smile. My friends grinned and nudged each other, but I was oblivious to them and to everything around me. I danced duty dances with some boys my age, blindly following the routine of fast song–slow song–slow song–fast song, and when my best friend's brother brought me a glass of Coke I could barely drink it. I had thought Kon had forgotten about his request but, sure enough, as the party was winding up he came up to me and we danced. Never have I wished so hard that Meatloaf would just go on singing. Looking back I wonder whether he had done it just to make himself look good in front of Diya. But then I loved him even more for being nice to a gawky eleven-year-old.

My love for Kon ended when he cheated on Diya, who discovered scratch marks on his back. I didn't even know what scratch marks on someone's back meant, but my best friend told me about it in such hushed, horrified tones that I knew it had to be a bad, bad thing. I tore up his pictures and the letters I'd written to him because his cheating on her meant he'd cheated on all of us. As for Diya, she started dating my best friend's brother soon after.

As a kid it used to drive me crazy that when we got to the

end of a fairy tale it'd always say, 'And they lived happily ever after.' Ma tells me I'd follow her around the house, whining 'And then what happened?' until she would finally have to make something up just to get me off her back. It's still the same way. When I get to the end of a book or a movie, I always like to think about what could happen with the characters afterwards. And I'm a sucker for sequels—even the really bad ones, like the sequel to *Gone with the Wind*, what was it called? oh yeah, *Scarlett*. Even though I know it's by a different author and Margaret Mitchell would probably be rotating in her grave at the very idea of it (and possibly more, seeing as it is the worst book I've ever read), it still allows me to be happy as I reach the end of *Gone with the Wind* that it's okay, Rhett doesn't really leave Scarlett, he goes back to her and they have a daughter.

So, yeah, I spotted Kon coming out of Big Chill at Khan Market the other day and I got really excited at the thought that it would be a good way to end that story and I wouldn't have to keep wondering what had happened to him. I'd always believed that I would recognize his face anywhere. But, dude, he looked so different that it took me a while to place him. Obviously he couldn't wear his hair long forever, but it was cut really, really short. And he was fat and he wore a shirt and a tie, which he tugged loose as he talked into his BlackBerry. A plump woman with streaked hair and in denim capris stood next to him jabbering into her phone. They were obviously together, because as soon as he got off the phone, she dragged him into the grocery store. For a brief moment he looked at me, appreciatively I like to think, because I was wearing a particularly pretty kurta and was humming to myself and checking out shades in a shop window, but obviously he didn't recognize me. Why would he? He didn't know what an important role he had played in my life. We never know, do we? We're so obsessed with keeping all the people in our personal 'dramedy' shows where we want them to be that it never occurs to us that we might be playing a rather important cameo in someone else's life. I didn't say hello to him either. And then Topsy called and I slipped into Barista to meet her, and Kon and his wife vanished into their life—and that was finally the end of that chapter.

Michael once told me that my habit of idolizing people had developed because I've been searching for a father figure my entire life. 'Because your own father's been absent most of your life,' were his exact words, as he peered into my face. He has a way of peering, Michael does.

Not that he's a psychologist or anything, no. His parents run a travel agency and Michael's been helping them out since he was in school and all through college, and as soon as he graduated—BA Pass, Bhagat Singh (Evening)—he joined them. Now the travel agency, which by the way is called LeeZure, some kind of play on 'leisure' and the dumbest name I've ever heard for a travel company, is doing rather well. Lots of foreign tourists and all that, and Michael takes off every couple of weeks for Udaipur or Ellora or Mukteshwar. Lucky bastard.

Many of our acquaintances think Michael and I are dating, or have thought that Michael and I were dating, but truth be told I've known him for two years now and nothing's ever happened. There was one time when a whole group of us went out at night and wound up later in a car, waiting for my friend Farah and her boyfriend to buy smokes, and he kissed me briefly and I kissed him back and it went on for longer than I'd intended it to. But we talked about it the next day and agreed that it had been a stupid thing to do. I shouldn't even have kissed him back, considering we had been eating seekh kebabs and our mouths smelt of onions and beer, a yucky combination.

It's just luck that we're good friends; I don't think we would've ever spoken to each other again otherwise. I suspected he might want to walk down that road again, though, because there were too many awkward silences in the conversation, and I was careful to keep the exchange light and steady.

Michael's not the sort of guy I'd normally be attracted to. He's very, very sweet and he'll be there for me in a pinch, but he's just, um, not my type. I'm not really sure what my type *is*, but I can accurately identify what *isn't*. Which is a start, I guess. I like the guys I date to be slightly, well, if not arrogant, confident at least. You know, sure about themselves and their place in the world. The thing about Michael is that he's very eager to please and for some reason he's more than eager to please *me*. Still, Michael and I are really close and the whole time post-Cheeto when I was super-depressed, he met me once every week for coffee and guidance.

In fact, it was Michael who suggested I go out of town for a bit. 'You need the break, yaar,' he said. 'You're looking bloody dead these days.' It was a good idea, I thought. I was due for a short leave, and since I didn't care any more about Shruti yelling at me at work I figured I might as well go. 'I need someone to travel with though,' I told him, and his eyes were all shiny and he grinned wildly at me and I knew immediately that he had been rehearsing this conversation in his head for some time. 'Well, I'm taking some Americans to Manali this weekend on a four-day trip. Come with us, and you don't even have to spend any money.'

'Oh, Michael, that's damn sweet of you, but won't your parents mind?'

'No, no, why should they mind? They've told me for so long that if I want to take a friend I'm welcome to. Please, it's our company after all.'

Since I couldn't think of any other excuses—'please promise not to hit on me' not being an appropriate thing to say—I said okay and we left that weekend.

Topsy was all for it. 'Manali, dude. Think of how much fun you'll have! Do lots of shopping, okay?'

I think she was secretly quite thrilled because it wasn't a weekend her parents were supposed to visit and Fardeen, who is a pilot and was in town that week (*and* his parents weren't), could come over and spend a couple of days with her. So she gleamed at me while I packed, even made me sandwiches and a cup of coffee.

If Topsy's parents *ever* found out what she was up to in Delhi, they'd come straight down from Meerut and take her back, and immediately get her married off. She hasn't *mentioned* Fardeen to them yet, let alone the fact that he's Muslim, which had seemed like no biggie to me till I met Topsy's parents. They're ultra-conservative people. We have to clean out all the ashtrays and hide the alcohol in the kabadi stuff when they're here. All Topsy's female relatives, and I'm talking about age sixteen up, are either married or prepping to be married. Topsy's parents are the 'liberals' among the lot: they want to find her a groom who will appreciate the fact that she has a degree. She's doing her mass comm degree here, and every week her father mails her details of some Shaadi.com dude, settled abroad (naturally), who is looking for someone with a college education.

'Beta,' her mother told me the last time she was here, massaging her own feet and sighing, 'we will not always be there to look after Timala, no? We must provide for her, so that, god forbid, if anything happens to us, she will be okay.' That's Topsy's real name, by the way. Timala. She hates it. 'Some old aunt of mine told my mother it was an auspicious name,' she told me once, rolling her eyes, and taking deep drags of her cigarette. 'It means a musical instrument. Auspicious, my ass. It hasn't brought me jack-shit.' But if you see Topsy around her parents, you'll never think she's the same girl who lives with me. She pulls out all the salwar-kameezes her mother bought for her to wear to college. Godawful things they are too—all shiny and brilliantly coloured. She wears her gorgeous hair constantly in a ponytail and speaks in very soft polite tones in a mix of Hindi and English. I don't know how she grew up the way she did, but she says it was boarding school and the Internet that changed the way she looked at things.

It was a little harder getting people at work to accept my sudden decision to get away. Shruti raised one of her almost vanished eyebrows when I told her. '*Two* days? I don't know, Arshi. There's a lot of work to be done.'

It's hard to describe how nasty Shruti was to someone who hasn't worked with her. She was fat, but not the kind of fat that makes a person look jovial and sweet. She was the kind of fat that mean old sows are, with beady eyes and immense power, and you know they're constantly plotting how to knock you over and eat you. Shruti, as far as I knew, was unmarried and single. According to the office gossip she'd fallen wildly in love with her boss when she was a lowly intern, but that affair had ended badly when his wife found out. I found it hard to imagine her as an intern. Shruti, all eager and wide-eyed, getting coffee and making photocopies and possibly tripping over herself to ass-kiss her boss. Actually, I could imagine the ass-kissing; she still did it around the CEO when he stopped by occasionally to check whether everything was on the up-and-up. She had some friends at work—I use the word 'friend' loosely here. These were basically people trying to suck up to her and in grave danger of turning into mini-versions of her. Shruti ate her lunch in her room, alone at her desk, cooing to someone on the phone. If she had a boyfriend, I often thought grimly, then men were really much weirder than I had imagined. She used to come to work at eight or nine in the morning—our official reporting time was ten, but we could make it ten-thirty if we liked—and then she'd start calling us on our cellphones: 'Where are you? Are you still sleeping? Get into office. Right now!' like it was some national emergency, when really it was nothing more than the fact that she felt insecure without people to boss around. Also, she never said hello when she called you. She'd start her conversations with a noise, like 'Hmmm, Arshi, are you on your way to work?' I'd make it a point to say 'Hello Shruti' and end the conversation with 'Goodbye' but my gentle hints never seemed to work.

'I've finished the press releases I was supposed to do over the next week,' I said meekly.

'What about the Gulzar event?'

'Yamini said she'd handle that for me. I'll be away for just two days.'

'Hmmm . . .' Her mouth got all scrunched up. I wondered if she knew how ugly she looked when she made that face. Then her eyes narrowed. 'The press conference for Levi's?'

'That's not due for three weeks!' I squeaked. I could see the look of triumph on her face.

'No, I don't know, they want the brief presentation by next Monday. And I'd really like to have a look at it before that.'

'I'll be back next Wednesday. I can do it then.'

'No, you know what? Just finish it up today before you leave. Have it on my desk by tonight.' Then she turned around and answered her cellphone which had been ringing its stupid head off.

I slunk out of her cabin. No point explaining that I still had to pack. She'd probably just dismiss it with a wave of her stubby fingers. I smoked a rapid cigarette on the balcony and then just as rapidly put together the presentation—assigning what would go in the press kits, doing the damn release and, worst of all, calling all those bloody journos and confirming whether or not they would be there. And, naturally, since the event was three weeks away, they refused to tell me one way or the other. 'Ya, Arshi, we'll see,' said the polite ones; the rude ones just said to call them again, a day before the actual event.

The team working on an event scheduled for the next day shot me sympathetic glances from their desks. No one usually stayed beyond six p.m. at work, seven max, unless you were working on a big-deal account, when you stayed till midnight or longer. But after your event was over, you got to take a day off. By ten p.m. I had mailed Shruti the press release and the rudiments of the press kits. Home, free!

It wasn't too bad, fundamentally. I mean, a lot of people had a really good time. But having the right job is like having a good relationship: you either click or you don't. And if you don't, you can go on being with the person and going out with them and all, but there will come a point when you're at a nightclub or a party and you're hammered out of your brains because you're so bored and your 'boyfriend' asks if you're ready to leave and you realize that you're suddenly depressed and lonely because you don't feel anything at all for him; you really want to be one of those slow-dancing couples who are dancing to the closing songs being played. He'll keep asking, 'What's wrong?', or 'You okay?', or, worse, he'll be silent as well and you'll be thinking, 'Well, hallelujah, at least we feel the same way about something' and then he'll try to make out with you before he drops you off. By this point you're so tired, so drunk and so depressed that you go through the motions and wake up the next morning with a furry coating on your tongue and a feeling of utter doom in the pit of your stomach.

That is what a bad job is like.

3. in which there's a pool party and i meet a hot boy

IT WAS HOT, VERY hot. Actually 'hot' is probably not the right word to describe that day. It was muggy, the way only Delhi can be muggy, weighed down by the kind of oppressive sultriness that makes your clothes stick to your skin and no matter how many times you bathe a fine film of sweat gathers in your armpits and your cleavage and at your neck, and everyone and everything becomes unbearable.

Our flat was not air conditioned; Topsy's parents had bought her an ancient cooler which gave off small electric shocks and spat water at us when we slept in front of it on the living room floor, so I had bathed and stretched out under the fan for a bit to cool off and feel the water evaporating gently from my body. I still hadn't decided what to wear to the pool party Fardeen was taking us to later that night. It was about seven p.m., the sky just turning into twilight pink and shades of purple, and we had agreed to go for the party around nine. It was early for a party, but Fardeen had a morning flight the next day, so we'd have to leave the party latest by one in the morning.

I was in no mood to meet new people, particularly after the

Manali debacle, which I had still to get over. What had started out as a pleasant enough journey with Michael and his three joint-rolling American clients had quickly swung from drunken brawls between the brother–sister duo Cute Louis and Sour Rachel and my attempts at staving off the not-so-subtle advances from their companion Horny David to my general irritation at the ignorance they displayed about India. As though it's all about beggars and arranged marriages and dowry deaths. It was almost like reliving my snappy interactions with Barbara, though those turned out to be quite entertaining at times. And that wasn't all. On our second night at Manali, Michael, looking sad and sloppy around the edges from too much drink, said the one thing I had been dreading since I had agreed to go on the trip: 'I like you, Arshi . . . *More* than a friend. And I don't know how you feel about it, but I'd like to take this relationship to the next level.' I tried to be gentle about telling him I didn't want to date anyone for a while now and I wasn't surprised when he leaned forward and kissed me, and even though I didn't feel anything, anything at all for him, I kissed him back. I was lonely, I guess, and I just wanted contact, any kind of contact, with someone who liked me. When his breathing got deeper and more ragged I stopped and pulled away. 'No, Michael,' I said, and he nodded and left. We spent the remainder of the trip being very polite to each other. It was as if that night never happened. Anyhow, it had all been too much and I was glad to get back to Delhi, where Topsy was treated to all the details over a smoke and a special vodka cocktail she'd rustled up for me. Michael didn't call me for almost a week after that and when I called him he sounded awkward and embarrassed, so I let it be.

I got off the floor to consider my clothing options again. I tried on my pink halter top in front of the mirror, standing in profile and raising my arms so my stomach looked semi-flat.

The top was beautiful, except that I didn't have a basic cotton strapless bra to go with it. I have to be in the right mood to wear the right underwear and since I wasn't in 'party' mode I didn't want to bother wearing a particularly pretty bra, all cleavage and lace.

Men believe in the myth that women wear all sorts of lace-and-wire underwear all the time, that their panties are always either thongs or g-strings or pretty little briefs with bikini straps. That is so not true. If any of the men I've dated saw me on a regular work day, when I knew there was no chance of any action, they'd be quite surprised. Normally I save the really sexy underwear—of which I have perhaps two or three pairs—for a night out or a date or some special occasion. Otherwise it's old, holey Jockeys, with the waist rolled down so you can't see them over the waistband of my jeans, and regular cotton bras with no underwire or lace. Underwire bras chafe at my chest when it's hot and I've worn them for a while and there's always an angry red line around my boobs when I take them off. And then of course if you don't wash underwire bras properly or you squeeze the water out too hard the whole damn cup gets bent out of shape. Half my underwire bras have little holes in them where I have snipped the stitches and pulled out the crescent-shaped plastic, which makes my breasts look somewhat lopsided—one side all perky and in your face, and the other, well, almost there. Luckily, so far I've almost always known when I was going to get some, so I've had on my silk and satin feminine ones on all the right days. Cheeto did get to see me in my holey Jockeys and an ancient bra with a pink stain from an old T-shirt on one strap in uneven blotches once or twice, but I was so comfortable with him that it hardly mattered.

Sometimes I think that the 'comfort' thing is the basic problem with all adult relationships. When we stop acting like we're unique from our partners, the *opposite* sex I mean, then the enigma vanishes and we become regular people, the girl next door, a cousin, the girl who sat behind you in class. Who really wants to be that, and lose all the allure of being an unfathomable, extraordinary *woman?* It's feminism of a different brand, I guess. It was so much simpler when we were younger, in the in-between years, just beginning to realize that *we* were different from *them*. I remember how terribly tongue-tied I was around boys when I was in school, but it wasn't such a big deal because all of us girls were, really, as were the boys around us. We girls were still coming to terms with being 'young women' and the fact that our classmates, whom we had previously played with and shared lunch with and screwed up our noses at for being sweaty or loud, were now creatures to impress. During the first couple of mixed outings we had, I could never eat around them no matter how often I'd eaten from their tiffin boxes before. Heaven forbid they thought of me as unfeminine or, worse, a *hog*. So, suddenly, as they stuffed their faces, got pizza cheese on their chins and gave each other high-fives with every loud burp, we girls concentrated on looking pretty and smelling lovely and being inaccessible divas on our squeaky-clean pedestals. It all sounds very *The Rules*-y, but if you think about it those relationships were so much more functional, perhaps because we were keeping the mystery alive and growing.

My friends were the same way. One never brushed her hair in front of boys, the other shone her lips with gloss every three minutes and constantly adjusted the straps of her newly acquired training bra, and the third wept for a good forty-five minutes when she accidentally stained her school uniform. Being unused as we were to being 'women' or, actually, even girls, distinguishable by things other than the obvious, menstruation was a big pain in the ass, even more than it is now. Oh, sure it allowed the girls who got it first to lord over the girls who still hadn't by putting on big-girl airs but, as active twelve- or thirteen-year-olds, what with sports and homework and all that, we always forgot to change the bulky sanitary towels on time anyway. Luckily enough, our school uniforms were a darkish colour and we covered up the unfortunate stains by pretending we had sat on ink, or, if it was winter, wearing our maroon pullovers tied around our waists.

Anyway, it was around this time that I got my first real 'boyfriend'. He was in my class, in my section, and he wasn't one of those scary all-rounder types, but a bit shy, a little on the fringes of the popular kids' crowd we hung out with—just as I was. We started out by talking about homework and school, always on the telephone because we hardly spoke to each other in school. He called me almost every evening, much to Ma's amusement, and our phone conversations generally ended with him mumbling 'So' and me saying 'Uh-huh?' Then he kissed me at Deepti Raman's birthday party after an energetic round of Truth or Dare, when it was his dare to kiss a girl. I heard later that he and the other boys had rigged it, but I was too embarrassed to say anything to him. Still, playing at dating was great fun because we sat next to each other at movies and he held my hand, stickily, and we kissed gently a couple of times. He did try a little tongue-kissing, thanks to Hollywood, but stopped when I firmly dissuaded him. Then we broke up, mutually—he told me his studies were getting interrupted and I was a little bored anyway—but we stayed friends. Later he started dating one of the other girls in our group and I didn't really think anything of it.

Now, though, there's this unspoken code that specifies that you can't flirt with your friends' ex-boyfriends, former crushes or fuck-buddies. I don't quite get the concept of a fuck-buddy, though, and I certainly don't think it works in an Indian context. Sure, we're second-generation liberated and all that, but there are still people among us who talk about rape victims in the most uneducated way, saying things like they had asked for it because they had dressed attractively and were walking alone on a deserted street and what not. In short, the accusatory finger points straight at the woman, always, and I'm not sure it's about to change. It's not really the twenty-first century in many parts of India, and it's not just the small towns I'm talking about. Sometimes when I'm travelling and I light a cigarette, the way people look at me it's almost as if I were dancing around naked, ringing a bell in their ears to draw attention. In Delhi itself if a woman is thirty and opinionated and lives alone, she's either a slut or one of those terrible Indian women who doesn't need a man and is therefore, definitely, a lesbian. With attitudes like this, is it any wonder that women in Indian urban societies still stifle orgasms and are yelled at in school for wearing skirts that end above the knee because it would mean attracting 'male attention' which would make you, well, 'dirty', 'Westernized' and 'loose'?

I moved away from the mirror to dig out the turquoise blue sleeveless top with little pink and blue flowers embroidered diagonally across it, which I'd recently picked up at the export-surplus market in Sarojini Nagar and chose a comfortable cotton bra to wear under it which wouldn't look too grotty when I got wet. I was bound to be thrown into the pool and emerge dripping, holding my top away from my standing-at-attention nipples, which would only draw more eyes to my chest. It happened every time. I picked out a pair of shorts to go with it, and floaters. Finally it all looked right.

While I was trying to smooth my hair down around my ears, Topsy emerged from her room wearing nothing more than a sports bra and shorts. Unlike me, Topsy is free and open with her body. In the summer, during power cuts, she strips down to her plain cotton panties with just the tiniest bits of lace around the crotch and shrugs out of her bra and walks around the house eating an apple, or sometimes just lying down on the cool floor waving a newspaper over her body. Initially it really freaked me out, this display of naked skin, and I would run around looking for a towel or something squealing 'Topsy! Come on! Put on some clothes!' But she would continue to lie there, eyes closed, asking me to 'Just chill', and she looked so cool, so comfortable, that soon I would strip to my bra and shorts and lie down next to her.

Next to Topsy I always feel large and chunky. Not that I'm much bigger or taller than she is, but she has a certain elfin grace, what with her fluttery fingers and her tiptoe walk and her perfectly flat stomach and the way she shakes her head to move her hair gently from her cheek to behind her shoulder, like a girl in a shampoo ad. Tonight she was wearing a twisted copper armband with a huge green stone in the centre on her golden upper arm. Her hair was brushed and gleaming and she had made two little braids and coiled them around her head to keep it from getting in her face. I noticed the stud in her bellybutton gleam and even though I have a navel piercing too, I felt bloated and fat, like a troll with greasy hair and a snarly voice. Even the silver rings I had worn on my recently pedicured toes suddenly felt wrong.

'I feel fat,' I said sadly.

Topsy looked me up and down and nodded decisively. 'Well, you don't look fat. You look great, Arsh, better than great. I wouldn't be surprised if half the men at the party hit on you.'

I made my 'aw' face and grinned. 'Thanks, but no thanks.

I'm through with men, completely. One hundred per cent finished.'

'What you need is a fling to get that stupid Cheeto out of your head.' She contemplated me closely and then turned towards the bathroom. 'You also need some bronze body glitter. It'll look good on you.'

With deft, quick movements, she strategically dabbed the shiny powder on my face and in the hollows of my neck and cleavage. That's another thing I don't get about Topsy. She's so very touchy-feely. Really. She thinks nothing about hugging someone she's met for the first time, and I'm talking about a full-body hug, where every inch of you is in contact. In the same situation, my body cringes and is stiff and awkward. When she's with her friends, she rubs her head against their shoulders, like a cat, or holds hands, or links arms, and around Fardeen she's like a vine, because she's constantly twined around him. Once at a party, one of those really loud, really crowded parties, I spotted the two of them in a corner. Topsy was sitting in the crook of Fardeen's arm, gently stroking his torso, and he was murmuring something to her while he ran his fingers through her hair. They looked so private, even in that crowded room, that I felt like I was being rude by just looking at them.

Just as she finished, a single ring sounded on her cellphone: Fardeen's signal for us to get ourselves downstairs, pronto. Topsy hurriedly examined herself again in the mirror and dumped her stuff in my shoulder bag. Bags don't go with her personality, she claims. She carries a jhola-type bag to college because she has to and the first thing she does when she gets home is dump it on the nearest available surface. Normally when she's going out she stuffs her phone, wallet and keys into her pockets, or Fardeen's, and hooks her glasses on the neck of her T-shirt or top. On the other hand, I can't go anywhere without my bag,

not even to the local Mother Dairy or grocery store. I feel, I
don't know, naked without it. In fact, I feel the same way if I
leave the house without earrings on. Topsy says these things are
like my security blanket, which might actually be true.

'So whose party is this anyway?' I asked Fardeen in the car.
'Will there be anyone I know?'

'You might, you never know,' said Fardeen. 'It's one of
those huge-ass parties where *everyone* is invited.'

The drive to Chhattarpur was surprisingly quick considering
it was a Saturday night. The Gurgaon-bound road has heavy
traffic around then, what with all the weekend revellers heading
that way.

Pretty soon we were pulling up in front of an ornate gate
that led to a sprawling farmhouse—with not too many cars
outside.

'Ohhh, it doesn't look like too many people have come,'
said Topsy.

She and Fardeen exchanged concerned looks and then
Fardeen glanced at me and said, 'Relax, it's still early, I'm sure
more people will turn up.'

I loved them for that. I knew they were both anxious that
I have a good time and enjoy myself. It had hardly been a few
months since Fardeen had seen me lounging in my pyjamas for
three days straight, emerging from my bed only to go, tottering
a bit, to the bathroom. I hadn't realized, you see, that a *boy*
could do this to me, that I would feel this bad about anything.
It was as if someone had taken a giant iron brand or something
equally red hot and pushed it straight through my stomach and
my liver and my intestines, pausing to take a quick flick at my
lungs, so that while the pain was constant and daily, sometimes
there would be bouts worse than before, which would leave me
almost breathless with agony. Anything could trigger it off, a

song, a phrase, the smell of a particular cologne, anything at all. I wallowed in the pain, because I didn't know what else to do. I couldn't even weep, because it felt like my eyes had been forced permanently open and a fan had been held right in front of them till every bit of moisture had evaporated. It was only when Topsy finally shook me out of bed and made me go to work that things got slightly better. After that I'd kept myself busy and occupied, doing stuff like going for the Manali trip or taking on extra work just so I didn't have to *think* for a while.

'I'm sure it'll be fine, guys,' I said, smiling at them. 'Let's go check it out at least, no?'

Topsy linked her arm through mine and we walked into the gate, past the guard (who confirmed that our names were indeed on the guest list) and into a huge, practically empty house. A television set was blaring in one of the rooms and a sleepy servant soon emerged to direct us outside through the kitchen. Here we stepped on to a paved path that ran around a sprawling lawn and broke off at a corner to lead to a decent-sized pool. Neat hedges edged the path and had been strung with fairy lights, as had a few large trees further down the lawn. Beyond that was darkness but I suspected the lawn stretched over a few more acres, at least. Two larger lights fitted at strange angles at two corners of the pool made the water shimmer alluringly. A bamboo shack with a thatch for a roof had been constructed to one side of the pool. On a table under it, amidst flickering candles, stood rows of glasses and bottles. I could see only two other people on a seat swing on the other side of the pool. Another guy was swimming in the pool and pulled himself out as soon as he saw us.

'Fardeen, my man!' exclaimed the guy, as he walked over to us, dripping, smiling warmly. I noticed he had a bit of a pot-belly over the waistband of his Hawaiian shorts, which was printed with blue and white flowers. He was obviously the host, because after a gingerly one-arm hug and a clap on his back, Fardeen turned him towards us.

'This is Akshay,' he said, then to him, 'Topsy and Arshi.'

'Nice to meet you,' Akshay grinned. His teeth were so super-straight I almost asked him which dental surgeon he frequented. 'You guys are nice and early. Come, I'll get you a drink.'

We went over to the seat swing, occupied by a guy strumming on a guitar and a girl swaying next to him. She jumped up as soon as she saw us and giggled at Akshay.

'Oooh, Akshay, you're all wet, baba. Do you want me to get you a towel?'

She was, I noticed, exceedingly thin. You could see her ribs jutting out between her almost non-existent breasts, and the bones in her shoulders were so sharp they looked like they would cut through her pale skin. Her eyes were enormous and rimmed with black circles, and the tapestry of veins on her face made it look like they had been painted on. She noticed me staring at her and tilted her chin away from me and up at Akshay.

'You want a drink, baba? I'm going to make myself one.'

'No, no, you sit. And I don't think you should be drinking any more.'

'Oh, Akshay, you're soooooo silly. It's not like I'm going home or anything tonight, no?'

Akshay smiled dismissively at her and went off to get us our drinks. The girl trotted off after him. When he returned, he plonked himself down next to the guy with the guitar.

'Sing us a song, man, you're the piano man,' he said, laughing.

'Fuck off, Akshay,' said the guy, but he was smiling too. He had a nice smile, with deep dimples that appeared and disappeared with every movement of his face, and a neat little French beard running from the sides of his rather lovely mouth to his slightly pointed chin. He was a little on the shorter side, barely taller than me (and I'm not very tall), I thought, though these things are hard to tell when someone's sitting down.

'Guys, this is Kabir,' said Akshay, waving towards him. 'Brilliant photographer by day and extraordinary musician by night.'

Kabir made a flamboyant gesture with his hand like he was taking a bow, and we cheered.

'With an introduction like that I'll have to sing, won't I?' he said, looking at Akshay.

'Arrey, why do you think I was flattering you in the first place?'

'Bastard!' he said, but he started to strum idly on his guitar.

The skinny girl returned to the swing with a drink in one hand and started to massage Akshay's shoulders, who looked mildly embarrassed by the gesture.

Kabir had by now launched into one of my all-time favourites, Extreme's *More than words*, and he did it well, too—all the drumming on the wood of the guitar between chords and an improvised riff or two, which made us feel even more like part of the audience at a music concert. Normally, I get quite annoyed when people start singing at parties. Oh it's pleasant, enjoyable even, when you're outdoors and moderately drunk and someone is singing old Hindi songs and you tilt your head back and watch the stars (whatever stars you can see in Delhi's orange, polluted skies anyway). What irritates me is when, at a house party where there are only four or five people in the first place and the conversation's been quite animated, someone says, 'Shh, shhh . . .' because some dude is about to sing with his eyes closed and everything. I make it a point to keep my eyes down during these performances, because I'm scared that if I make eye contact with anyone at all I'll start to giggle. As it is my phone inevitably rings at the choicest moments, drawing annoyed looks from the friends of the singer, who've been sitting close to him murmuring, 'Wah, wah.' They see me as this anglicized chick who doesn't know the value of classic ghazals—and perhaps I don't. See, my Hindi has never been stellar. We spoke in English at home, my parents and I, and I barely scraped through in Hindi (which I studied as a 'second language') at school. That's what it's always been for me—my 'second' language. I can speak Hinglish rather well, and watch Hindi movies with comprehension, but when I speak the language, I directly translate it from the English sentence in my head, which doesn't always work because you have to keep in mind things like the gender of the object you're talking about and grammatical nuances.

When Kabir was done, Fardeen whistled and I clapped and joined the raucous requests for an encore.

'This musician's tired,' said Kabir, standing up and peeling off his white T-shirt. Oh he had a *hot* body. His stomach had just about missed having a six-pack, but it was taut and firm and there was a hint of downy hair running from the base of his chest and vanishing into his shorts. It was much like what Cheeto had once referred to as his 'happy trail', and it was certainly making *me* happy now despite the tiny pangs of guilt flashing about in my head for leching at a hot guy while thinking of the recently-ex boyfriend. I caught myself staring and looked away, feeling the heat spread over my cheeks and ears, only to catch Topsy's eye. She winked at me.

'Who's coming for a swim?' Kabir asked, raising an eyebrow at us.

'Not me, man,' said Akshay. 'I just got out.'

'Not me either,' said the skinny girl. 'I'm too tired.'

'I'll come!' said Topsy, getting up and dragging Fardeen to his feet.

The three of them turned to me. There was *no way* I was getting soaked and wet-haired in front of this guy.

'Um . . . not now,' I said, smiling weakly, but Topsy made her impatient face, mouth twisted, eyes rolling heavenward.

'Come *on*, Arshi, don't be boring.'

'I'll join you guys in a bit, I swear,' I whined, but by then Kabir was already hooking my elbows with his arms and pulling me to my feet.

'Yeah, come *on*, Arshi,' he said, mimicking Topsy's tone, and by the time I was done with being shy about his hands on my body and my heart beating so very loudly that surely he could hear it, he had run towards the pool and thrown himself in.

I walked up slowly, watching Topsy splash Kabir and Fardeen who were falling all over themselves trying to duck her.

'The ball! The ball!' yelled Kabir as I approached.

I found a small yellow plastic football lying near my feet and threw it in. Then I stood by the pool for a bit debating whether it was too late to go back. Before I could, though, someone grabbed me around the waist and tossed me into the water. I emerged sputtering and saw Kabir and Fardeen give each other high-fives.

'Pig!' I screamed, but Kabir saw I was laughing and swam over to me.

'You're on my volleyball team,' he said.

'We're playing volleyball with this yellow thing?'

'Well, we are now.'

'Okay, but I should warn you, I suck.'

'That's cool 'coz I'm good enough for both of us.'

I made a face at him, he grinned at me, and we started to play. Well, at least Fardeen and Kabir did. Topsy and I didn't do much more than squeal and make wild grabs at the ball when we could see it and right after it flew over our heads. In a bit, when Fardeen noticed we were kind of being left out, he grabbed Topsy and made her climb on his shoulders.

'Now we're unbeatable!' he crowed and Topsy did a little victory dance, while he held on to her ankles.

'Hah! That's what you think,' said Kabir and tried to hoist me on to his shoulders. Only, since we were about the same height, it was tough for him and most embarrassing for me. Finally he said, 'Okay, I'll swim underwater and you climb on to my shoulders quickly, okay?', and before I could say yes or no he had vanished and I was in agony because *oh my god!* what if my bottom looked gross from down there? He was up between my legs rapidly enough though, holding on to my shins, and we played a loud, noisy game.

In a while Topsy announced that she wanted another drink, so we got out of the pool. Uncomfortably conscious that my hair was forming weird rat-tails all over my neck and face, and that my blue top looked practically black now and clung oddly to my body, I pulled at the curly strands that surrounded my face and hoped that Kabir wouldn't notice. When we got back to the bar, there were a few other people there, some of whom Fardeen knew, and Topsy and he started chatting with them. Meanwhile, Kabir headed back to his guitar, and I sort of hovered so that if he looked at me like he was thinking 'Oh, what is she doing here?' when I followed him, I could just pretend I was actually heading for Topsy. Well, he saw me lingering and beckoned me over to where he was and I casually strolled over trying not to reveal how happy, happy, happy I was.

'Tell me about yourself, Arshi,' he said, pulling me down beside him.

'Umm . . . what do you want to know?'

'Something. Anything. What you do, where you grew up, what your favourite colour is . . .'

'Well, my favourite colour is leaf green. Ooh, and fuchsia.'

'Really? Mine too!'

'Really?' Okay, no wonder he was so cute. He was obviously gay.

'Noooo. But I would've guessed fuchsia is yours. You look very . . . fuchsia.'

'What does that mean?' I asked, laughing.

He smiled too. 'Like an unpronounceable colour.'

I swatted at him with my hand, 'Actually, I'm very easy to figure out.'

'I'm sure,' he said, looking me up and down. 'You look like one of those kids who had those fancy colour-pencil boxes. You know what I'm talking about? With colours like burnt sienna and fuchsia.'

'Burnt sienna is such a great name for a colour.'

'Maybe, but what used to piss me off most was that the colour they called "flesh" was always this really gora shade of peach.'

'Ah, so *you* were one of those kids . . .'

'How do you think I knew what fuchsia was?'

'My Barbie doll used to have a fuchsia dress which I loved.'

'You had a Barbie?'

'I'm allowed to have a Barbie! My mother never bought me one, so I had to wait for birthday parties and look all deprived and whisper "I don't have a Barbie doll, aunty." It worked like a charm.'

'Hmmm . . . manipulative!'

'And proud of it.'

'Did you have those male Barbie dolls too?'

'They were called Kens. And no, actually, no one gave me one of those. My Barbie had to date GI Joes that came up to her hip.'

'That must have traumatized her.'

'Oh, it put her off dating forever.'

By this time we were both giggling, and such a feeling of general well-being took over me that I was alarmed. The last thing I needed was to feel emotion for anyone ever again. Okay, perhaps not ever again, but not for a really, really long time. But it was such a perfect moment, that I mentally added it to my photo album. Some day, this moment, this party, this guy would be special. No, wait, not special. Just a fling.

From there the conversation rolled steadily on, punctuated only by our visits to the bar to refresh our drinks and grab some hot kebabs and assorted munchies that had at some point been brought out of the kitchen. We spoke about what I did and what he did (freelance ad photography), where he had grown up (in Delhi mostly, like me, before his parents sent him to Doon in Class 9), how he knew Akshay (his best friend from school), where we wanted to be in six years. And delicately, carefully, we broached the subject of our respective 'social statuses'. Mine was easy, I reasoned, as I said 'Oh my ex-boyfriend and I went there' when he brought up some pub which had an 'awesome' live band playing, so he would get the message. But it seemed to be tougher than I'd thought.

'Oh,' he said, and took a sip of his beer. I waited.

He checked on his guitar. I waited.

He waved to some friends, and I began to think that bringing up Cheeto was a mistake after all, because clearly, *clearly* this boy was taken.

And then he said, 'Umm . . . are you seeing anyone now?'
Bingo.

'No,' I said, sweetly. 'Are you?'

'Nooo. As in I was, but I don't really want to be in a relationship right now, you know?' His eyes searched the crowd and landed on the skinny girl. Oh, so she was the ex, and it must be tough for him, because she was so evidently into this Akshay guy.

'I'm not looking for a relationship either,' I said firmly and a little voice inside my head cheered.

Then another little voice came on, more insistent. *Don't get too attached.*

I'm not.

But it seems like you are.

Really, I'm not. Hello, I just met this guy.

That's what you always say.

Relax, would you? I'll worry about it later.

No, no, worry now, worry now. Why put off the pain that you're inevitably going to feel?

The voice was getting ridiculous. I shushed it and turned back to Kabir.

'I'm glad you feel the same way,' he was saying. 'There are so many women who're all like, oh, commit, commit!'

I was still mentally patting my own back for the way I was carrying this conversation off. Dude! So nonchalant! So like I didn't give a fuck! But I said sternly, 'I don't know what kind of women you're meeting, dude.'

'Yeah, maybe they're all weird and screwed up.'

At this point, I noticed his hand gently drift to my back and rest there, not doing anything, just . . . resting. I smiled secretly to myself. Perhaps this was the fling that Topsy had been so insistent I have. And he was so cute too, way cuter than that fuck-face Cheeto.

We spent most of the evening talking except for one point when I had to pee and excused myself. Walking through the large, empty house—practically on air because he had told me to 'hurry back' and I thought that was surely an indication that he was hitting on me—I reached the bedroom where the loo was located, only to find the skinny girl there, weeping quietly.

'What's wrong?' I asked, trying to quell my happiness a little and sound concerned.

'It's my feet,' she wailed. 'They're really hurting me.'

'Did you cut yourself?'

'No, but the heels are so high, they've given me blisters.'

I tried not to raise my eyebrows. 'Um . . . why don't you just take your shoes off and go out barefoot?'

'Could I do that?' She stopped crying, almost instantly. The tears practically rolled back into her eyes.

'Sure,' I said, smiling a little. 'It's a pool party. Casual and all, you know.'

I went into the bathroom and when I came out she had kicked off her big red shoes with ankle-straps and the close-to-five-inch-high pencil heels. 'Oh my god, that feels so much better.' She smiled at me and said, 'My name is Esha.'

'I'm Arshi.'

'Oooh, that's a pretty name! What does it mean?'

'It means heaven,' I said, rolling my eyes to show how dumb I thought it was.

She kept smiling. 'That makes it even prettier!' Then quickly changing the subject, she said, 'You see, I'm a little shy of going barefoot, my feet are so large.'

She extended one long, bony foot.

'That's nothing. Mine look like Bigfoot's,' I said, placing my floatered foot next to hers.

'You're funny,' she giggled, and then abruptly asked, 'How do you know Akshay?'

'Um, my friend Fardeen? He's his friend from school.'

She mouthed an 'oh', then quickly asked, 'Do you think he likes me?'

I laughed. I couldn't help it. She was so charming, a little like a very cute six-year-old who knows that if she says or does certain things the grown-ups will lap it up. Esha seemed to know her brand of childlike charm very well, and she knew how to work it. Usually girls like that annoy me, but Esha was so bubbly and so frail, like she needed to be protected, that it was hard to feel annoyed. She reminded me of a cat. Now cats really know how to work their stuff. Dogs get guilty expressions on their faces as soon as they've done something wrong and run off to hide under the dining table, waiting for you to discover the damage and scold them. Cats, on the other hand, walk casually around the mess, looking up at you, their mouths forming silent meows, and butting your legs with their head. And they have such an expression of injured innocence on their faces, it's like they're saying, 'Who, me? Would I lie to you, baby?'

'I don't even know Akshay,' I protested.

'Ya, but you've seen him with me and all . . . you must have some idea.'

'Okay, well, ya, he seems to like you enough.'

She smiled a smile of pure pleasure and sat down on the bed, bringing her knees up to her chin. 'He's so cute, no? I met him at a wedding reception and I've liked him ever since.'

'Oh, I thought you knew him through Kabir,' I said.

'Oh, no. I met Kabir through Akshay.' She looked at me mischievously. 'You like Kabir, no?'

'I just met him!' I said, startled.

'You do! You do like him!' She sprung up to do a little dance and then said kindly, 'It's okay. He's a damn nice guy. His ex-girlfriend was a bitch and a half though.'

'Really? How come?'

'Oh, you know, yaar, the usual, all like ultra-bitchy and ultra-pricey and all. So he dumped her, oh, two–three months back.'

'He dumped her?'

'For someone who doesn't like him, you're definitely asking a lot of questions,' she teased, as she rubbed gloss on her lips and offered it to me. I shook my head.

'Ya, anyway, I didn't like her much. She once told me I was too skinny.' Esha scowled briefly and ran her palm down her stomach. 'You know what I told her?'

'What?'

'I said, my *mother* told me you can never be too rich or too skinny. She just made a face.' She linked her arms with mine and started to walk towards the door. 'I hope you *do* start dating Kabir. We can double-date!'

Outside, Esha looked around for Akshay. 'Oh, there's Akshay. I'll just tell him where I was. He would've worried.'

Akshay didn't look worried at all. They never worry, these boys we love. They keep us on tenterhooks, just by their unconcern. We spend our days agonizing over them; at nights if we're out together we try to make them jealous by flirting with someone else. But they rarely seem to care and at the end of the evening just a casual arm around our waists or a murmured 'Ready to leave?' can make us weak in the knees. This is it, we think, this is the night they've realized they do need us after all, this is the night we will make out and they will whisper the sweetest of sweet nothings in our ears, only they won't be nothings; they'll be deep, meaningful somethings.

Everyone, I've gathered, has a power role to play in a relationship. And the one who has the power will try his or her hardest to keep it. Why should they tell us they love us, these boys? If they do, it will mean that an entire afternoon of not responding to calls can't in fact be made up for with just a 'Hello sweetie'. Before Cheeto, there was a boy called Ranvir in my life. He was quite a bit older than me and pretended he was wiser, and he had an on-again–off-again girlfriend whom he wasn't willing to let go of just yet. Of course, he brought out the most pathetic part of me, the part that needed to be reassured all the time and, of course, there was no reassurance forthcoming. Because, if he were to tell me that I was special, he would lose the edge, wouldn't he? It would mean I could stop *pretending* to be so damn happy and upbeat all the time and actually feel that way; I wouldn't be the needy one any more and he wouldn't have the upper hand. But, I would keep thinking, it takes so little to make me happy, and surely, surely he knows this and surely, surely he's not fucking with me when he says he doesn't know where we stand? Neediness kills. Somewhere within our souls something dies every time we are needy and the boys we care so much about are dismissive of it.

Topsy and Fardeen came up to me. 'You good to go, babe?' asked Topsy, yawning.

'Already?'

She grinned, 'Yes, yes, I know you and Lover Boy have a lot of talking to do, but you and *I* have a lot of talking to do too.'

I made a face at her. 'Give me five seconds, I'll just go say bye.'

Kabir was sitting by the pool with two other women when I approached him. Perhaps if I kept telling myself he was a player it would make it easier not to get attached, I thought. Or, maybe not. His face lit up when he saw me and he got up and came towards me. 'Where've you *been*? You took *forever*.'

'I'm sorry,' I said, thrilled at feeling his arm around me. 'I met your friend Esha. She was having a little crisis with her shoes.'

He rolled his eyes, 'Esha has several crises every day. It's nothing new. That girl just talks and talks and talks.'

'Anyway, I'm leaving.'

'So soon? No, you can't go!'

'Um, actually Topsy and Fardeen, whom I came with, are leaving, and they're my ride home.'

'I'll drop you,' he said, leaning in and nuzzling my neck.

I started at the sudden rush of warmth that filled my body. 'Another time. I promise.'

But as he walked me towards the gate, it struck me that there perhaps might not be another time. After all, he hadn't asked for my number or anything. Maybe he was just bored at this party, maybe I was just someone he could have an interesting conversation with one evening and never see again. At the gate, I waved bye to Akshay and Esha who insisted on wrapping her arms around my neck and squeezing hard.

I turned to Kabir and gave a little smile and said, 'Well, bye then.' He reached into his pocket and pulled out his cellphone, wrapped in a plastic bag (to keep it from getting wet, he explained quite unnecessarily), and asked for my number, which I gave, not daring to look at him, my eyes fixed on my curled toes.

'I'll call you soon. We'll do coffee or something, okay?' he said, kissing my cheek.

I nodded. I couldn't speak.

4. in which i visit my mom

I SPENT MOST OF my childhood wanting to be 'normal'.

To be 'normal' was to have a mother who had long hair and was mostly in a sari and called you in from the park as soon as it got dark, and a father who came home from work at a bank or a government office and loosened his tie and patted you on the head. A 'normal' dinner was a silent, dal-chawal affair at the dining table, where your mother piled hot phulkas on to your plate and your father responded to questions in grunts and occasionally asked you how school was. Sometimes your father would have guests over from work and then your mother would swing between feeding you and carrying ceramic bowls brimming with munchies into the living room, where the guests sat on a large sofa with a Rexin cover and velvet cushions opposite a glass cabinet with assorted books and knick-knacks arranged in it. I wanted to be like the 'normals' because it seemed like such a safe way to be. In my eyes their lives were superior in every way to the one my family lived. Including a longlist of relatives—taya–tayi, mama–mami, chacha–chachi and innumerable cousins—whom I never tired of hearing about. I would watch them with their brothers or sisters and feel defiantly lonely, longing for a sibling, at least, but my mother laughed every time I broached the topic with her.

My parents and their group of friends, all young, working couples (some unmarried), met often for dinner at each other's places. Many of them didn't have children, but the few who did carted their kids everywhere, like my parents did me. We kids had a sort of gang, and were kept busy in a separate room from the one in which our parents sat, with food (mostly pasta in white mushroom sauce), and soft toys, because our parents disapproved of violent ones (guns) or stereotypes (Barbie dolls). Unlike the 'normal' parents ours wore jeans with kurtas and smoked stubby Goldflakes, with the ash growing endlessly at the tip. Our houses were minimally done up, with messy bookshelves, wicker chairs and old divans to sit on. To us kids our parents' friends were never 'uncle' or 'aunty'; they were Deepa or Raghu. Now, of course, having boho parents is very much in vogue, but then it was something that made the other kids snicker and made me blush wildly, especially when my parents visited my school for a PTA or some other function. My parents attempted conversation with the others (who were mostly bankers or housewives), but my father usually looked bemused and my mother had to sneak outside quite often for a smoke.

My parents' marriage, I realize now, had been shaky then as well. They weren't happy for a very long time but they stuck it out for my sake and, well, I guess because the legal bit of getting divorced was a pain in the ass. Oh, of course there were happy times. I remember our family trips and falling asleep in the backseat of the car listening to them dissect their work and their friends and each other's families, hearing them laugh, and feeling safer and more secure at that moment than I have ever been. I suppose it's just that Ma and Dad would have made better friends than spouses.

I'm not particularly fond of Barbara. In fact, I'm quite
indifferent to her, as you might have guessed, but I'm glad my
father has someone in his life—though I must admit it felt a
little odd going for their wedding. Barbara wanted very much to
have it in Delhi, but my dad put his foot down and they finally
had a quiet ceremony in a church in Iowa, where Barbara's
sister lives. My three aunts attended it, with their kids and my
grandmother. And I was there, as a bridesmaid. (No one else
seemed to think it was weird being a bridesmaid at your dad's
wedding.) My mother had been invited as well, but she didn't
get leave at the last minute. Barbara's family and friends filled
one entire pew. They were mainly from the Midwest, and all of
them had Barbara's slow, deliberate way of speaking. Her
father, a stocky, worried-looking man, walked her down the
aisle, while her mother caught me in a huge hug and told me
that I now had to call her Nana and her husband Pop. 'Because
that's what everyone calls us, dear,' she said at the reception
after the ceremony, smiling so I could see the lipstick stain on
her teeth. I had grandmothers of my own, Dadi and Ow-ma,
which is what I call my mother's mother; no grandfathers, but
I had never felt their absence. And now I was to be related to
this lot, this loud, back-slapping set, with not even *one* good-
looking step-cousin whom I could flirt with? I smiled politely at
her and slunk away to a corner table to read *The Bell Jar*, while
everyone else danced and drank.

My mother, however, has not shown any desire to marry
again or be with anyone since she and my dad broke up. Oh,
sure, loads of sad bachelors, mostly friends of friends, have
come over for dinner but she treats them all kindly and at the
end of the evening, just as kindly, shows them the door. It's not
that they're not good people. One Old Faithful, which is what
I call her persistent suitors, used to turn up every week from the

time I was thirteen to the time I was twenty, bearing chocolates for me. At first I was rude to him but then I began to see the amusing side to it and happily accepted the chocolates while my mother rolled her eyes at having to entertain him again. 'Once is enough for me, Arshi,' she said one time after fending off another Old Faithful all evening at a cocktail party. 'They *breathe* all over me, and besides, I don't want any more children. Why get married?' I laughed and told her she should be happy she was still hot, but she said she'd rather be fat and have a moustache if it meant they'd leave her alone.

I went to visit Ma on the weekend after the pool party. I was glad it was Sunday, Sunday afternoon really, because then the road to Manesar isn't as jammed with traffic as it otherwise is.

I don't think of the Farmhouse (which is what the house is called now, after years of trying to think up imaginative names have come to nothing) as home like I do our old place in Green Park where Ma and I moved shortly after the divorce was final and my father had left for the US. Now *that* was home, even if it was a rented apartment with only two bedrooms. We had the terrace to ourselves and a giant veranda, which we filled with potted plants and used to dry our washing. The drawing room was done up in an ethnic style, with lots of earthen stuff, softly lit lamps, and bright, embroidered floor cushions strewn around on the floor. The walls were lined with bookshelves. The only gadget was the TV which stood in one corner and we covered it up with a pretty cloth to make it look like it fit in.

Shifting into that apartment had initially got me very depressed. Suddenly, we were a truncated family, sitting in an apartment that was tiny, much smaller than our previous one, and there were boxes everywhere, and dust, and all we had to eat was Maggi noodles. It seemed like everything I had taken for granted and everything that had so far brought some semblance of normalcy into my not-so-normal world was rapidly vanishing.

'Cheer up, sweetie,' my mother said, coming in from the veranda which she had been sweeping clean. My job was to unpack the boxes that said 'Books', except I was sort of opening the cartons and pulling the books out, but not really putting them anywhere.

Her gentle, comforting tone was too much to bear. I pushed the books aside and burst into tears.

'Oh, Arsh, it'll be okay, you'll see,' she said, holding me close and stroking my hair. No one can stroke my hair like my mother does. I love the feel of her small hands, the soft, pale palms smelling of Nivea and cigarette smoke and the lingering fragrance of Charlie. 'Tell you what. You go to school tomorrow, and by the time you come back, I'll completely transform this place. You won't even know it! And then, this weekend, we'll have a housewarming party and you can call all your friends and show off the house.'

'Really?' I said, between sniffs.

'Really,' she smiled. 'And now let's forget about the rest of the unpacking and go out and get some dinner. Where would you like to go?'

'Could we go to Nirula's?'

'Sure! Just let me get my bag, okay?'

That night we slept on mattresses in the living room, and the next day when I returned from school the boxes were gone and the apartment had become home. Ma had put the basics together. Floor cushions in the living room, new curtains over my bed, paintings on the walls. Even the kitchen looked like a kitchen, with the groceries and spices and tinned stuff all in place. We ate out again that night, but Ma almost fell asleep over her pizza. She kept her word about the grand housewarming party, too. She divined a maid, almost out of nowhere, she made salad and fondue and mushroom soup and bought the bread I liked, with the crumbly crust, to go with it. Two of my closest friends were even allowed to stay the night and they whispered admiringly to me, 'Wow, your house is so *nice*, Arshi.'

'Isn't it?' I replied, gloating.

Now there was the Farmhouse. Normally I have this love–hate thing going with the Farmhouse, because essentially I'm a city person. I thrive on action, on people moving rapidly around me, on drinking with music turned up to deafening levels, even on traffic jams. So I guess a weekend of being away is all I can take. But I do like going to the Farmhouse, because it's peaceful and allows me some space to think and at the same time it's bustling with activity because of the school my mom runs, I get good food, and also, yeah, I get to be mothered a little bit.

The house itself is large and thanks to its high ceilings and the two coolers Ma's had installed in the living and dining rooms, deliciously cool waves of air waft through it at all times. My own room has a second-hand air conditioner, but the electricity situation in Manesar isn't too stable yet and the air conditioner doesn't run on the inverter. There's also a permanent water problem. We have a bore well, with a pump, but that's temperamental too, so we have to have back-up plans for water supply, just to be safe, and every morning the first sounds in the house are of many, many buckets being filled up to last through the day. Besides, as my mother keeps telling me, the Farmhouse is our own, as in it *belongs* to us. Mom's school—Devi, it's called—is also 'recognized' now by several NGOs, which keep the donations going. She has staff now, working at the school, two or three college students who study social work and do their internship there and occasionally work in the neighbouring villages as well. The school is very popular among interns, especially idealistic young girls who think my mother is the epitome of liberated Indian womanhood.

I must admit, though, that I love the drive to the Farmhouse from our place (Topsy's and mine) because it takes me past the Tughlaqabad Fort, which I've always wanted to explore but have put off over and over again thinking it's just around here anyway. But the sheer expanse and scale of the fort, its crumbly stone walls arching towards the sky, the rolling hillocks within, the half-broken walls that speak of age-old construction fascinate me. I often imagine that in some past life I've inhabited such a fort, been a part of the nobility, for sure, because what else could explain my connection to brick and sandstone? I imagine myself bathing in large sunken tanks, peering out of the windows of a palace in Old Delhi, and even as a soldier, positioned high on the turrets, peering into the distance to spot enemy cavalry. Driving past the fort with the music turned up, and the road ahead practically empty, I feel as though I'm in a movie, like I'm suddenly watching myself driving my rickety Fiat Uno against the grand backdrop of the ruins. It's humbling, that feeling.

I'm lucky to have my own car to get me to the Farmhouse whenever I want. Ma insisted I take driving lessons about three months before my eighteenth birthday, so I could get a licence as soon as I turned 'adult'. Mostly, I sucked at my lessons, and for a while my licence was just something I showed off to my college friends. But then commuting by bus from Manesar to Delhi University's South Campus became a pain and I finally began to drive my mother's old Fiat Uno around the village, with the kids running after it, laughing every time I got stuck in a pothole. Finally, I managed to drive it, unsupervised, to college. In celebration, my mother bought herself a Tata Sumo, hired a driver for it and gave me the old Uno to use. The Uno is charming, but it does have distinct disadvantages, like heating up horribly if I drive it for too long without stops, or only letting out wisps of fresh air from the air conditioner even if the blower is on high. That weekend it stalled twice and both times I had to get out and pour water into a hole in the hood, which I presumed was where the water went. (I've never got around to figuring out the car's inside workings, though my mother still insists I should know the stuff in case I get stuck on the road after dark.) It worked, though, whatever the hole was, because the Fiat gave a complaining gasp and started again and after about half an hour I was finally, finally pulling into the Farmhouse, feeling happy to be home.

Since it was Sunday the small outhouse where Devi usually took place was quiet. I walked into the house, past the colourful office and into the den where my mother was talking to a woman from the village.

'Sweetie!' she called, waving me down so she could kiss me hello. 'You look so thin.'

That's her standard greeting. There was a time when I wasn't exactly fat, but pretty plump, and every time she sees me Ma insists on referring to that phase, telling me how 'healthy' I used to be and how I'm clearly not eating right any more. She insisted on getting me some mango, right then, because I looked starved of fruit and other nutritious foodstuff. 'You're going to get vitamin deficiency at this rate,' she said sternly.

I ate some of the delicious mango and went up to my room. I dumped my stuff on the bed and checked my phone again. Why hadn't Kabir called, *why, why, why?* I hadn't stopped thinking of him since the party and Topsy had liked him too. 'I think he's into you,' she'd said knowingly. It was even clear we were from similar backgrounds. See, as a kid of parents like

mine, I never fail to recognize other members of my tribe. I
know it from the references they make, the casual relationship
they have with their parents, and the connection is made almost
immediately. I do have friends who weren't brought up like I
was, but they are few and far between, and I've long since lost
touch with the few friends I had in school, except Deeksha. It
gets weird after a point. You start ignoring phone calls, you
might meet them at some school reunion function, but the
conversation will be stilted and you wind up feeling depressed
that someone who used to be a close friend just doesn't *get* you
any more.

Take Topsy, for instance. Her family is the complete
antithesis of mine and sometimes this annoys me. Like her
whole thing with Fardeen. She knows for a fact she can't be
with him, or marry him, and it bugs me to see how easily she
accepts this. Actually, not *easily*, because I know it hurts her that
she can't be with Fardeen forever, but I hate the way she
pretends a major part of her life doesn't exist when she's around
her parents. I asked her about it once, my voice breaking with
irritation.

'It takes so little to make my parents happy, Arshi,' she told
me, her hand on my arm. 'If I was to bring home a boy, a
Muslim at that, it would be like a slap on their face. Why should
I cause them so much pain for nothing?'

'That's what you and Fardeen are? Nothing?'

She shook her head and her eyes filled with tears. 'You
know we're not. But Papa even said to me before I came to
Delhi, "If you find someone, even if he's not from our
community, it's okay. As long as you don't defile the family and
find a Muslim boy." And what do I do? I find a *Muslim boy*.'

'Topsy, dude, this is the twenty-first century!'

'Some things are passed on, no, from generation to
generation.'

'Yes, but things change.'

She smiled sadly at me, 'Some things never do.'

Topsy does have some traditional ideas. She hasn't slept with Fardeen, for instance. I know, because she's told me she's saving herself for her wedding. She knows if news gets out about her and Fardeen, it will spoil the marriage prospects of her beloved little brother, and several cousins, even if beloved little brother is living it up in Mumbai. And there are some things she gets from having grown up in a close-knit joint family. Her affection. Her way of making two cups of coffee in the morning when she wakes up and then coming into my room, all smiles, to give one to me. Her way of bringing back something for me every time she goes to Meerut. In fact, the rest of her family is just as inclusive. For her cousin's wedding in Delhi, I was made to run around as much as she was, the little kids called me Didi, the older ones helped me choose an outfit and sang songs while we had our hands covered in mehndi. And they thought nothing of it. I was Topsy's flatmate, her family in Delhi, and they decided to love me for it. I guess that's something I could appreciate them for, after all.

Over a quiet dinner that night, I told my mother about Kabir.

'Why this fixation with finding another boyfriend?' she asked me.

'It's not a fixation, ma. It's just that I don't want to be alone . . . And I really like this guy.'

'Oh, sweetie.' She smiled at me over the methi-aloo. 'You're so pretty and talented and you have so many friends. You'll never be alone.'

'Talented? Hah! I have no talents.'

'You know you were always very good academically. Perhaps it's time to consider going back to college?'

I shook my head. 'I can't go back to college. Not now. What would I study there? Besides, I'm so sick of my life, I hate it, I really do.'

'Of course you can go back to college, or at least contemplate getting a different job. You're just staying in this PR job because it's easy and it's a habit.'

'Oh, you don't understand.'

We cleared the table, Sunday being the maid's day off, and went into the living room to watch *Desperate Housewives*.

I thought she'd forgotten the entire conversation, but just before I went to bed Ma said to me, 'Your father is eventually going to retire and come back to India, you know. You might as well go for a stint to the States while he's still there.'

'Maaa,' I said, rolling my eyes, 'we've had this discussion.'

'Just think about it. You could do another master's, and you'd be happier.'

'I already have a master's, ma. Fat lot of good it's done for me.'

'I'll look into some options for you.'

'Ma, you're not listening. I do *not* want to go back to college. Now, good night.'

'Good night, darling. Give me a kiss.'

I entered my room and found my way to the large window that overlooked the vegetable patch behind the house. I pressed my face against the warm iron mesh of the window, spitting out intermittent dust as I smoked into the night. Then I quickly sprayed my room with deodorant before snuggling into bed so the smell wouldn't stay.

5. in which we meet significant others

IT HAD BEEN A little over a month since my disastrous trip to Manali and I hadn't seen Michael since, though our conversations were now back to normal. I had been quite wrapped up in obsessing about Kabir and work had suddenly gone into overdrive so I hadn't worried too much about it. In the interim, he had managed to meet some chick at a friend's wedding and started to date her and the last time we had spoken he had gone on and on about how *wonderful* she was and how he just couldn't wait for me to meet her.

Now I'm not too crazy about meeting a friend's significant other. It always turns out to be a bit of an ordeal because I'm expected to relentlessly analyse and deconstruct and perform complex body-language-decoding brain functions while the friend's eyes constantly beseech me for approval—and if I have a bad feeling about the person I'm tempted to say 'I told you so' when things go wrong instead of just lending a sympathetic shoulder.

I used to have a friend who was dating a married man while we were in college. The two of us weren't terribly close, but we belonged to the same group and occasionally hung out at one of the many nightclubs we had begun to frequent as an expression of our newly gained 'adult' status. My friend had met this man while interning at the company he ran—well, not ran, but was a partner in. He used to supervise her presentations and stuff, and they went out for lunch a lot. The lunches soon became occasional drinks after office, then one thing led to another and they fell 'passionately in love'. At least that's what she said.

The first time she brought him to one of our gatherings, we were at TGIF celebrating another friend's birthday. They walked in together, my friend and this somewhat portly man, his salt-and-pepper hair pulled back into a ponytail, with a salt-and-pepper (well, to be completely honest, it was more salt than pepper) beard to match, his arm around her waist. We had been really curious about him and all of us stopped our munching and conversation to watch them walk in. She must have sensed our collective anticipation, because immediately her laugh grew more defiant and she greeted everyone loudly, with much-forced gaiety, as she slid across the leather booth, patting the seat next to her and smiling coyly at him.

'God, he looks like her *dad*,' whispered one of the girls at our table. I too wondered what had attracted *this* friend of mine, the youngest in our group, to a man so much older than us. I mean, we had had hypothetical discussions about Older Men it Would be Acceptable to Date but they had always been the Richard Gere/Sean Connery types, not someone who looked like someone else's dad—well, if you took off the ponytail, at any rate.

'Do you like him, Arshi?' asked my friend, a little plea in her voice.

'Sure,' I said, smiling, because I did. I did like him. He was charming, and had a warm smile and an easy way of fitting in in a crowd of people more than twenty years younger than him, which was rather endearing. By the end of the evening, we were all completely bonding with this guy. He was sort of playing the role of Father Confessor-slash-Babysitter-slash-Old Wise Friend, and we were so totally okay with it. Yet, every now and again, I couldn't help wondering if the situation was—shall we say— a little *odd*. I mean, he was forty-something, with a wife and kids and a business to run, and we were nineteen and the Great Indian Rock Festival and career options were the hottest topics of discussion among us.

What amazed me was that we were, all of us, accepting this man and treating him as one of us. Theoretically, I would be totally against dating a married man, especially if there were children involved, but here I was, making conversation, teasing and being teased, as if it was any old boyfriend of a friend I was being introduced to, you know? Where had my sense of moral righteousness disappeared? Perhaps it was different meeting someone face to face, experiencing a situation in real life as opposed to in the 'Never Have I Ever' drinking game, where you drink to stuff you *have* done, as in, 'Never have I ever wanted someone who was married'—I never drank to that.

Perhaps, our reaction was triggered by the way my friend looked and behaved around him. She seemed even younger than her eighteen years, her voice was high and childish and her eyes danced around at the rest of us. She had positively blossomed. It got me thinking. Never mind his family, never mind that by the time she reached the age when she'd want to settle down, he would be in his dotage. It was probably completely worth it just to be the object of the kind of devotion he seemed to have to her, just to be taken care of, when all the boys we knew were fucking around or making statements like 'I can't commit right now' or 'I need space' or 'I need to figure things out'.

They did break up though, a year or so later, after I had watched her grow from starry-eyed and glowing to bitter and jaded. Her eyes got harder over the months, her mouth tighter, her statements more and more cynical. He promised he would leave his wife but couldn't and then there was a messy, messy break-up and she was briefly shattered by it.

But even at nineteen, I hadn't felt as awkward about meeting my friend's married 'boyfriend' as I did now about meeting Michael's new girlfriend, Chhaya. Oh, I was so *not* looking forward to it.

We had decided to meet at Mocha in Greater Kailash, which I loved, because they made the best shakes ever and because you could smoke there, even though all the seating was indoors. Plus they always had really funky music playing in the background, and that was always good in case you were stuck for conversation. I was done with work early that day, and since we were supposed to meet at six I got there around five-thirty, chose a book from the in-house bookshop (which was unusually generous about letting you read the books as you sipped on something, as long as you didn't spill), ordered myself a cold coffee and curled up in a snug velvet couch to read.

Michael was late, very late, which was completely unlike him. It must be this Chhaya, I told myself bitterly, Michael had never been late before. I called him and he sounded breathless and apologetic and I just said, 'Yeah, yeah, hurry the fuck up,' and hung up.

They arrived when I was almost through with both the coffee and the book. Michael gave me a hurried hug and then proudly stepped aside to present the girl who was with him. 'This is Chhaya,' he said, his eyes sparkling with love.

Chhaya was pretty ordinary-looking, I noted. She was wearing a sleeveless blue top and blue jeans and had huge eyes, dusky skin and a little mole high up on one cheek. There was an anxious expression on her face and I'm ashamed to say that inwardly I quite relished the fact that I could make someone feel anxious.

'You're Arshi?' she said, smiling nervously. 'I have heard so much about you. It is so nice to finally meet you.' Her voice was soft, her English slightly accented, the kind you'd expect from someone who didn't speak the language at home. I was already judging her, and she was steadily losing points. I made a mental tally in my head, so I could elaborate on them to Topsy later in the evening. But then her eyes rested for a nanosecond on Michael, and I thought, 'Oh, now I get it,' because they shone with affection for him. In fact, in everything she did after that— the way she shot glances at him every time she spoke, the way she smiled happily at him when he pulled out a chair for her, the way she waited for him to sit down before sitting down herself—she reaffirmed how deeply she felt for him.

Arshi, stop being jealous and bitchy, I chastised myself. *These two are so obviously into each other. Michael's happy; be happy for him.*

We started to talk, about me and about Michael, generally catching up and pausing to update Chhaya about who was who. I told him about the pool party and Kabir, how the guy still hadn't called me and how convinced I was that he never would.

'Come on, yaar,' said Michael, 'like who *doesn't* call you?' He turned to Chhaya, who looked a little mystified by this exchange and said to her, 'Don't you think Arshi looks like the kind of girl who'd be warding off calls from boys all day?'

'Yes. Yes, she does,' Chhaya said with a smile, and I felt awful about thinking mean things about her, because she really seemed like a good person.

She didn't say very much through the evening, but there

were some moments when she stopped being shy and was full
of adventure and confidence.

Once, when I was smoking a cigarette, she asked, 'Can I
have a puff?'

'A drag,' I corrected her and handed her the cigarette.

'No, what are you doing? You don't smoke,' Michael said
immediately.

'One drag . . . so I know what it's like?'

'No,' he said firmly and took the cigarette away from her.

I couldn't help the pang of envy that clutched at my heart.
With Michael and me there was none of this kind of stuff.
Michael had made some noises once about my smoking, but all
that it resulted in was me laughing and blowing a carefully
directed stream of smoke into his face, which made him cough
and made me laugh even more. Chhaya actually *cared* about
what he thought and what he felt; I mean, she cared enough to
make it a model for her own behaviour. I even offered her the
cigarette again when Michael went to the bathroom, but she
shook her head. 'He doesn't like it when I do things like that,'
she told me.

What got Chhaya really animated, however, was the
boutique she ran with her sister. 'The label's called Perky Wear,'
she gushed. 'That's because my sister has a baby whom we call
Perky and she was born just before we opened the boutique, so
we thought it was a good name.'

'What kind of clothes do you have?' I asked.

'Oh, mainly Indian, office and party wear.' She pointed to
her top. 'This one's a Perky Wear.'

'It's doing really well, isn't it Chhaya?' said Michael, beaming
at her. 'You should check it out, Arshi, they have some nice
salwars.'

'Silly, salwars are the bottom half,' laughed Chhaya. 'You
mean kurtas.'

'Arshi knows what I mean,' said Michael.

I nodded and said, 'But I'm so broke, I have no extra money to buy clothes and stuff.'

Chhaya said shyly, 'If you come, we would give you a discount, of course.'

She was just being generous but I suddenly felt guilty for making it look like I had staged the conversation just to get a discount. Guilt is such a strange, non-emotion kind of emotion. It makes you obsess, over and over again, in a loop, and even though you're feeling terrible about what you did to someone else, in the end it's still about what you did, which makes it very narcissistic somehow. And I am the guilt *queen*. I find ways and means to make myself feel guilty about *every*thing. 'You're so *easy*,' Topsy keeps telling me, because all she has to do is snap slightly when I'm insisting on something and I let her have her own way because I feel bad about it otherwise.

Michael seemed different around me this time. Very—I don't know—very platonic all of a sudden. It should have made me happy, not having to shy away from a knee-brush, or to think twice before making the most insignificant statement so it wouldn't sound like I was leading him on. But it made me feel strange, slightly at a loss, because—I have to admit—I quite enjoyed the attention. Now, when Michael spoke to me his words were not as measured as they had been in the past, his eyes weren't always scanning my face for a little extra emotion and, in fact, while he spoke to me his hand lazily tangled itself in Chhaya's hair and he massaged the base of her neck with his thumb and forefinger.

This is a good thing, I reminded myself. Now I could concentrate on being 'just friends' with him, which I really, really enjoyed, and not get annoyed at his overanalysing every word that left my mouth. I began to feel very mature; super-cool and super-grown-up.

'We should go, jaanu,' said Chhaya, checking her cellphone and looking at Michael, who nodded and then quickly glanced at me to see if I'd noticed the 'jaanu', because he knows full well that I'm not a great believer in calling people things like 'sweetie' or 'darling' or 'honey' or whatever. The most I can do is 'babe', 'baby' when I'm feeling particularly affectionate, but usually I stick with names, given names, and not loving derivatives. But I noticed how that little word seemed to make Michael proud; his shirt swelled just a little bit and he stood up, pulling out the chair for Chhaya again. Michael was made to be a boyfriend, I figured, as I put my things back in my bag. He was happiest when he was doing stuff for someone else, when he could make his affection known by simple gestures like brushing a strand of Chhaya's hair away from her cheek and then, just as casually, letting his hand rest on the small of her back. And she glowed under it, too, became all soft and radiant—and suddenly, despite my jealousy, I knew they made a great couple.

I got out of Mocha, kissed Michael goodbye and gave Chhaya a half-armed hug, which she returned with a tighter squeeze than I'd expected. 'You guys have to come over soon,' I told her, and she nodded vigorously.

'Definitely. I will get Michael to bring me. I am so glad to have finally met you.'

Michael lingered long enough for me to give him the thumbs-up and say, 'She's very nice. Way to go.' Then, with a parting hug and a huge smile, he walked her to his car.

That night, *finally*, my cellphone flashed a strange number and I answered it with my heart in my mouth.

'Hello?'

'Hi, is that Arshi?'

'Ya?'

'Hi, Arshi, it's Kabir. Not sure if you remember me . . . we met at the pool party?'

Was he kidding me? Did he not realize I had been obsessing about him for a good week and a half now? No, wait, not a good week and a half, a *terrible* week and a half.

'Yes, yes, I remember you. I thought you'd forgotten me!'

'Nah, dude.' He was smiling, I could tell. It's knowledge I've gained from stealthily visiting one of those online forums which, every now and then, tell you how to keep a guy from getting bored with you and stuff like that. It once said that you should smile when you answer the phone because it reflects in your voice. I'd tried it a couple of times, but all I got was 'What's so funny?' in an accusing tone, so I stopped.

'I've been busy,' he continued. 'Lots of work came up suddenly and I haven't had the time to call anyone.'

'That's okay. I've been really busy too.'

'Anyway, I was wondering what you're up to.'

'Me?' I paused in front of the mirror and did my Marilyn Monroe pout, 'I'm not doing anything. I just got back from coffee with friends.'

'You've got a pretty active social life, huh?'

'Not really. It's just that this close friend of mine wanted me to meet his girlfriend. You know, the whole approval thing.'

'Right, right. Achcha, what are you doing tomorrow?'

'Well, work I suppose.'

'Do you want to catch a bite or something after that?'

I looked in the mirror and gave my reflection a high-five. 'Sure, that sounds great. Where?'

'Well, I live in Jor Bagh, so I was thinking either Khan Market or the Defence Colony market?'

'Def Col's really close to my office.'

'Excellent. Def Col it is then. See you around seven?'

'Okay!' I said and hung up—after which I danced crazily around my room, ending with a neat dive on to the mattresses that served as my bed and whooping and kicking my feet in the air.

When I was sixteen or seventeen, I had decided to have a Valentine's Day party. The party was (as with most of my parties) expressly for this boy I knew, with liquid-brown Labrador eyes and a way of murmuring even the most mundane things into your ear that made you feel all tingly. My basic POA for such parties was to call up the boy in question, casually ask him what he was doing that weekend and then say, 'I'm having a small get-together at my place on Saturday . . . you could come if you're free.' The 'occasion' varied, depending on what month it was. March parties were for Holi, August for Independence Day, October for Diwali, and since this party was in February and fourteenth was the only available Saturday, this was to be a Valentine's Day party. The boy I had a crush on that February was someone called Pranay, whom I had met at an inter-school singing competition at a fest organized by another school (both our schools had reached the finals in the Western Music category). We were both spectators, cheering for our teams. He bought me a Coke from the canteen when I was standing behind him in the queue and generally flirted with me the entire afternoon, which ended with him scribbling my number on his palm.

My 'get-togethers', or GTs as they were referred to, were pretty popular. Getting other guests was never an issue. Deeksha, my best friend in school, who is now in Canada finishing some hotshot MBA course in international business, could be depended on to come along with a host of other friends from her neighbourhood. My neighbour Riddhima dropped in too, and occasionally brought one or two of her friends. Sometimes other people who needed a similar pretext to meet the people they had a crush on asked me whether it would be okay if they 'casually' invited their interests and, well, I mean who was I to come in the way of love?

Our apartment in Green Park was quite conveniently located for everyone to come, and much to my delight my mom, having already decided to quit her job when I finished school, had started to work part-time and travel quite a bit attending education conferences all over the country. She trusted me and the full-time maid enough to leave me at home though she did expect me to report every activity to her, especially when I was planning on having a party. Invariably, she raised an eyebrow and demanded to know whether there would be alcohol involved and I always lied and said no.

Of course, there was alcohol. You can tut-tut at underage drinking all you like, but we were in our late teens, already older by one board exam, and Coke just didn't do it for us any more. Many of my friends were sneakily smoking behind school buses and I even knew two boys who would pour Erasex into their hankies at the end of the last class every single day and lurk at the back of the classroom sniffing at the cloth maniacally till they were reeling. One scary day, Deeksha and I sniffed it ourselves, holding down one nostril and pulling hard at the fumes with the other, and the rush was unbelievable. We had already begun experimenting with cigarettes, but the mild head-rush nicotine gave you was nothing compared to this.

The first time I drank, at a classmate's birthday party, I had some imported white wine that his indulgent parents had served. Pretty soon the wine had run out and we were left—unsupervised—with the hard liquor, not so imported. Deeksha, who was with me, cocked her head at the selection and poured us Old Monk rum, two fingers' worth, and Coke. Both of us were quite drunk by the end of it, but in a strange, unpleasant sort of way. I began to get giddy and couldn't stop giggling, and Deeksha, I learnt later, quietly vomited in a corner and wound up having her bottom felt up by some strange boy who was there by himself swigging whisky from a bottle. I confessed a little bit of this to my mother in a moment of guilt—not the drunkenness, of course, but just the fact that there was alcohol—and she was briefly upset, wondering aloud whether she should speak to the parents of the boy, at which I panicked and begged and whined so much that she agreed not to mention it.

By the time the party in honour of Pranay came along, we were in Class 12, and had been secretly drinking for a while. Our batch had some confirmed potheads by then, who spent their time with red, bleary eyes, laughing strangely and strictly keeping to themselves. I was never really curious about marijuana, though. Sure, I had encountered it before at my house with some of my parents' 'out there' friends smoking reefers quite openly, but it was never something I felt compelled to try. We were still 'good girls', Deeksha and I, who didn't smoke and didn't go overboard on the liquor.

Valentine's Day was always a big deal in school, and this one began quite perfectly. Every year the eleventh standard would organize a Rose Day and arrange for flowers to be delivered throughout school, all through the day. The girls who were popular would have some ten flowers on their desks after lunch (the delivery was done during lunch break and the girls strategically emptied the classrooms leaving their bags unattended so that their secret admirers could slip cards in if they wanted to). In other years Deeksha and I sent each other flowers as a joke, but this Valentine's Day I received a genuine rose, from a genuine admirer. No matter that his voice hadn't broken yet and he wore his pants up to his armpits. Still, he liked me and I was quite thrilled by the attention. It was going to be a perfect evening, all the signs pointed towards it. The thought made me so happy that I beamed at the boy who had sent me roses, causing him to follow me to my bus every day after school for the next two weeks till I got Deeksha to gently disillusion him.

Pranay turned up for the party that evening—with his *girlfriend*. I spent much time dabbing at my eyes in the bathroom, Deeksha consoling me with, 'Chill, he's not worth it.' But what I remember most about that evening is the sense of possibility it held even if nothing that I'd expected came out of it: How I'd dressed up in my best sleeveless top and how we played Truth or Dare, just as I'd planned, how Pranay made excuses to come up and talk to me, how I flirted back shamelessly and how Pranay's girlfriend regarded me with jealous eyes.

Nowadays, the happy thrill of anticipation involved in preparing for someone new in my life is invariably thwarted. And the bizarre thing is *I'm* the one who does the thwarting. It's like I'm my worst enemy; I can burst my bubble with more flourish than anyone else. I'm a proficient Self Bubble Burster. So, if I've been planning a special evening for a while, or really looking forward to something, my thoughts will begin to follow a familiar pattern: *Ooh, I'm so excited* → *Wait, what if things don't go according to plan?* → *Oh, what's the point? Nothing in my life ever does* → *This evening sucks.* I kill it, all by myself, with no help from anyone at all, simply by expecting too much out of it— because nothing, *nothing* lives up to what I have already built up in my head.

These days I've adopted a simple mechanism to deal with this regressive thought process. It's a small part of what I call my Hangover Zens, which are certain very wise, very cool philosophies that come to me only when I'm drunk and which I then tell Topsy about with my eyes half shut. Or, more likely, the next morning when I'm replaying the events of the night before in my head and hiccuping violently as I recall something unspeakably dumb I've done. Anyway, so I'm usually lying in my bed groaning *ohnoohnoohno*, when a brilliant thought flashes through my brain. That's a Hangover Zen at its best. One of my favourite HZs, the one that helps keep those bubbles in my head from bursting on me is DO NOT EXPECT ANYTHING. Sure, it's hard to implement, but it's like a mantra you have to keep repeating in your head, over and above the loop of depressing thoughts that kick in as soon as you sense something good is about to happen. The key is to time it so that you begin with *Ooh I'm so excited* and skip immediately to *Don't expect anything*. It works, with time and practice. I haven't quite mastered it yet, but I'm so committed to perfecting it that, soon enough, I'm certain to become almost Buddha-esque.

Needless to say, this was exactly what I was doing as I rushed into the Defence Colony market on that Friday. I looked like shit, I knew. I was tired, I smelt of smoke and coffee, and my hair was in its final I-give-up stage. When did I get to being like this? I used to look so put-together in the past, with hair that was always brushed, eyes that always had kajal on, not strange raccoon markings from rubbing at them, and I used to smell *good*, all the time. Seriously. In college, I was one of Those Girls, the kind who carry kajal sticks and lip gloss and perfume in their bags. Oh, and a hairbrush. So if I had to meet anyone after college, all it took was a little pick-me-up in the bathroom and I was fresh 'n' fine. And this was bad even by my current standards, especially since Kabir was seeing me for the first time since the pool party, where I was all dressed up. Well, not all dressed up, because I hadn't bothered to shave my legs or my arms and it was just too hot and humid to get waxed, but it was dark then and chances are he hadn't noticed all that. I quickly checked my face in the rear-view mirror, pushing down the tufts of hair on top of my head which now looked like they were playing a football match.

We were meeting at one of the many cheap alcohol places in the market, frequented by broke college students and people who were having extramarital affairs. I loved that he had chosen it; it was my absolute favourite among the shady drinking joints in the city. As I rushed in, I saw Kabir sitting at a table looking intently at his cellphone as he punched in a text message. Oh, he looked so *good!* I felt a jolt of part-happiness-part-fear flash right through my heart: What if he had forgotten what I looked like? What if he were to regret meeting me at all? But when I reached him and he looked up at me and smiled, dimples flashing, and he stood up and leaned forward to kiss me on my cheek, his hand resting lightly on my shoulder, I was completely undone.

A few hours and three drinks later, he told me he thought I was amazing and that he was very, very attracted to me. I stammered a ditto, mentally congratulating myself on the success of my lately discovered HZ: How wonderful it is to not expect anything and how wonderful it is to get the very thing you were trying so hard not to expect.

6. in which i talk about summer and first times

SUMMER, FOR ME, HAS always proved to be the coming-of-age season. From being twelve and skinny and growing brand new breasts, to realizing my parents' marriage will not last forever, to being sixteen and knowing that people change, that friendship and loyalty and love are all subject to change, and in another couple of years, the discovery of the most momentous of all experiences—sex; it's always been about summer.

That summer, the summer that followed my eighteenth birthday, I was dating a boy called Amar, whom I sincerely believed I was in love with. I liked the way we looked together and I liked that he liked that we were a couple. He had access to a car, which was important, and normally our random groups of friends would congregate at his house before we went out somewhere. This was the summer after our board exams, right before we joined college, so we were free and footloose, not really worried about where life was taking us. I tried not to think about the fact that Amar had been accepted by a college in the UK, though we continued to get sentimental after a few drinks and proclaimed our love for each other and swore we would *never ever* lose touch.

Amar and I had been daringly progressing from making out to heavy making out, till it seemed like the room would explode from the intensity of our desires. I had had my hand down his pants, even if I hadn't *looked*, and he had learned about the spots on my body that made me moan (softly, because his grandmother was in the next room). Even on those sultry summer days we seemed to get the mirrors fogging up and we couldn't stop touching each other no matter where we were, even in public places. Even a gentle hand brush or a casual arm around the waist brought on delicious tingles at the thought of the secret hickeys hidden away on our bodies. I adore hickeys, love bites, really. I love the way they advertise, just like a pregnancy, that you've recently been wanted. I love the way you can look at them later, touch the raw red-slowly-turning-purple bruise, and feel all fluttery with the sudden gush of memory. Although, I wonder now, could you call them love bites if no love was involved?

We had, of course, planned the grand 'becoming adult' ceremony, both of us being virgins. We'd gigglingly bought condoms—Durex Super Thin, if memory serves. He'd looked at me and said, 'So, we're really going to do this?' I'd squeezed my eyes shut (the painful stories I'd heard from my girlfriends playing on and on in my mind) and said, 'Yes, we really are.'

I wish I could tell you it was beautiful and pleasurable, but it wasn't. The pain I felt (so much worse than the first time I'd used a tampon), his apprehension about hurting me, because though I tried to hide it, it showed on my face, and his discomfort mixed with his desire—not pretty. We almost stopped several times, but persevered nevertheless, and finally we were done, virgins no more. I rolled over, naked and sweaty, and lit my first postcoital cigarette, a tradition I didn't know then would become mine, with different men, in different beds. So even though my thighs hurt and I was sore in areas I didn't know existed in my body, I felt like quite the diva, straight out of Hollywood, talking to the man lying next to me in a slightly husky voice, blowing smoke rings into the air.

That evening we went for a walk to a hidden-away park in Amar's locality, free of ayahs and children and people out for their evening jogs. Amar bought some roasted chana from a vendor, and we sat on a bench there, not talking, not even looking at each other, just enjoying the moment. I wouldn't describe it as happiness; it was beyond happiness, the kind of feeling that makes your stomach clench and your eyes prickle. The kind of feeling that's so overwhelming it scares you. The kind of feeling you cannot express in words. My legs felt as though they would not hold me up any longer, and I knew I was glowing because I could see it reflected in his face. All I wanted at that moment was to be alone with him, sitting silently in that park forever.

Did I really love Amar? At that time, I thought I did. I'd had my share of teenage crushes and brief intimacies, but with Amar it was the flush of 'first love', hand-holding love, love that transcended 'relationship talks'. And it made that 'first time' all the more special. It stays with me as a happy, fulfilling, sepia-tinted memory, even more so because our break-up was amicable—in a saner, not-so-drunken moment we had realized that since he was leaving and we didn't know when we were going to see each other again there was no point in swearing undying love for each other. In so many ways that memory has made up for the boys afterwards: the ones who try to force things you don't want, the ones who expect you to do all the work, the ones—and these are the worst—who don't call you back after the first time you've slept with them.

Of course, as the time for him to leave came closer, the sex quickly lost its resonance. In fact, I had never enjoyed it that much. What I loved more than the act itself was the cuddling afterwards, and when my friends spoke of multiple orgasms I nodded wisely, pretending I had been there, done that. In reality, I was wildly jealous of them for being able to let go and *really* enjoy the sensation of having another person so close to you watching you lose control.

By last summer, though, I was pretty much done with most of my 'firsts'. The only 'first' last summer held for me was that it was the first time I felt jaded. I know, I know, twenty-five is hardly an age to be world-weary. But I didn't expect anything out of turning twenty-five, nothing at all. Suddenly my life had ceased to be a wonderful surprise and had instead become something that had to be endured.

Take my career, for instance. The first month I worked, I was so elated to see an actual pay cheque with my name on it that I went out and splurged on coffee for me and two friends. The very next month I was cribbing that I didn't earn enough. Within the next few months Shruti managed to take away all that I had once enjoyed about the job, which wasn't very much to begin with, except that I got to meet new people. That she took care of by moving me from meeting clients to pure media management, where I would be briefed by another colleague, Shruti's Golden Boy for the moment, Ankur, a tall guy with a grossly prominent Adam's apple and a lisp, and a way of sucking up to Shruti that the rest of us found nauseating.

Ankur was, in fact, getting married this summer. His parents had found him a girl, though I'd always suspected he was gay. I was the youngest employee in my office, unless you counted the two interns who'd joined fresh out of college and spent a lot of time on the balcony talking softly to each other. Everyone else was married, with kids and all, and I preferred to steer clear of them. Ankur was the closest to me in age, and the only other unmarried person in the office, but I just didn't like him. He had a high-pitched laugh, snuggled up to the other men, especially by the water cooler, and clapped his hands in a strange way when he was excited about something. He was popular with some of the journalists I met, especially the fashion reporters, who loved the way he was bitchy and cloying at the same time. But what really put me off was his annoying habit of referring to me as 'Baby' (as in, 'Everything all right, baby?') and putting his arm around me, which made me shudder inwardly. It was all I could do to restrain myself from kicking his teeth in.

Of course, since he was a colleague, and since Shruti the Horrible loved him so much, all of us had to contribute towards his wedding gift and ensure we attended the ceremony. For once Shruti got her huge butt moving and personally bought a rather humongous antique Ganesh which weighed a tonne and cost even more for Ankur and his soon-to-be bride. Not my idea of the perfect gift, but I didn't say much because everyone else was ooh-ing and aah-ing over Shruti's *wonderful* taste.

The wedding was in Pitampura, way out in northwest Delhi. Like most inhabitants of cities who get bound by the address they live in, I'm a complete 'south Delhi' person. None of my friends lived in west Delhi except for Michael and he came to this part of town pretty often, so I saw no need to venture further, north, east or west, unless I absolutely had to. Or unless it was to visit my mother. Not being very familiar with the area I was quite relieved when Dhiraj, one of the few co-workers I could actually stand, offered me a ride. He would be going with his wife and their two daughters and I had a distinct suspicion that I was being invited to accompany them so I could keep an eye on his kids. From what I'd heard from Dhiraj himself, they were holy terrors.

Dhiraj's wife, Mandy ('short for Mandira', she told me), was a lawyer, now mainly working on freelance assignments. There was some office gossip about the torrid love affair she and Dhiraj had had, how she came from a really, really rich family and her parents had all but disowned her for marrying Dhiraj, who was decent enough but not really up to their 'standard'. Another more malicious rumour was that she had been pregnant with their first daughter and so he had had to marry her. Whatever it was, you could still see some vestiges of glamour in Mandy, though now she looked faded and plump.

Their kids had matching names, Samara and Tamara, like many other siblings I know, though I always find it slightly odd when parents give their children matching names. Like Manav and Manavi. Or Tina and Rina. Or Dimple Kapadia's poor sister—Simple. And her daughter Twinkle. What are these people thinking, I wonder. And you can be sure their homes will be like that as well—matching coasters, matching cutesy figurines, matching cushions and sofa upholstery—even a Labrador with a matching coat and basket. Samara was three years older than Tamara, but they were dressed in identical purple ghagra-cholis, with purple hair bands holding back their hair. The minute I got into the back seat, they started to squabble over who would sit next to the other window. I tried to slip in without crushing my sari too much, ready to slap them if they sat on my pallu. I had taken great pains for over three-quarters of an hour to drape the damn thing properly and get both the pallu and the pleats to fall correctly.

'I was sitting there first!' said the older one.

'But I also want a turn,' whined Tamara.

'Mamma! Tell Tamara I was sitting here first!'

'Mamma! Didi's not giving me a chance!'

In the midst of this confusion, the Pepsi Tamara had been

clutching (why in the car, I wondered, on the way to a party?) upturned and spilt—of course—all over my sari. The two girls stopped fighting immediately and turned to watch the dirty stain spread over the pale blue silk.

'Two slaps I'll give you two,' yelled Mandy from the front seat. 'You should be ashamed! I can't take you anywhere!' She twisted around in the seat, reached over and whacked Samara hard on the arm. Samara started to wail, and Tamara did too, out of sympathy. My head hurt as I desperately dabbed at my sari with a piece of tissue paper.

'I'm sorry, Arshi,' said Mandy after she realized she couldn't hit both the kids with her seatbelt on. 'We'll find some soda there and I'll clean it up for you. And I'll give it to my drycleaner afterwards.'

'No, no, that's fine,' I said. 'I'll just hold my bag in front of me and hope no one notices . . .'

Mandy now turned to her husband. 'I told you not to bring both of them, no? I said leave them at home, they don't know how to behave, and did you listen? Now turn back, we'll drop them home.'

'But, Mandy,' protested Dhiraj. 'We're almost there, I can't drop them all the way back home.'

She seemed to accept this and was silent for a bit. Then she turned to the backseat again, 'If I hear one more choo out of you two, I'll slap you really hard, I swear. Samara, no more teasing your sister, it's because of you this has happened.'

I used two fingers to rub the aching spot between my eyebrows. Was it any wonder I felt jaded? I had not been able to hold on to a single relationship for a very long time; in fact, my longest relationship had been with Cheeto and *that* had only lasted ten months. Nothing seemed to have progressed with Kabir either, although we were friends now. *This* was obviously what my future held as well: screaming kids, a distant husband and a memory of once being hot. Either that, or dying alone and unloved. There seemed to be no happy middle path.

The gang from work mostly clung together right through the evening. Spouses, a few children, the men drinking Scotch or beer, the women feeding the children snacks and occasionally sipping their hideously coloured soft drinks which the waiters were carrying around, were spread across three adjoining tables. Shruti was the centre of attention at one table, making loud conversation. I got myself a Coke and made one last attempt to rub the stain out of my sari. No luck.

Ankur's younger sister, whom I had met at the office when she and Ankur had come by to drop off the wedding invitations, bustled by, her arms overflowing with marigold garlands. She represented another part of Delhi, the part I seldom interacted with, where tradition battled with modernity, where she could carry off a sari and jeans and tank top with equal panache, and where even though her hair was fashionably streaked and styled the purpose of it all was to land herself a wealthy man, from the same sub-caste and preferably based abroad. People like me kept a distance from these families, and they had little intention of doing otherwise. Their sons wouldn't marry me, a strange mongrel with blood from two parts of India and, worse, a 'modern' girl, who held no value for tradition or family ways. Their daughters saw no need to be friends with me either. What could I offer them? No future kitty parties, no company for jewellery shopping, no bitching about how hard it was to get a manicure appointment, and no older brother that they could have a love–arranged marriage with.

As the crowd moved towards the dais to watch the ceremony, I saw Mandy still struggling with her daughters. Tamara had Samara's hair band in her hand, and Mandy was doling out slaps and promises in equal measure while struggling to keep the two apart. I was feeling quite sympathetic (and also, yeah, I had no one else to hang out with), so I went over to her.

'Hey, want some help?'

She looked up, still frowning, and then painfully erased the frown as she saw me. 'Oh, hi Arshi. No, no, just . . . these kids are driving me mad. God knows where their father has gone.'

I spotted Dhiraj in the crowd and pointed him out to her. She waved to him. 'Samara, Tamara, go to Papa now. No more fighting, okay? No more fighting and I'll get you ice cream.'

Samara and Tamara looked at each other and sprinted off towards Dhiraj, startling him as they suddenly grabbed his hands.

Mandy sighed and turned to me, 'Did you manage to get the stain out of your sari?'

'No,' I said. 'But it's okay. I'll give it for drycleaning.'

She sighed again. 'Don't have kids.'

'They're cute, you know.' I pulled out a packet of cigarettes from my bag. 'And they'll grow up soon.'

She eyed me and my smoke hopefully and said softly, 'Would you mind if I bummed a cigarette off you?'

'Not at all.' I handed her the pack and watched as she lit up, inhaling deep.

'It's been forever,' she said, opening her eyes and smiling at me.

'I know. I can tell.'

'I stopped smoking before Samara was born and then started again. I couldn't help it. She was a sweet baby, but just so stressful. She's like that now also, always wants her own way.'

I laughed. 'She's so pretty. Both of them are.'

'Oh, my khandan is famous for that . . .' Then she noticed

me smiling and quickly added, 'No, no, I'm not being vain. My dadi had seven sisters and only two brothers. In their generation no one wanted girls, you know? And my great-grandfather just said he was happy to have so many girls because they were so beautiful they raised the izzat of the house. No dowry, nothing they had to give.'

'Wow. That's incredible.'

'You can't tell now, but I used to be very pretty too. People used to ask me on the road whether I wanted to be a model. I *was*, before I got married.' She rubbed furiously at a spot on her hand which grew red.

'Why did you give it up?' I asked. Funny, I'd never thought Mandy would be so open with me about her past. I was, after all, her husband's colleague, someone she had only met at the occasional cocktail party. But she spoke like someone who had been waiting a long time to be heard.

'I had to give it up. My father told me, "Beta, don't worry about marriage. Go abroad, see the world." But I met Dhiraj and I thought this was the life I wanted. My friends . . . now one is a CEO, one is a lawyer, and they're all looking for someone to marry. I tell them to enjoy their lives.'

'This isn't what you want any more?'

Just then Tamara came back to her mother, tears in her eyes, looking whiny and tired, and slipped into her lap, resting her head against Mandy's shoulder and slipping a thumb into her mouth. Mandy quickly extinguished the cigarette and put her arms around her daughter. Resting her chin on Tamara's head, she said, 'What happened, baby?'

The moment had gone, you could tell. She was absorbed in her daughter's voice, rubbing her little back and arranging the chairs so that she could put Tamara to sleep. She laid the child down, pressed a kiss on her forehead, ruffled her hair and stood up.

'Chalo, I must go find Dhiraj. It's late, the children are tired. We should go.'

I waited with Tamara for them to return. Samara clung to her father's arm as Mandy scooped up her sister, murmuring to her, and then we made our way through the crowd to say our goodbyes. I watched as Tamara was transferred from Mandy's arms to Dhiraj's before Mandy got into the car to drive us home, how Mandy rested her hand briefly on his arm and how they seemed to gain definition from each other through that simple gesture. Mandy, Dhiraj's wife; Dhiraj, Mandy's husband; together, parents of Samara and Tamara, making sure that at the end of the day they would be acknowledged for that, if nothing else. If they died tomorrow, one or both, they wouldn't be known as PR executive or one-time model with chance to travel the world, they'd be parents, married people, with a family they'd created themselves.

It made me kind of sad. If we are put on this planet with the aim of figuring out who we are, and the only way we can figure out who we are is through someone else—either the person we wind up with or the person we create—then what hope does my generation, my we-don't-need-nobody-dude generation, really have?

I said as much to Topsy when I got home. She was oiling her hair, something she does dutifully for herself, out of habit, leaving coconut oil fumes all over the house. I had objected to it so vociferously that she had switched to almond oil, or used olive oil sometimes. Once in a while she oiled my hair for me, like her mother used to for her, warming up the oil in a bowl and rub-rubbing at my scalp with strong fingers, turning each tendril of hair into a potentially flammable item. But most of the time I didn't have the patience or the energy to sit around waiting to have a hot bath at the end of the day, a warm towel wrapped around my head so the oil would seep into the roots. Back in Meerut, Topsy has a family masseuse: an old lady who comes bright and early on Sunday mornings. Each female member of the family past puberty is then pushed awake and made to strip down to functional cotton undies and sit in the sun, while the old woman does her thing. Babies are brought out, massaged thoroughly with oil and made to lie in the sun, the older women of the family use the time to gossip and oil each other's hair while they're at it, and the teenagers who are being massaged for the first time quickly forget their shyness in this communal nakedness.

'It's like a rite of passage,' Topsy told me once. 'Like the first time I got a malish. I was thirteen, I think, and had seen my older cousins and my mother going off every Sunday morning while we slept on. I had just returned from boarding school the previous day and I really wanted to sleep but my mother woke me up and took me to the terrace. I was a little shy, you know, sitting around in my chaddis in front of everyone, but it turned out no one was really paying attention. It was the first time I really sat with the adults, heard them talking about recipes and my cousin who was going to get married, and they actually asked my opinion on things. I felt so grown-up for, like, the first time in my life.' She sighed, stretching her body, 'And really, Arshi, a good massage is addictive. I wish I could get such good malish in Delhi.'

I sat down next to her, lit a cigarette and told her about my evening: if nothing else, Topsy retained one thing from her small-town roots—she loved to talk about weddings. When I told her what Mandy had said, though, she dismissed the story. 'Some people don't really know what they want, ever,' she said. 'I feel bad for them.'

'Oh, like *you* really know what you want.'

'I do, eventually.' She adjusted the steaming towel on her head and looked at me. 'I want to be a teacher and marry a good guy and have two children, one boy and one girl.'

'What about the other stuff, like the more important stuff? What about your goals and ideals and things like that?'

'These are my goals and ideals. I'm sorry if they're not as ambitious as yours, Arshi, but this is the way I was brought up.'

It dawned on me that as the weather got hotter, Topsy had become more prickly. She was still sweet tempered and funny and willing to socialize like she had been before, but over the summer she had grown edges that I had never noticed before. She became alternatively clingy and withdrawn, twisted her mouth and raised her eyebrows more often, and on many nights when I returned home she would silently open the door and then, just as silently, return to her room, clicking the door firmly shut behind her. Occasionally I'd try to talk to her, gently prod her to unburden herself, but her responses were either muted or too bright. Sometimes she'd shake her head at me and say, 'Nothing's the matter, I just want to be left alone'; at other times she'd laugh hysterically: 'Really, Arsh, stop stressing, it's probably PMS or something.' I left her alone, not just because I knew she'd come to me on her own if she needed to vent, but because I too wanted to be left alone.

Cheeto and I had been done for about four months and it was beginning to seem like everything—all the rituals Cheeto and I followed, the private jokes we shared—had happened to other people. I couldn't see myself doing those things any more: calling someone right before I went to sleep, making my plans according to his, worrying about a whole other set of people, like his friends or family, and then, just as instantly, not being bothered about anyone else at all. I had come to enjoy depending on no one but myself, and I had once again begun to believe in the sense of *possibility* each day held, the feeling as I got out of bed that today might be the day when something marvellous and magical will happen to me. Yet, while I sprayed perfume in my cleavage and flirted with many, many people, Saturday-Night Loneliness never really left me: You know, when it seems like everyone you know has a plan, an agenda, an arm to dangle from and you stick your chest out and wear aching heels and smile at random pretty boys who, even if they kiss you, aren't going to be there on Sunday morning when you wake up with a hangover.

I spilled my loneliness woes on to the Gmail compose page and got a stern reply from Deeksha: *Stop focussing on boys so much. Think about your career, spend some more time thinking of YOU for a change.* I didn't reread that email (though, often, when I'm bored I dredge out old mails and read them), because hmmph, what did she know? She had a hot French-Canadian boyfriend called Jean-Luc, whose *pictures* she had sent me as part of this same mail! If Jean-Luc had broken up with her, I can bet anything that Deeksha would send me long, sad notes telling me that nothing was okay. How easy it is for people who are in love to be complacent; how easy it is for them to forget what it feels like to not have anyone special.

Which brings me to Kabir, as it must, I suppose. Although Kabir and I had become what can be called 'good friends', it seemed distressingly as though we had tucked away the conversation in which he'd said he was attracted to me in some corner of a drawer, not to be addressed for a while. We regularly went out for coffee together, sometimes for drinks or dinner or a movie, and we'd never run out of topics to chat about. Although, because I mostly talked and he listened (yes, I did check on and off for the glazed look of disinterest and boredom, and, no, it wasn't there) he knew stuff about me that I had a tough time telling other people, even Topsy. When we entered a party together, people would look from him to me and back to him, assuming we were a couple and neither of us corrected the assumption. We would be shoulder to shoulder, having our own individual conversations, but every now and then, we would be compelled to exchange glances. It struck me that these looks were not of smouldering passion, but of two people who have been together a long time, the kind of look that said 'Let's go home', or 'I'm a little bored with this person I'm talking to', or 'If you drink any more of that, you won't be able to drive'.

Yet, he never tried to touch me, not once. Not even when I hopefully kicked off my shoes under the table and stretched out my legs so that if he wanted to play footsie my foot would be right there, ready and waiting and accessible. What did he *want* from me, I wondered. Were we to remain 'just friends'? Was it possible for a guy and girl to be in a platonic relationship, especially when they admitted they were attracted to each other?

One evening Esha and Akshay joined us for dinner and the conversation was very stilted, not like it normally was. Esha talked most of the time, Akshay and Kabir teased each other and me, but I was silent. I was terribly apprehensive that evening. It had been all very well meeting them earlier, but now I was meeting them with *Kabir*, and what if they sensed how very much I liked him? Or how every part of my body yearned for him? Maybe they'd make fun of me when I wasn't around, joshing Kabir about it, and he'd roll his eyes and say, 'No way, guys. I made the mistake of telling her that I was attracted to her once when I was really drunk, and now she's so annoying.' Oh, but that couldn't be. He called me almost as often as I called him, he made plans for coffee and dinner and parties . . . he *had* to want to be with me, right?

Kabir looked over at me several times during that evening.

Eventually, when Akshay had left for the bathroom and Esha was on the phone, he reached out and put his hand on my arm.

'Hey,' he said.

'Hi,' I whispered back.

'Are you okay? You've been really quiet.'

'I'm awkward around new people.'

'You've met them before.'

'Ya, but that was different.'

He didn't ask me how it was different, and I was grateful for that. He just smiled and squeezed my arm again, 'Relax, okay? Don't think so much about whether people like you or not.'

I looked at him, my eyes filled with love. It was like one of those evenings when you're out with someone and they've just said something that makes you either laugh really hard or look at them intensely and say, 'Me too.' And then you realize that at that moment you've fallen a little bit in love with them, even though you may not feel the same way the next morning. Then Esha returned from her phone conversation and, just to prove to him that I was okay, I started a loud energetic conversation with her about my college days and my professors.

At the end of the evening Akshay and I were getting along like old friends and Esha stored my number in her phone, telling me she would call me the next day and we'd all meet for coffee. And I turned to Kabir and saw a look of pride on his face and felt foolishly triumphant.

7. in which my best friend comes back to town

DEEKSHA'S MOTHER CALLED ME around the end of August. Deeksha was coming home, she told me; did I want to go to the airport to pick her up? 'Yes!' I squealed into the phone. What a cow! I had got a mail from her barely a week ago and there had been no mention of her returning to India at all that year!

Deeksha and I became friends in Class 8, when she had just moved to Delhi from Jakarta. Her father was an ad film producer who frequently did stints abroad. Deeksha herself had been born in Paris and knew about six languages, including French. All this made her very foreign and very alien to the rest of the kids in school. She said 'off-ten' for 'often' and knew very little Hindi, which made everyone giggle and pass snide remarks around her in Hindi class. The teacher, who was a complete bully, made it considerably worse by habitually mocking the students who didn't know the language, while her pets smirked from the front row.

It would have been all right if Deeksha had acted all cool and standoffish and shown off her fancy pencil box and strawberry-scented eraser and put everyone in their place, but she was just too eager to please, doling out foreign chocolates and inviting everyone to a large party at her house within the first few months of being in school. The kids ate the chocolates, laughed at her strange accent and didn't go for the party. I'm a little ashamed to say I didn't either, but I felt sorry for her, sitting in class during lunch break, eating ham sandwiches with trimmed crusts, her smile a little broken. So one day when it was raining and we were all indoors during the break, I sat next to her and we got talking. She was quite plump at the time, with a wide face and large, slanting eyes. I was intrigued by her stories. She had been to so many places, seen so much of the world, and she could translate the French passages in *Jane Eyre*, which I was reading then, with such ease. She giggled when I exclaimed about this, biting the corner of her lip and covering her mouth with her hand.

In Class 9 our sections were shuffled and I wound up in the section that didn't have most of my friends, but had Deeksha in it. We decided to share a desk. She let me use her fancy stationery, told me about London and Paris and New York and Jakarta, and, in return, I invited her home for lunch and for my birthday party and made sure my friends spoke to her. Soon they became her friends too. In fact, by the end of it, she had many more friends than I did because she was infinitely more charming. But it was the time that the two of us spent alone that I remember the most, sprawled on the bed or on the floor in her room or mine, reading quietly, or listening to music on my ancient cassette player or her dad's fancy CD player, which we weren't allowed to touch but played anyway when he wasn't home.

Her parents, older brother and younger sister considered me part of the family. I would land up at their place very often for dinner when I was in college, and talk to her sister about school, her brother about politics and her parents about my life. I guess it's because my own family is so tiny that I love large families, especially the feeling of *belonging* to one, teasing each other at the breakfast table and being in on the private jokes and everyone just, you know, looking out for each other. It's incredible, it really is. Topsy's family is large too, like I've mentioned before, but it's a different sort—less like a private party and more like one of those Hindi soaps. Still fun, though.

After Class 12, Deeksha went off to the US for college and has never really been back to Delhi since. Oh sure, she's come, her accent more pronounced than ever, for flying visits over a week, but since her family prefers to spend summer abroad, she usually joins them wherever they are.

On the way to the airport in the middle of the night, I thought about us, Deeksha and me, the incredible connection we had, the sort I've rarely found with friends I've made after, and how inseparable we used to be at one point. I had cried so hard the night she left for the US that I almost made myself sick. Leaning over the pot in her fancy bathroom, I had rested my head for a second against the tiles and wondered if anyone would ever know me the way Deeksha did. I love my new friends dearly, but it's comforting to be around people who already know your stories, who can cut through the bullshit and tell you exactly what they think of you, who know when you've made a mistake and love you just the same.

Deeksha's brother, Saurabh, was driving, with their younger sister, Devyani, beside him, while I sat in the back seat.

'I'm so looking forward to Deeksha coming home,' said Devyani, hugging herself with pleasure. 'It seems like so long since we've seen her.'

I leaned forward to hug her. Devyani was all of nineteen now, in her first year of college, and I remembered how she used to follow Deeksha and me around everywhere till Deeksha got really annoyed and threatened to slap her. I had once asked Deeksha whether the three of them had been adopted, because they looked so unlike each other. Saurabh was tall and gangly, with a wide mouth and eyes set close together, and the only one of the three who wore spectacles. Deeksha was fair and plump, had very straight hair and slanting eyes, though she lost her puppy fat and actually became quite curvy by the end of Class 10. Devyani, I realized, was rapidly turning into the beauty of the family, tall and delicate with perfect features, almost model-like. Deeksha had shut me up and claimed she and Saurabh looked like their father's side of the family, while Devyani resembled their mother, but you had to be from the family to spot the likeness, I suppose.

We pulled up at the international terminal, parked and waited, wilting outside in the sultry heat. Sundown had not affected the temperature by even a degree; there was absolutely no breeze and the air was stifling and oppressive. We watched the glass doors slide open for the foreign-returned travellers to exit, their noses wrinkling instinctively, their mouths already gasping at the moist, stuffy air. Uniformed chauffeurs stood in a huddle holding up placards with names written on them in large letters, and there were touts and beggars and taxi drivers, some smoking desultorily, others taking a nap inside their vehicles. As the crowd started to pour out, I saw families returning home from foreign holidays rushing to hug the people who had come to receive them; couples, obviously back from their honeymoon, looking shy or cosy; lots of foreigners, mostly backpackers, who looked around alert with interest at the sights and sounds that were so obviously new to them. 'We're in Injah!' I heard a small boy exclaim as he jumped into the air, his arms raised. His parents looked less thrilled, though, as they ushered him into a taxi.

Saurabh and I stepped out for a smoke, sharing a cigarette, as Devyani balanced herself on the divider, rocking back and forth, her eyes scanning the faces of the arriving travellers. Saurabh and I have always had a strange relationship. We've never been close, really. He's four years older than us and, at twenty-nine, believes he Sees All and Knows All. But if I think about it he was like this even at seventeen, when I first met him. My most abiding memory of him is listening to Pink Floyd for the first time in his room, which was lit by a single lamp, the red lampshade casting a strange light on the walls.

Deeksha and I had been listening to Madonna, singing along to *Papa don't preach* and acting out the music video. We were taking turns at being Madonna, firmly lip-synching 'But I made up my mind, I'm keeping my baby.' This time I was Madonna and Deeksha was the father of the baby, and she waggled her finger at me which I thought was hysterical. We were cracking up when Saurabh came in and said, 'Don't you guys have anything better to listen to than that junk?' Deeksha shrugged and so did I and he sighed and asked us to come into his room. He played *Comfortably numb* and *The wall* and since our musical taste at this time was Boyz II Men and Ace of Base with Bon Jovi tossed in when we felt daring, we didn't quite know what to make of it. After one side of the cassette had played, Saurabh looked at us and asked us how we'd liked it. 'It's . . . nice,' offered Deeksha, and I nodded. He beamed. 'It's incredible how everyone gets Floyd, generation to generation. When you're a little older, you'll understand what they really mean.' We made a rapid exit, a little thrilled that Deeksha's normally very aloof brother had spent so much time with us, but when we got back to Deeksha's room we put on Madonna again and tried on some new clothes Deeksha had bought.

Saurabh was currently teaching at Delhi University, a trainee lecturer straight out of JNU and all the girls in the first year had a big crush on him. I could imagine him as a teacher, looking excited about Chaucer and running his hand through his beard when he was trying to make a point. Devyani had been teasing him relentlessly about it, and I giggled as he protested.

'Look, there she is!' cried Devyani, and I quickly flicked away the cigarette and stepped on it. Deeksha didn't approve of smoking, though we had once smoked a surreptitious joint in her bathroom, crushing the 'right amount' of hash ('the size of the Nokia switch-off button' as one of her friends from her colony had directed) with tobacco and filling it back into the cigarette we'd emptied with great difficulty. Of course, we got very stoned and thirsty and hungry, and polished off two large chunks of Brie and quite a few packs of Maggi which we cooked ourselves. Her mom caught us binging and proceeded to give us a stern lecture about how she had bought the groceries just yesterday and would now have to go to the store that stocked imported cheese again and if Deeksha and I had wanted to eat cheese we should have stuck to the Britannia cubes since we didn't know the difference anyway. In our stoned state Deeksha and I thought the word 'Britannia' was the funniest thing we'd heard, and all the while her mom was talking to us, one of us would say 'Britannia' and the other would say (eyes round, mouth wide), 'That is *such* a great word' and we'd fall over each other, laughing. I think her mother caught on, though, because she abruptly stopped talking and said, 'Deeksha, Arshi, I'm really disappointed in you two.' 'Why, mom?' asked Deeksha, trying to look like the picture of innocence in between snorts of laughter and, of course, this made me laugh even more, until finally we got a hold on ourselves and went to her room where we spent the evening yelling 'Britannia!' at sporadic intervals.

Deeksha was walking steadily towards us, and there beside

her, talking to her, was the Jean-Luc of her photographs. When she spotted us, Deeksha broke into a run and threw her arms around Saurabh first, letting him lift her up and spin her around, while Devyani tugged impatiently at their clothes. Then she turned to Devyani and gave her a massive hug. I hung back, a little shy of intruding into family time and also feeling strangely apprehensive about meeting her after so long. What if Deeksha had changed, what if our relationship had changed, what if she was completely different, and why had *no one* said *anything* about Jean-Luc coming with her?

Jean-Luc was, by the way, phenomenally hot. In the snaps Deeksha had sent me, his eyes were always squinted against the sun. In one of them, obviously taken inside her flat or his, he looked like he had just woken up. His face was puffy, his eyes half-closed with sleep, but he was smiling as he stretched out his hand towards the photographer. In person he was tall and black-haired and green-eyed, with the slightest stubble on his squarish jaw. I felt conscious of my slightly faded T-shirt and car-whipped hair and instinctively crossed my arms over my chest. Deeksha, who had seen me by now, came over to me, her eyes brimming with joy. We kissed each other and she slipped her arms around my shoulders and pulled me into a hug. We rocked for a while, and a wave of relief swept over me because I immediately knew that things were pretty much the same after all.

'Oh, I have to introduce you guys,' she said, wiping away the tears from her eyes. She had always been the 'Little Miss Crybaby' of the family. Anything could set her off—sad movies, happy movies, books, a loving statement, a back rub. I smiled at the memory as Deeksha strode over to Jean-Luc. 'Guys, this is Jean. Jean, this is my brother, Saurabh, my baby sister, Devyani, and my best friend in the whole world, Arshi.'

Jean stepped forward, smiling. 'It's so nice to finally meet all of you. Even though I feel like I know you already because Dee tells me so many stories.' Saurabh shook his hand, Devyani and I grinned widely, already a little bit in love.

'Gosh, it's so good to be back in Delhi,' said Deeksha, casting a happy look at the touts who edged closer to us with hopeful glances. 'Jean, sweetie, this is the city I grew up in.'

I noticed Jean's nostrils gradually wrinkling upwards and his grey T-shirt already had a patch of sweat on it. Delectable, really, the way it clung to his body. 'You'll get used to the heat,' I told him. 'Everybody does.'

'Wow. I never expected it to be so, so . . . clammy,' he said, giving me a wry smile.

Deeksha rubbed his back affectionately, 'I warned you it was going to be really hot.'

'Let's get to the car,' said Saurabh. 'You guys must be exhausted.'

Deeksha and Jean exchanged looks. 'We're tired, yes, but really excited. Do you think we could stop at the Marriott or some place and get some coffee before we go home?'

'Ooh, yes, let's do that,' squealed Devyani. I didn't blame her. There was this feeling of celebration in the air, of happy anticipation. I must confess, however, that I did feel slightly envious. Suddenly, I wanted to be the one returning home with news, to look and feel different and gaze with fond eyes around my home city.

Deeksha linked her arm through mine as we started walking towards the car and gave me another kiss on my forehead. 'It's so good to see you, Arsh. I told Saurabh, when I called home to tell them I was coming, to get you to the airport.' Her eyes shot sideways, where Saurabh and Jean were having a conversation, both lugging suitcases. 'He is nice, isn't he?'

'He seems amazing,' I said. 'And really cute! But how come he came with you?"

'I'll tell you later,' she said with a mysterious smile as we reached the car. Deeksha sat in front with Saurabh and chose a radio station on the system and soon the car filled with the rhythmic beats of *Kajra re*. Deeksha swayed and clapped and did some bhangra moves with her shoulders and hands. Then she twisted around to look at us and said, 'God, how I've missed this music.'

'The language sounds really difficult to understand,' said Jean.

'Oh no, it's very simple. I'll teach you while you're here.' I snorted, remembering how terrible her Hindi used to be.

'What?' she said, turning to me and swatting at my arm, 'Shut up! My Hindi's great now.'

'I'll help!' said Devyani, giving Jean-Luc a toothy smile.

'That would be very nice,' said Jean, resting a hand on top of her head.

Devyani looked like she would burst with delight and I couldn't help giggling. Deeksha said archly, 'I come from a family of hotties, my dear, but remember which Sharma you love,' and everybody laughed out loud as Devyani crossed her eyes and stuck out her tongue at her sister.

At the Marriott, Deeksha hurriedly ran her fingers through her hair as she got out of the car. 'I really need the loo. Arshi, come with me?'

Once in the bathroom, she washed her face and brushed the tangles out of her hair, letting it fall over her shoulders. 'God, I look a mess.'

'No, you look lovely,' I said, noticing for the first time under the bright lights how her skin had completely cleared up, her eyes were shiny and liquid and, perhaps because she was so happy to be home, little sparks seemed to burst off her skin and fill the air.

By the time we returned to the coffee shop Saurabh had ordered a round of cold coffee, which Jean was cautiously sipping. Saurabh lit a cigarette and I looked apprehensively at Deeksha as I reached inside my bag for my own, but I needn't have bothered. Deeksha had pushed her chair back and was leaning forward, her eyes sparkling. 'I have something to tell you all,' she said.

'You're getting married,' Saurabh countered flatly.

'*Yes!* Yes, I am! How'd you know?' Deeksha's smile stretched all the way across her face now, but she had caught the tone of her brother's voice and her eyes looked hopeful. I was dying to say a million things at once, but I figured I'd think this over first. Plus, Deeksha looked a little bit like she used to look in school before she made any friends, her smile on the verge of being broken. It's funny how our pasts confront us in so many different ways. I crossed my fingers underneath the table. Please don't screw this up for her, I told Saurabh silently.

'Well, because it's fucking obvious. You show up with your boyfriend, unexpectedly, what else could it mean?'

I could see Deeksha's jaw clenching but she managed to say, quite calmly, 'Since we both chose Indian companies for our internship and will be here for four months, we thought we'd get married while we're here.'

'That's fantastic!' said Devyani, jumping out of her chair to hug Deeksha who patted her distractedly on the arm. She was still looking at Saurabh. 'You could at least be happy for me,' she finally said, her lower lip quivering.

'Why *should* I be happy for you? You're twenty-five, you're in the middle of a degree, the first guy you meet you decide to marry? Grow up, for fuck's sake.'

Deeksha was crying by now and wiping away the tears with the back of her hand. Jean put his arm around her and I reached over and squeezed her knee. Saurabh puffed resolutely at his cigarette and looked away defensively.

'I think it's fantastic that you're getting married,' Devyani said again. Deeksha gave her a watery smile. 'Me too,' I said, though I wasn't really sure that Saurabh didn't have a point.

Deeksha glared at Saurabh, 'You're *always* like this. I'm sure Mummy and Daddy will be very pleased.'

'I'm sure,' he said, taking a final drag and signalling for the cheque.

The drive back was very quiet. They dropped me home and I leaned over to hug Deeksha goodbye. 'It'll be okay,' I whispered. 'Call me tomorrow.'

'I will,' she said. 'Love you.'

'Me too.'

As they drove away I suddenly felt I had been thrust into adulthood by default. Why, oh why, did everything have to change?

8. in which i go to kabir's house

IT'S FUNNY HOW SO many things in my life function like the computer, and yet the functions that would actually be of any use to me are clearly missing. There's no Edit/Undo so I can take back all the things I should never have said or done, nor the Control-C/Control-V that would copy-paste the best times of my life again and again and again. No Control-X to take out times that I wish had happened in another life, or to another me under totally different circumstances. No Back-up folder for my drunken moments to be stored in so when I'm groaning the next morning at the excruciating pain in my head I don't have to whine, 'Umm, what happened *after* I had those three tequila shots?' Instead, there is the perpetual recurrence of the 404 error. For instance, I'll be trying and trying to get someone to hit on me or to at least respond to the attention I'm giving them, but no, I'll get a 'Page Not Found' or a 'This server is down, please try again later'. Then there are all the 'Shut Down' messages. And it's not a gentle Windows reminder that says 'Your computer is shutting down, please close all windows', but a loud siren that shrieks 'ABORT! ABORT! ABORT!' and proceeds to do exactly that while I'm gasping out a 'Wha-huh?'

The time had come, as you might have guessed, when I needed a seriously effective computer function to give the Kabir part of my life a slight nudge.

Kabir came over to our place a lot. I suppose it was reasonable, given that I lived alone and he didn't, and that we, Topsy and I, had a large stock of alcohol in the house, thanks to Fardeen's frequent flying and getting us stuff at duty free. He wasn't senior enough to do the international rounds yet but he had friends who had friends, which ensured a constant supply. The alcohol came to good use, too, because Topsy's the best bartender ever. She has a natural feel for what goes with what. 'I only make drinks for people I love,' she told me once. 'Otherwise they don't turn out right.'

Usually, when we had people over, we just sort of put all the bottles on display and let people help themselves; often, people brought their own stuff, and just drank from that bottle. But sometimes, when Topsy would be talking to someone, listening to how he or she had had a fight with someone, or how excited they were about a new job, she'd suddenly look at them all wide-eyed and say, 'What're you drinking?' Then she would reach out for their glass and, even if they protested saying they didn't want to drink anything other than what they'd served themselves, she would pour the drink down the sink and make them something new and exotic. One summer, she served mango panna with gin, pre-mixing it and sticking the bottle in the freezer, so when people came, she served them about three inches of it, topped with crushed ice, and they loved it. The next time we were invited to another party with the same crowd they asked us to bring along some more, but Topsy substituted the panna with Rooh Afza and poured the cocktail into ice trays. In the evening, right before we left, we popped the cubes into an ice bucket, made Fardeen drive madly so they wouldn't melt and, once we got there, Topsy asked for a blender, crushed the flavoured ice and served it in short, fat glasses on a bed of mint leaves and lemon slices. It was gone in less than half an hour, all of it.

But those were party drinks. Topsy concocted stuff for just the two of us, too. Last winter, she made hot rum toddy almost every night, stirring Old Monk with hot water, honey, lemon and a tablespoon of milk over the stove, till the whole house smelt warm and safe, and when I got home, she'd pour me a glass, right before dinner and sometimes before we went to bed. It made for quite an alcoholic winter. Later, when I broke my toe, she plied me with 'cast shots'—lots of tequila with nimbu-paani and rock salt and just the tiniest bit of sugar. She lined them up on the bed at the Farmhouse, and we took turns downing alternate glasses till I had to go pee. Of course, since I couldn't stand straight, she practically had to drag me there to keep the cast off the floor, almost collapsing under the weight.

Kabir was not into cocktails like we were, nor into beer or vodka, which we stocked in plenty. Whisky was his drink of choice, and the very first day he visited he brought over a bottle of Teacher's, which he said we should keep just for him. Topsy loved him, almost as much as I did, and we developed a grand ritual of packing up the bottle and putting it away in our linen drawer after he left. Occasionally, if Kabir hadn't been over in a while, I'd tell Topsy sadly, 'The whisky bottle's still full' and she'd say, 'It'll be empty soon.' It became like a code between us, so if he was coming over and she wasn't home I'd send her a text saying, 'Whisky's finishing,' and she'd reply, 'I hope it's not going to finish tonight.'

It struck me as slightly odd, however, that though he was over so often, Kabir hadn't once asked me to go to his place. It's never a good sign when a guy doesn't ask you to his place or to hang out with his friends. It could mean: (a) he's embarrassed to be seen with you in public; (b) he doesn't see you fitting into his comfort zones; or (c) both of the above. This was not looking good.

I asked him about it one day, pulling nervously at my lower lip. 'Kabir? How come we never go to your place and hang out?'

He was hunched into the fridge looking for ice for his refill, and looked around in surprise, 'I never thought about it. Your house is so great, I like hanging out here.'

'Yes, but it seems weird that you've never asked me over.' My voice began to sound whiny and I stopped.

'We'll hang out there next time. Okay?' He smiled his gorgeous smile. 'You should've said something before.'

'I didn't think about it before.'

He leaned over and ruffled my hair and, in a voice that was full of affection, said, 'Come over on Friday. Have dinner at my place.'

'Yay! Okay, for sure. Don't ditch, all right?'

Kabir had a terrible habit of making plans, promising to come over, only to call at the last moment and tell me he was busy and couldn't make it, leaving me fancy-underweared and cleavage-perfumed and miserable. Each time I'd tell myself that the next time I'd definitely tell him to fuck off and that he should never take anyone for granted the way he did me, but he'd just have to call and say 'Don't be mad at me' or make another plan for me to melt back into a little puddle of longing. I wanted to own him, to possess him, to carve my name on his stomach with my tongue, but more than that I wanted him to want to own me. I knew it was crazy and unlike myself and, more importantly, it was ridiculous, because he hadn't even *kissed* me yet. I wondered if he was playing girl games with me:

You know, when someone wants you and even though you're just as attracted to them you keep them dangling, send them subtle and not-so-subtle signals, sometimes of love, sometimes of indifference, while you laugh crazily inside your head.

But by the time Friday came along I was feeling more positive. Platonic friendship, here I come! Who said a guy and a girl couldn't be 'just friends'? Sure we could. I was an empowered woman after all, and I didn't have to make out with every guy I met. Plus, Kabir was a great friend and would probably suck at being a boyfriend. So even though I put on sexy underwear, I didn't wear a thong, and I chose an average work T-shirt instead of a strappy top. I was so okay with this.

I didn't know very much about Kabir's family except that, like me, he was an only child and his family had to be rich because they lived in Jor Bagh. Jor Bagh is a beautiful, planned residential area almost in the heart of the city, inhabited mostly by the old moneyed families of Delhi, expats and foreign diplomats from the various embassies. It's very green and very quiet, and the only activity that takes place is in the evening when the ayahs come out to walk children and dogs and gossip to each other. Since I seldom visit the area except for a rare stop at the two shops in the market that store imported foodstuff like pork and cheese, I got a little lost finding Kabir's house till I finally spotted his battered green Gypsy parked outside a formidably barred gate.

Kabir had told me once—and that was probably the only time he ever mentioned his family—that his dad was a 'cold, uncaring bastard' and that his distance from his father was his flighty mother's fault. 'As soon as I was old enough they packed me off to boarding school,' he told me, rolling the remnants of his whisky in his glass. 'Not that I'm complaining. The sadness in that house was beginning to kill me. They're really the Ice King and the Ice Queen of the world.'

'Does that make you an Ice Prince?' I'd asked, smiling a little to lighten the conversation.

He'd smiled back, a weird crooked smile I hadn't seen before. 'I am, actually, come to think of it.'

I parked my car outside the gate, feeling very self-conscious about how shabby it was, and walked up to the guard. He was wearing a uniform—a striped shirt, with blue trousers and a grey beret. I had never known anyone before with a uniformed guard for their house. He looked at me doubtfully, checked on the intercom with someone inside if I was expected and waved me in. In the driveway I noticed a shiny black Mercedes and a shinier blue Chevrolet Forrester parked one behind the other.

I concluded the uniform was a running theme in Kabir's grand mansion when I saw the maid, who held open the door for me, dressed in uniform as well, a striped salwar-kameez with a blue dupatta running diagonally across. She looked uncomfortable and sweaty. I was beginning to feel very underdressed, especially when I saw our reflection in the glass doors of the living room, where she paused and then changed her mind and ushered me into a little room beside it. It was very tastefully done up, with low coffee tables, a piano and some really striking art work on the walls. You know, the kind of contemporary stuff you can pick up only in New York or London or some European country. I sat stiffly on the plush couch placed along one wall as the maid asked me whether I wanted 'Coke, Di-yat Coke, nimbu-paani, cuppoochino.' I opted for Coke and asked her where Kabir was. 'He'll just be down,' she said in Hindi, and exited rapidly.

I drummed my fingers on the table, flicked through a coffee-table book on dogs and accepted the chilled glass of Coke the maid brought me. I searched desperately for a coaster but there was none in sight. Finally, I set the glass on my knee, but the air conditioner was set on max and the glass was so cold I could feel myself getting frostbite. I should just go, I thought, this was a really bad idea. But here was Kabir now at the door, wearing shorts and a ratty old T-shirt, bless him. A Basset Hound stood next to him, watching me through dark eyes. 'Hi!' he said. 'Sorry for keeping you waiting, I was just tweaking some pictures for a client.'

'That's okay,' I said, smiling as I stood up and put the glass down, still coaster-less, on the table.

The dog bounded over to me and started to sniff at my jeans.

'This is Sasha,' said Kabir. 'She's my babe, aren't you, aren't you?' He bent down to scratch her head as she wagged her tail madly and gazed at him with adoring eyes. He was different in this house, I noticed. His voice was different, more brittle, and he looked more self-assured—but colder, like the Ice Prince was taking over. I shivered a little and he said anxiously, 'It's cold in here, isn't it? Let's go to my room, it's much cosier. And I want you to see my studio as well.' The Kabir I knew was back and I felt much better.

His room was all the way on the top floor. 'Not really a floor,' he explained as we walked up the stairs. 'More like a mezzanine, the wrong way round. Or an attic.'

Three flights of stairs up, we got to a huge, industrial-looking steel door with a 'Do Not Disturb' sign hanging officiously on the doorknob. 'My parents hate it,' he told me. 'It clashes with the rest of the house, but I fought for about a year till they gave it to me as a birthday present.' He held the door open and said, 'Ta-dah!' Sasha bounded in, panting heavily, and started to lap water from a bowl on the floor in the far corner of the room.

The room was gorgeous, done up in dusky blues and

greens, and a maroon carpet that stretched from wall to wall. There was a skylight, now open, on the wall above the bed which probably let in natural light quite beautifully during the day. Right now the sky was a little cloudy, probably just smog, and the dull glare of a street light was visible through the leafy branches outside. One wall was covered with three sagging bookshelves and a simple niche had been created in the corner for a fancy computer to which was attached a bulky professional-looking camera. Lenses of various sizes, cleaning material and batteries lay strewn around the computer. A plasma TV was placed in the opposite corner and on the wall next to it were three large framed photographs of a girl, reclining on Kabir's bed, with her arms behind her head, laughing. 'Who's that?' I asked, pointing, though I could easily guess.

'That's my ex,' said Kabir. 'She photographed well. Hey, I think you would too.'

'Are you kidding? I look horrible in pictures!'

'Not if they're taken by the right photographer.' He was already by his computer, unplugging the mammoth camera and adjusting the lens.

'Oh, ya? And how do you know you're the right photographer?'

'I just do.' He aimed the lens at me and looked up, grinning, 'Don't worry, this won't hurt.'

'I'm not scared,' I said, but crossed my arms over my chest.

'Don't look at me, okay? Go over and look at my books . . . you know you want to.'

I rolled my eyes at him and went over to his bookshelf, very aware of his body, half leaning, poised to start clicking, his eyes already arranging me against the furniture so he could shoot. I ran my eyes over his books. All the Salingers, nice; some books on photography, e.e. cummings, *Zen and the Art of Motorcycle*

Maintenance, hmmm; a phenomenal collection of Calvin and Hobbes, ooh, very good. My expressions must have changed while I browsed, because I heard him discreetly clicking away. And when Sasha came up to me, bumping her head against my legs, tongue hanging out, and then collapsing at my feet with a sigh, and I reached down to scratch her head, Kabir bent too, like he was anticipating my movements, and captured a shot just as I looked up and shook my head at him.

I moved from his bookshelf to his bed, leaning over to look at the spectacles on his bedside table. 'I didn't know you wore specs,' I said.

'You never asked.' There was a smile in his voice as he shot me, deliberately posing now, sprawled across his bed looking through the skylight, then bending over to take off my shoes. No one had told me how sensual this was! My movements had automatically become slow and deliberate, even when I ran my hand across my neck and over my hair to smooth it down. I can tell you without the slightest hesitation that there's nothing as incredible and as erotic as posing for someone you have the hots for, who has made you the subject of his art. *This* was why Kate Winslet had slept with Leonardo DiCaprio in *Titanic*.

Abruptly, he put his camera down, and I felt faintly disappointed because I had just about got into it. He reached out for my hand so I could sit up. 'Before I had my digital, I used to work with a manual Nikon,' he said, looking at me so earnestly I knew this was important. I quickly erased all dirty thoughts from my head and sat up. 'I still use it sometimes, though not often. Anyway, back then I'd made myself a dark room to process the negatives and it's still pretty cool. It's my most favourite place in the world. Any time I'm feeling stressed, or upset, that's where I go to hang out.'

'I'd love to see it,' I said, knowing this was the right thing to say.

'It's up on the terrace, but getting there is a bit of a pain.'

'How much of a pain?'

'Well . . .' His eyebrows danced at me, the funny scar in the middle of one moving up and down. I loved that scar, it made his perfect face somehow flawed, and very sexy. 'There's the boring way, which is going down and getting the keys from the watchman.'

'And what's the interesting way?' I made my eyebrows dance too, and he laughed.

He threw open the window and said, 'Climb on to this ledge and pull yourself up to the terrace parapet. I've done it lots of times, it's part of the deal.'

I stuck my head out of the window and looked down, 'Oh no. No way. I'm scared of heights.'

'I'll give you a leg-up. And I promise you won't fall.'

'How do you know I won't fall?' I asked, but I was already climbing on to the ledge, feeling quite thrilled at this adventure.

'Trust me, okay?'

I avoided looking down, like Kabir had told me, and placed my hands on the cement parapet above me. The cement was old and crumbly and scraped against my palms. 'I don't think I can do this!' I said through clenched teeth, turning towards Kabir.

'Here, put your foot on my palm . . . there you go, got a good grip? Aaannd, there!'

I hoisted myself on to the terrace and did a little victory dance, 'I did it! I did it!'

He pulled himself up easily, resting his weight on his forearms and swinging his body up so his knee met the railing and he straddled it. 'You mean *we* did it,' he said, blowing the cement off his palms.

'Right, okay.' I stuck my tongue out at him. 'Now where's this meditation room of yours?'

He took my hand, easily and surely, linking his fingers in mine instead of just clasping palms, and walked me towards a ramshackle cement structure on the roof, next to where clothes were drying on a line.

'Hang on, it might be a little dark in here.' He reached up to the low ceiling to pull at a wire and a single red bulb lit up inside. There were rows of wires pegged from one wall to the other, lines to hang developing pictures on and below them a wooden bench with empty trays on it. On a low stool by the door was a battered register and next to it Kabir's guitar, which I noticed like an old acquaintance you raise your palm up to greet with a 'Where have you been?'

'These are some photos I took ages back,' said Kabir, pointing to the ones hanging on the line. 'We were at a family reunion in Jaipur, and my digicam ran out of battery.'

I looked at them closely, curious to see what his family looked like, but there was only one shot with people in it, the rest were all of monuments. Even the one 'family' shot had them all standing against the sun so that their faces and bodies were dark, almost black, and behind them the massive stairs to the palace were prominently in focus.

'Did you do that on purpose?' I asked.

He nodded. 'Obviously. They were all like, "Kabir, take a picture, take a picture, no? You're the family photographer" and I got annoyed. I quite like it, actually.'

'So do I.'

There was silence after that; an awkward silence, I thought. I looked at the photographs again, trying to think of something to say so he wouldn't think it was a mistake bringing me here. This was obviously a big deal for him. Suddenly I felt like I knew him more and, absurdly, I wanted to hold him and comfort him. Did he play his misunderstood card on purpose, I wondered, just so someone like me, who thrived on that sort of thing, would want to mother him and yet always understand that when he pulled away it wasn't his fault?

'I'm glad we're friends,' I said, trying to fill the silence.

He raised his eyebrows again. '*Are* we friends?'

'Yes, of course we're friends. I mean, we hang out, we talk about ourselves with each other, that's what friendship is, right? Right?'

Without any warning he reached across, grabbed my face and kissed me.

We didn't talk much after that. I sat on his lap, and he played his guitar, just for me. We shared a cigarette and blew smoke into each other's mouths. It grew really warm inside the shed, and our palms were sweatily entwined, my fingers occasionally caressing his lines, his life line, fate line, his heart line, which I stroked with my thumb, feeling its slant across his hand, the bumps on his palm. Kabir ran his fingers through my hair, along my earlobes and the corners of my smiling mouth, and after I whispered in his ear that I couldn't believe we had just kissed, he reached out over and over again to kiss me, till my heart throbbed against his chest and my jeans were damp where I'd crossed my legs.

As I'd suspected, Kabir was a good kisser. He was sure of himself, his mouth was soft, his lips firm yet tender and teasing as he nibbled on my lower lip and, best of all, his tongue didn't dart around inside my mouth, nor play a battling match with mine, nor even plunge right in, towards my tonsils. Once, tentatively, his hand moved from my shoulder towards my breast, but I stiffened and he asked, 'No?' I shook my head and he stopped.

At some point we floated back to his room for dinner. I couldn't eat; how could I, when butterflies were romping around in my stomach and I felt little bubbles of joy drifting through my veins? There was another thing. Kabir was the first guy I'd been with since Cheeto, and it felt weird kissing someone else. My mouth was conditioned to Cheeto's, his messy kisses and the way his stubble pricked the sides of my mouth. Kissing Kabir was new, but so, so good. He smelt fresh too, the deodorant that he wore and the faint smell of soap on his skin mixed with the smell of smoke and something else that I couldn't quite put my finger on.

I have a theory about associating people and their smells. I believe everybody grows into their individual smells, smells that other people then associate with them, which is why all babies smell alike until they're about three or four. For instance, if I'm at Deeksha's house, I get whiffs of her light, floral talcum powdery fragrance everywhere. Well, it's not her smell, but rather the smell that goes into being her. It's on the bath towels, the upholstery, on her mother's saris, everywhere. Topsy's smell is all over her room, too, and if I ever borrow clothes from her, I know that when I slip them on, right before I pull the neck over my head I will smell a tangy mixture of orange, the perfume she uses, and the soap on her skin. Shruti the Horrible smells sickly sweet, of incense and jasmine and rose water, and it's enough to make me feel tense whenever I smell something similar. I wonder sometimes what I smell like. A colleague once told me I smelt the same every day and asked me what perfume I used. Since I didn't wear the same perfume every day, I think she meant the smell of my shower gel, which I use consistently. Cheeto had told me that I smelt delicious after a long day at work when I was sure my perfume had completely worn off. I said as much to him, but he snuggled his face in the back of my neck, inhaled deeply and said, 'No, it's you. It's your smell.' Indefinable they may be, but our smells are there, little signatures that people associate with us. Cheeto's own smell was warm and musky and once when he met me at the airport, after I had returned from a conference in Hyderabad, he threw his arms around me and I buried my face in his chest and breathed deeply and knew I had come home.

'It's getting late, I should go,' I said finally, reluctantly moving away from Kabir.

'Must you?'

I nodded and he got up to walk me downstairs.

'Can I ask you something?' I ventured, as I stooped to put on my shoes.

'Go for it.'

'Umm . . . so you and me . . . now what?'

He smiled, tilting his head to one side, and kissed me again. 'We'll see. Let's go with the flow for now.'

What was this, the flow? I hate the flow. I hate going with the flow. I'm not a go-with-the-flow type of person. But I didn't say anything, just smiled and leaned in for another kiss, afraid that if I said anything at all this would end right now and I wouldn't be able to bear it. Besides, he *would* fall in love with me; he had to. I was smart and funny, he had admitted he was attracted to me and I made it very evident how much I liked him. What was not to love?

9. in which i completely humiliate myself

I'D GOT TO WORK bright and early the next morning, having fought the temptation to dawdle in bed and dream about the previous evening. Since Ankur had got married and gone on leave, I had been given a sort of mini promotion, and Shruti wasn't so much on my case any more. I was simultaneously working on my second cup of coffee and a fashion show that was scheduled for that weekend, the first assignment I was handling completely on my own with no supervision whatsoever. One of the two interns in the office had been assigned to help me and I'd delegated to her the task of compiling the press kits while I checked on the arrangements at the venue and waited for it to be past noon so I could call the journalists. If you called them before that they would either not pick up the phone, or sound all grouchy to let you know you'd pissed them off. This was one of the first things Shruti had told me when I joined the firm. 'Never call a journalist before twelve, because most of them work late and come in to work around midday. Two or three o'clock in the afternoon is perfect, when they've checked their mail, had their coffee and figured out the day's assignments.'

As nasty as she may have been, she did have her moments of wisdom, Shruti did. This time it had been spot on. More so because, since these two designers were new, fresh out of NIFT, it was unlikely that any of the leading fashion journalists would come to cover the event, though I had dutifully mailed them their invitations. This event would be strictly interns and trainees at the magazines and newspapers, the ones who need the most buttering up because their egos are already a little bruised.

I had barely explained things to the intern and moved on to my own work when a mail from Ma popped up threateningly in my Inbox. It was simple and brief, and grammatically precise, as everything she writes always is. Each sentence began with a capital letter, the full stops and commas were in their proper places and I even spotted a semicolon somewhere. Basically it said that *if* I was interested, there were dates, beginning next month, on the GRE schedule. She had apparently been looking at some colleges abroad with good English programmes and had written to a few of them for brochures, so I should have a look at those too (a list followed). Meanwhile, there was no harm in my visiting USEFI, which was right next to my office anyway, and picking up an application form for the exam. She'd buy me the test prep book and with my intelligence it would be a snap. *Besides, Arshi, even if you don't want to study further this year, I believe the GRE scores are valid for about five years, so you can save them till you're ready to go. But I really think you should do this.*

I stuck out my tongue at the monitor. Subtle as a battleaxe, my mother. After I'd told her, and told her again, that I didn't want to take the test. Well, it's not like she didn't have a point. The score would be valid for a while, though I would check again myself to see whether it was five years or less. And I didn't want to be stuck here in a PR job for the rest of my life, unhappy, while my friends moved on with their degrees and

promotions and high-flying careers. But then, the job was finally
going well. And I could always quit and find myself another
one. As a journalist, perhaps. Or in publishing. Or I could teach,
seeing how I had my master's and everything. Or would I need
a Ph.D. to teach? Whatever it was, there *had* to be other options.
I loved living in Delhi, I loved living in India where everything
was changing so rapidly. I mean, I remember only about eight
or nine years ago when PVR Saket was an old rundown theatre
called Anupam, when Saket itself was the back of beyond and
McDonald's was something you dreamed about when you
envisioned 'abroad'. Everything was happening here now; there
were a million acceptable career options apart from the doctor–
engineer–civil servant triangle. Besides, I admitted reluctantly to
myself, what if Kabir fell madly in love with me and we started
to date? I'd definitely not want to leave him.

Just then Arjun Singh, one of the designers whose show it
was, called me. I could never think of him as plain old Arjun;
in my head he was 'Arjun . . . Singh'. He was not terribly
attractive, but he had the most pleasant temperament ever and
was very definitely gay. He was a bit of a people collector too.
Everyone who came into his orbit, and was funny and intelligent
and attractive, was instantly his new best friend. I had a feeling
I had been collected too. Not that I minded. He hosted the most
lavish parties, attended by beautiful, shiny people who drank
beautiful, shiny alcohol and wore beautiful, shiny clothes.

'My darling, you're like a kingfisher, my beautiful, naughty
kingfisher,' he crooned over the phone. 'I've been trying and
trying to call you, my kingfisher, but your phone has been
unavailable all morning.'

'That's impossible,' I said, smiling into the phone. It's hard
not to smile when someone's calling you a kingfisher. Try it
sometime. 'I've been receiving calls all morning, Arjun, you
must have dialled the wrong number.'

There was a loud sniff at the other end. Arjun Singh was prone to morning colds, something he had told me about over a cigarette we had shared after a meeting, as if it was a big secret. 'That's why I can never spend the night at anyone's house, darling. I get so insecure about my face in the morning. It gets all swollen and puffed up and my eyes are watery and I keep sneezing on and on.'

'That's awful,' I had said, truly sympathetic, because I was no stranger to being insecure in the mornings. I hate the way I look in the morning, voice hoarse from too many cigarettes, usually sniffling, eyes swollen.

'Arshi,' he said, 'I would really like to go over the model list for the show.'

'The model list? You're supposed to arrange your own models!'

'No, no, silly, where is your head today? I mean, the models who are coming for my show. The *invitees*.'

'Oh,' I opened up the document on my computer and read out some names to him.

'Too old or too young, darling. Where are the established names?'

'Umm.' I stalled a little and frantically scrabbled for the words with which to tell him the established models were all too busy to come, or just not interested enough. But he cut me off before I could begin.

'You must call Sheetal.'

'Okay,' I said, agreeably. 'Who is Sheetal?'

'*Sheetal!*' Now he sounded shocked. 'Sheetal Goenka. Only the most happening stylist-slash-model we've had in a long time. And my personal, very close friend.'

'Great.' I rolled my eyes, wishing I could get back to daydreaming about Kabir and our wonderful, fantastic relationship that I was sure would take off soon. This was so definitely not a fling. The previous night I had returned singing under my breath and floated up the stairs to our apartment. Fardeen was over so Topsy had been in a great mood as well. He had brought over some South African wine and they had listened to my story over a drink, Fardeen patting me on the back, Topsy hanging back a little looking at my glowing face and saying, 'I do hope you're being careful, Arshi.' 'I'm always careful,' I had said breezily. Then Kabir had called to make sure I was home safe and I saw Topsy and Fardeen exchange the raised-eyebrow-upside-down-smile look. I had bowed to them both and slipped into my room, locked the door and talked to Kabir, stripping into nakedness and feeling vibrant and feminine and very, very sexy.

'You know what?' My conversation with Arjun Singh was evidently not over yet.

'What?'

'You should come over tonight. My place. Sheetal will also be coming and I think you two will get along beautifully. And you can bring the invite with you!' He sounded delighted, like a kid who has figured out for the first time that the funny half-triangle thing is 'A' and it goes at the beginning of 'apple'.

'Oh, I don't know about that,' I said, alarmed. My mind buzzed with all the what-ifs. What if Kabir called and wanted to make some plan? And, since you never knew about these things, what if this Sheetal person was totally hot and I felt terrible about myself in her presence? Frankly, the last thing I needed at this moment was to feel unattractive. It had been so long since I had felt the strange bubble-like emotion in the pit of my stomach I associate with happiness, which leaves me incapable of doing stuff like eating, or even peeing, without feeling the pygmy-dance pulse through my veins.

'But you must come!'

'I might have plans,' I said, thrilling as I said it. Dude, *I* had *plans!* I was no longer the sort of person who accepted every single social engagement for lack of anything else to do, because I . . . Had . . . Plans.

'Please? For a little while?'

I sighed. I loved Arjun Singh but he was being a pain. 'Okay. What time?'

'Seven, darling, I'm so excited! I've told Sheetal all about you and how talented and hot you are.'

I did love Arjun Singh.

By five-thirty that evening Kabir hadn't called and I rang Topsy, agonizing. 'He hasn't even texted me, Tops! I don't know what to do-ooo!'

'Whatever you do, don't call him. If he wants to, he'll call you. Really, why are you giving him so much bhav?'

'Bhav': a word that cannot be translated into English. I've tried before but have only come up with 'importance', but importance doesn't even begin to cover all that the word does. It's a powerful word, bhav, like so many Indian words that have no equivalent in any other language. Like 'chayn', with a nasal ending, used to describe girls with whiny voices and a way of becoming completely helpless in front of guys that pisses the crap out of me, or even 'jootha', which basically means something that's been contaminated with your mouth and so can't be eaten or touched by anybody else. Bhav is by far the best of all these words. 'Not giving someone bhav' could mean not elevating someone beyond what they deserve, but it also includes the disclaimer: maintain a certain dignity in interactions between you and the person in question.

But Topsy was in a relationship, and she couldn't possibly understand that in today's world there was no such thing as bhav. If you liked someone, you called them. No two ways about it.

So I called Kabir, and regretted it instantly because he sounded so goddamned distant. Well, okay, not cold, but normal, like the previous evening hadn't happened, like he hadn't had strange, jumpy feelings in his abdomen while we sat in each other's arms and did all the other stuff. He was busy, he said. Could he call me later?

I called Topsy again, slightly weepy. 'You called him, didn't you?' she said. I could almost see her eyes rolling to the ceiling.

'Yes,' I admitted.

'I told you not to. Never mind, perhaps he really is busy. I'm sure he'll call you back when he gets a moment.'

'And if he doesn't?'

'Then he's not worth it.' God, I hated it when she didn't say exactly what I wanted to hear.

Sulking a little, I made my way to Arjun Singh's house in Panchsheel Enclave, another really posh area of Delhi, full of tall, leafy trees that shade the streets and the houses. The houses are massive, with gardens, driveways and huge terraces, and the rents are forbidding. Arjun Singh had a rich father and so occupied a large barsati with an attached terrace garden. Everyone who lives alone in Delhi always gets the top floor. I don't know what the logic is, but first-floor flats are more expensive than the topmost ones, even if the latter are way prettier. Arjun Singh had a cat called Philo, short for Philosopher, he'd told me.

From what I'd gathered, Arjun Singh's basic aim was to recreate a New York City lifestyle (well, the NYC lifestyle that people on TV portray anyway) and he's one person I know who actually manages to get most of it right. He even has a brick bar structure separating his kitchenette from his loft-style bedroom, which overlooks the sprawling terrace garden. Then there's the all-white living space, with a gigantic white leather sofa set opposite a 48-inch plasma TV and a few ethnic nods, like floor cushions with raw silk covers and curtains from FabIndia. I had been to his place only once before, to drop off the press release, and even in that short time I had been hugely impressed, because he had one of those fancy cappuccino machines and had his sleepy servant boy bring us coffee in two huge balloon cups, the kind that look like hollowed-out boobs with handles. And he had all these tribal figurines in the corners of the room and a whole shelf full of fancy miniature alcohol bottles. I had wanted to marry him right then, just so I could make that house my home.

Sounds of laughter drifted down to me as I walked up the three flights of stairs. I regretted having gone almost instantly, because if there's one thing that makes me uncomfortable, it's walking into a room full of people already in mid-swing. Not that I normally have much choice, because I'm invariably late, but I end up feeling that those who are there already consider me to be an intruder, someone who doesn't really belong and who's screwing up their merriment.

'Hello?' I called from the doorway, knocking loudly on the open door. I could hear strains of jazz as well. Typical. I wish *I* had a posh flat and a high-tech multi-speaker system to play jazz on, I thought sourly.

Arjun Singh appeared in a bit, holding a half-empty glass in his hand. 'Come on in, Arshi. Why are you standing in the doorway?'

I walked in nervously. On the plush couch opposite the TV sat a beautiful woman. Sheetal, no doubt. No, really, she was stunning, with bronze skin and delicate, arched eyebrows and pouty lips. Next to her was a tall foreigner, her blonde hair done up in a long, messy braid, also fairly attractive, wearing what looked like a sarong. I felt suddenly sloppy and alien and smelling of garlic from lunchtime—and completely judged—as the women flicked their eyes over me and prepared to smile.

'What'll you have to drink?' asked Arjun Singh. Then he turned to the two women and said, 'This is my Arshi. She's doing a marvellous job handling my event this weekend.'

I was? I smiled nervously and said, 'I'd like, um, a vodka with orange juice, please.'

'Coming right up.' He went over to the bar and I followed, not feeling comfortable enough to sit with the two beauties, wanting to hang on a little longer to the one thing that I was familiar with. He handed me my drink and, even as I chanted the don't-spill, don't-spill mantra in my head, I tripped on the dhurrie and felt my glass flying out of my fingers as I slumped to the floor. I heard the horrible crash-tinkle noise of glass breaking and at the same instant my big toe bent back, almost in slow motion, followed by, no, not a *snap*, but the *crick* of a bone that's not meant to be bent beyond a certain angle. The pain registered the very next second and my body went into high alert, screaming out to all my limbs. I gasped and my face crinkled.

I felt Arjun Singh's arms lifting me off the dhurrie, and looked up to see he had a slightly amused (how dare he!) expression on his face. 'Are you okay?'

'Yes, yes, I'm so sorry,' I managed through gritted teeth as I pulled myself up and noticed Sheetal the Lovely cleaning up the mess. She had a mop in her hand, which she was regarding disdainfully, and her foreigner friend was dabbing water on her white skirt, where my drink had spilt. I wanted to die.

'I'm so sorry,' I said again. 'Let me help you clean up.' I got to my feet but my toe gave a sudden stabbing throb as I rested my weight on it. I teetered, nearly falling again.

'What's the matter?' asked Arjun Singh, concerned.

'It's my toe, it really hurts,' I said, embarrassed at the first pricking of tears in my eyes. Don't cry in front of these people, Arshi. Don't.

Sheetal noticed my expression and turned to her host. 'Get her an ice pack, Arjun. And, Arshi, is it? Sit down, don't worry about the mess, it happens to all of us.'

'Usually with at least one drink down,' said the blonde snarkily.

I gave Sheetal what I hoped was an expression of immense gratitude and sat down gingerly on one of the low wooden chairs. Philo the cat appeared out of nowhere and started to lap up the vodka that had spattered near the white couch. 'That cat is an alcoholic,' laughed Arjun Singh, reappearing with a towel wrapped around several chunks of ice, which he handed to me and which I pressed against my toe, wincing as the pressure irritated the nerves again.

'Listen,' said Sheetal. 'It's probably just a sprain, but I think you should go home and rest your foot. Do you want me to call you a cab?'

'No, no,' I said weakly, thinking how anxious they seemed to get rid of me. This was perhaps the most embarrassing thing that had ever happened to me and I just wanted the earth to open up and swallow me whole. 'I have a car . . . just give me a second, I think it's already stopped hurting.'

I sat for a bit, still blushing and hot under my armpits, feeling my heart and my toe pound all at once, while the three of them cleaned up and got themselves refills. Arjun Singh offered me a drink, but all I wanted was a glass of water and my mother, so I refused. They quickly got back to their conversation about common acquaintances and who was up to what. Feeling very much an outsider, I handed Sheetal her invite to the show, gave the blonde an extra one I happened to have with me, and left.

My toe actually didn't hurt all that much that night, but the next morning it was the size of a large plum and approximately the same colour, and I couldn't put any pressure on it at all. I called out to Topsy, who took one look at it and bundled me into a cab, calling my mom on the way to the hospital. It turned out to be a hairline fracture. All my life I'd managed to escape broken bones. Once I'd tripped and fallen down a flight of stairs and landed on my nose, but had miraculously come away with slight bruises. Another time a basketball had flown at my face in school and in fending it off I'd bent my little finger so it dangled hideously from the side of my palm, but that was only a dislocation. This breaking of bone, even if it was a crack, was most definitely a sign of old age.

'Only essential walking,' boomed the doctor, cheerfully encasing my foot in a green fibre-glass cast. I took his statement as indication that I needn't go in to work for two weeks and held the phone at arm's length through Shruti's several tantrums. Meanwhile, my mother whisked me off to the Farmhouse where she made me go through all the research she had done on the GRE, and I spent most of the following two weeks leafing through the study material she had gathered, in between daydreaming about Kabir.

I did make it to Arjun Singh's show that weekend. I felt as though I ought to, even though my intern helper had capably filled my shoes and managed the entire event on her own. I watched as the models sashayed down the ramp, wearing clothes that could only be described as, well, safe. I'm not a big fan of huge, crazy outfits like swansdown stuff, or what looks like three pieces of cloth tied loosely together, but Arjun Singh's designs were downright boring: skirts cut till the knee, pleated and plain, in various shades of grey and pink; light V-necked T-shirts and cardigans in complementing pastel shades worn over them. The models did their best to make the clothes look out there and sexy, or maybe that was Sheetal's contribution; I had heard she was styling the show. They wore vivid make-up, the music was just right and Sheetal had clearly experimented with the look as much as possible, because some of the models had their T-shirts rolled up, exposing the midriff, the skirts pulled low over the pelvis and, in one case, the cardigan was wrapped around the model's head. Sheetal herself walked the grand finale, waving out to the crowd and then to Arjun Singh, who appeared bashfully beside her. She stood on tiptoe to give him a kiss on his cheek making cameras in every corner of the room click and flash. 'Sheetal is my wonderful muse,' I heard him gushing to someone later. I waved at Arjun Singh, but I guess he didn't see me in all the rush, because I was sitting in a corner with my leg propped up on another chair. And then I went home.

We didn't really keep in touch after that, Arjun Singh and I. I realized his was a world I wasn't ever going to be a part of and I guess he realized the same about me. It didn't make me sad, not like you would think, because I didn't really want to *belong* to the moneyed, glamorous set. I liked to be around them, yes, I craved for their lifestyles, sure, but it would mean too much hard work—not to mention an entirely new wardrobe. And also, though it sounds most elitist and snobbish, I felt I was above them in some way. Smarter, perhaps, less self-involved. Which goes to prove the exact opposite, I suppose.

10. in which i wonder why i care so much about what other people think

I STOOD ON OUR little balcony surveying the construction site that had magically sprung up the night before right opposite our house. If you searched all over Delhi, you wouldn't find a single patch of land that no one lived on or at least used to park their vehicles and claimed as their own. This particular construction site had begun with just a light bulb hanging from a tree and an old lorry stacked with bricks, and now brick, cement and huge wicked-looking iron rods sticking out of the ground, just waiting for someone to fall and impale themselves upon them, were transforming it into a real house. The dust from the construction activities was everywhere. I could feel it under my rubber chappals, in my mouth, gritting against my teeth, and each morning, our maid, Gita-didi, swept huge piles of black, grey and sepia heaps out on to the staircase. We had been forbidden by our landlady from smoking on the stairs and so we never really felt like it belonged to us, like our apartment did, and we had therefore told Gita-didi that keeping it clean wasn't really our headache.

Gita-didi was pretty much responsible for the tiny bit of

normalcy in our lives in the teeny apartment. She was a skinny, small woman, with a soft voice and large eyes, who ran our house with efficiency and élan. She would arrive in the morning, ringing the bell several times till we woke up, groaning at being pulled out of bed to let her in, and then stand over our beds and holler, 'Didi, wake up, you'll be late for office/college' (depending on whom she was speaking to), while we struggled to get a few more seconds of shut-eye. Usually this would be followed by me sticking my face out from under my sheet and mumbling, 'Coffee,' which she'd bring in and place by the pile of mattresses that served as my bed. After that she'd pop her head in every now and then and say, 'Your coffee is getting cold, didi, wake up.' She also kept an eye on our household supplies, keeping us informed when we were low on Ariel, or needed to get more sugar, or rice, or bread, or eggs. Topsy gave in to her bullying more often than I did, accepting without question Gita-didi's constant demands and giving her money to buy more groceries. Unlike Topsy, I had grown up in Delhi and had developed an innate distrust for anyone else handling my money, so I usually stocked up on the groceries myself. But we both agreed that we loved her—well, not loved, but we needed her, and in certain cases, need equals to love.

We didn't always have Gita-didi working in our house, though. When we first moved in we had employed a young girl called Asha, who came highly recommended by our landlady and was a little pricier than what we had budgeted for. But when we opened the door on the morning that Asha was to come, we were confronted instead by another woman, dark and barrel-like, who said her name was Shanta and she—and only she—worked in all the houses in this neighbourhood. I didn't like her attitude and told her as much, but Topsy, always anxious to have things done quickly and smoothly, said she could come and work for us. So she did.

Being from families where maids were always considered as part of the family, people you trusted implicitly, both Topsy and I we were a little careless with our stuff. I used to hide my cash in my underwear drawer, and Topsy had one thousand-rupee note on her at a time, which for her was as good as being broke because she hated to get change for it. Since she didn't believe in wallets, she would slip it out of the pocket of one pair of jeans and into another. One day, after Shanta, whom Topsy and I secretly called Moti (which can be pronounced in two ways, the one with the softer 'th' sound meaning 'pearl', and the other with the harder 't' meaning 'fatty'—three guesses which one we chose!) left the house, I rooted around my drawer for some money and found it, *all of it*, gone. At first I thought I had taken it out to spend and lost it, but the next morning Topsy woke me up looking haggard and panicky to tell me that her precious thousand-rupee note was missing too. Since we both hated confrontations, we did a little back and forth about who'd ask Moti about it, and Topsy said since she had once fought with the milkman over getting back incorrect change it was now my turn to set this right.

I waited with growing trepidation for Moti to appear, and she did, looking as casual as ever. I went up to her as she swept the middle of the room and left the dust in the corners, my heart in my mouth because, dude, she was seriously immense, and said, 'Um, Shanta, we're missing some money.' Instantly she dropped the broom and began to wail: How, *how, how* could we accuse her like this? 'I have three children,' she screeched, banshee-like, 'and you can check me if you want to.' Her hands flew rapidly to her pallu, loosening the sari so her tight blouse began to open slightly and her massive bosom heaved.

'There's no need for that,' I said, backing away, and fled.

Of course, Moti quit, taking with her her son the car-cleaning guy and her daughter the maid who cooked for us, and devoted her days to telling the neighbourhood workers, the chowkidar, the mali and the other maids how we smoked and had heaps of empty bottles of alcohol and never woke up on time in the morning. Finally she was employed by the guy living opposite us and had a fine time sweeping the mess from his house on to our welcome mat. Gita-didi told us of this in hushed tones, shaking her head in amusement over Moti's antics. Topsy and I rolled our eyes, but secretly I wondered what the neighbourhood now thought of us, strange, scarlet women, who brought boys home, drank a lot and sometimes returned home at three or four in the morning. I don't know why it bothered me, but it did.

It's always been a problem for me: I care too much about what people think. Earlier, I used to be worse. I couldn't even go shopping without someone coming along and telling me what looked good on me. I didn't trust my own judgement, I suppose, so I relied on how people around me reacted to me in order to define myself.

Esha, who had become a fairly good friend over the past couple of months and had visited me when my toe got fractured, taking special pains to do stuff for me like baking a cake one day or bringing over three Disney DVDs the next, was the kind of person who *didn't* give a flying fuck about what people thought. She seemed the sort who'd care about that kind of thing, but once I got to know her I discovered she was impulsive, affectionate and totally unselfconscious. Over the past months she had rapidly diminished from skinny to brittle, enough for people to stop and stare at her. One time, when we went out dancing, she wore a very short halter top which rode up over her stomach, showing a tiny pot-belly with a thin layer of hair on it, which, frankly, was most unappealing, but she didn't care.

She even had a huge birthmark, a brown, messy patch, on her back, right below the nape of her neck. She usually wore her hair down, covering it, but sometimes she'd scoop it all up in a messy bun and people would repeatedly glance at the blotch, but she'd just go on drinking her cranberry Bacardi Breezer and laughing at something someone said. If it were me, I'd constantly be anxious about people commenting on how weird my birthmark looked, and I'd shy away from meeting people, like I do when I have a pimple. But Esha just tilts up her chin and looks people right in the eyes till they stop turning to look.

'You don't care what other people think, do you?' I asked her once, in wonderment.

'No,' she said, simply. 'Why should I? I care about my friends and their opinions and I think about what they say, but at the end of the day it's my life.'

She was so different from me that it surprised me that we were friends at all. It also surprised me that year how many of my close friends were people I had met only in the last year or two. Except Deeksha they were all relatively 'new friends', people who hadn't known me in braces, hadn't attended my sixteenth birthday party, had no clue who my secret celebrity crush was. Take Topsy, for instance. We had met through another friend, whom I had sadly fought with later, one of those tiny fights that escalate into something huge till eventually both of you are tired of slanging around abuse and oh-you-did-that-to-me-three-years-ago kind of accusations. This fight was particularly ugly because the 'friend' in question brought all her friends into it, people who had been my friends as well at one point and who were now forced to take sides. She was smart and a campaigner to the core, and I didn't want to bitch about her even if we weren't friends any more, so they wound up hating me with a vengeance that had me quite surprised. I had never thought I was capable of being disliked quite so intensely. I like to think of myself as a fairly likeable person, honest and friendly, fun and loyal, and to suddenly be called things like 'bitch' or told 'You're the worst friend ever because you're so fake' is not fun, because it makes you rethink everything you put into a friendship in the first place.

My 'new friends' weren't like that. They were far more mature, and though we got annoyed at each other sometimes we were always able to discuss things in a civilized manner later on. That was the year we were all *stretching* a little bit, forming our characters, figuring out what was okay and what wasn't, all over again, just as we had when we had hit our teens. And the real reason these new friends were such good friends, I figured, was because they met me the way I am now—as a finished product so to speak. Unlike the friends who had been around forever, with the exception of Deeksha, they didn't have a previous image of me in their heads to measure the present me against, so they didn't end up uttering that most profound of statements: 'You've changed.' The friends who have seen me through adolescence and my first crush and getting my driver's licence and all didn't really grow with me. And I didn't grow with them. So there we were, each at our individual crossroads. When they looked at me they saw images of the Me That Was and tried to tug me down their road, because once upon a time when I was a different person I would certainly have followed.

Anyway, so Topsy was living in a PG at the time and I was looking to move out of home. She seemed fun in a quiet and smart kind of way, and I particularly took to the way her eyes grew huge and she began to nibble the skin around her thumb when she was being attentive, and the dimples that appeared on her cheeks when she smiled. When I proposed we share a place, she looked at me deeply, like I was under special scrutiny—

something she still does when I make a suggestion she's not sure about—and then she smiled slightly and nodded, 'Yes, that sounds like a good idea.'

Only, I wasn't sure whether she was joking or not. I mean, sure, she *sounded* serious, but people did this a lot in Delhi, tossing out plans they had no intentions of sticking to. 'I'll call you,' I said and she put her hand on my arm and leaned in close, making me a little nervous at this invasion of my personal space. She wasn't going to *kiss* me, was she? 'I think we should go house-hunting on Sunday,' she whispered into my ear. Just then Fardeen had appeared from behind us. That's the first time I saw Fardeen and I couldn't figure out what someone as pretty as Topsy was doing with someone who looked, well, all right, but definitely not her male equal. But when Fardeen came with us on Sunday to help us look for a house, I instantly saw what a great guy he was and wanted him to hug me forever and take me home and adopt me. Seriously, he shines. Not like Topsy does—she has a different radiance, more sparkly; Fardeen's is like a glow, an aura that surrounds him. Being around him is comforting and reassuring, like eating an ice cream and knowing you don't want to be anywhere else doing anything else right then.

After a lot of searching for the perfect house—we grew increasingly afraid that it didn't exist and got grouchy with each other and cross with the broker—we found a little flat that was certainly not perfect but nearly so, and moved in and lived happily ever after.

Or not . . .

It was getting colder in Delhi, which was usually a happy time for me. Summer made me feel hot and unattractive and slothful but winter was my season. I loved snuggling underneath a quilt; I loved the acrid smell of woodsmoke; I loved the mild sunshine and basking in it every time I went into the balcony for a smoke. This was my weather, the time I felt the most energized and happy.

But Topsy didn't seem to be enjoying the weather this year as much as I was. It couldn't just be PMS any more like she had claimed so many times. The tension that had existed between us and in the house for the last couple of months just seemed to continue. She watched the changing sun with eyes that grew narrower as I sung around the house and pushed her into going out with me. When she stubbornly refused, I went out with other people, occasionally with Kabir, who kept me doing a weird yo-yo dance with his alternating I-love-you, I-love-you-not responses. On the days he loved me, I loved everyone and I loved me too. On the days he didn't, he told me I was wasting my time, that he'd never date me seriously and I should find someone else. When I'd get weepy at this he'd get irritated. I'd hate myself for continuously calling him only to hear him get more and more short with me, and then I'd get pissed off at him and go out and flirt desperately with someone else. And the next day he'd call me as if nothing had happened and say 'Hi' in his special voice, the one I knew he used only with me, and I'd melt, frolic in it, convinced that now, surely, he was falling in love with me. With Topsy practically unavailable for rational discussion and general venting I found thoughts of Kabir crowding in on me.

11. in which you meet
our neighbours

TOPSY AND I RARELY saw the other people who lived in our building. The only reason I knew they existed was from their garbage bins which sat outside their apartments waiting to be emptied, which I noticed every morning as I made my way down the stairs on my way to work. They appeared to be mostly single and working, or people who had migrated to Delhi to study, like Topsy, and their garbage cans always contained empty packets of Maggi, and eggshells, and the little plastic packets milk comes in. Easy food, food that tastes like it does at home without too much effort. There were two couples in the building as well, and their trash was more organized—big green plastic bags tied securely at the top and taken out of the garbage bin, not just left there for the kuda-wala to empty out. Occasionally, the dog that roamed the street the house was on would take it upon himself to gut their garbage bags, especially those belonging to the posh husband–wife lawyer team who lived on the first floor. Then I would spot potato peelings, onion skins and mango seeds, food that took time to cook. Since their air shaft was connected to ours, I'd sometimes come home to delicious smells wafting from the kitchen, and I knew it couldn't be the college boys downstairs, because eggs, however they were cooked, could never smell like that. On those nights I'd have fantasies about knocking on their door, being invited to sit on a plastic-covered sofa and being fed stir-fried vegetables with bread from the Oberoi Charcuterie instead of the regular Harvest Gold you got at the nearby grocery store. Or of the wife offering me a Margarita (I had spotted a fancy bar in their living room on my way up one day), while the husband made biryani, which we'd eat off glass plates, with little glass bowls of raita on the side, and finish with dessert, something she had made at home, like caramel custard.

Our trash, since you ask, was usually Domino's boxes, stacked high, one on top of the other. Or aluminium foil from kebab rolls. Occasionally we'd cook, when the maids were absent and we were too broke to order in, and on those days our trash would be piles of potato peelings, potato being the only vegetable Topsy and I agreed on. And one night a week there would be empty bottles of liquor, Old Monk or Smirnoff or White Mischief, or very many bottles of beer. If the kuda-wala was shocked by this he never said anything, and for the longest time in between we didn't have a next-door neighbour, so technically he was making the trip only for us and came and went as he pleased. So, as I exited the house one morning, I was quite surprised to find a bottle of whisky in our trash. Topsy and I certainly didn't drink whisky, and Kabir hadn't been over in a while. As far as I knew, we had the one bottle of Teachers stashed away waiting for Kabir to empty its contents and I had seen it lying half full in our linen drawer just the night before, so this couldn't be it.

We had had a bit of a party the previous evening when four or five of Topsy's friends from college had landed up, impromptu.

I had been sitting around watching *Jerry McGuire* on HBO for the hundredth time, sniffling at the scene in which Jerry reclaims Dorothy, in my track pants with the hole in the crotch area, and was quite embarrassed at the sudden appearance of all these people. But Topsy made me a drink and patted the floor next to her. Thankfully, these kids—they were all Topsy's age, some even younger—turned out to be smart and entertaining, so after a while I pretty much forgot about the sadly situated hole in my tracks and helped them polish off about three-quarters of a bottle of Bacardi which they had brought with them. These kind of parties were common at our house; they happened once or twice a week. ('It has this vibe,' Esha had said, as she sat comfortably cross-legged on the rug one day. 'It's really, you know, a chilled kinda place.') We had a rule about our friends, though; if they weren't common friends, or were people we thought the other wouldn't get along with, we would confine them to our own rooms. That worked out okay because very often I'm just not in the mood to meet new people and engage in PC, and neither is Topsy.

Anyway, to return to the Mystery of the Whisky Bottle. The previous night I had gone to bed a little before everyone left, pleading an early morning appointment, and as I stood there on the stairs I grew crosser and crosser at the thought that someone had finished *our* whisky bottle, our *Kabir* whisky bottle, which I hadn't even pulled out the night before. I called Topsy outside. She had just washed her hair and emerged towel-clad and disgruntled. 'Someone must have drunk it, no?' she said, her tongue clicking against the roof of her mouth in exasperation.

'But no one drank any whisky last night,' I pointed out.

'Well then, Arshi, it must be an old bottle! Why do you unnecessarily have to call me out here in my towel?'

'It's important, dude, whose bottle is it? We don't have any empty whisky bottles.'

'Um, actually, it's mine,' said a male voice, and Topsy shrieked and vanished into our flat, banging the door behind her.

I looked in the direction of the voice, which had come from the doorway of what I had thought was the empty flat next to ours, squinting at the dark form of a rather fat man lurking sheepishly behind the screen door.

'Sorry,' I said, not sounding the least bit apologetic because I was pissed off at this dude standing there eavesdropping on our conversation and staring at us. 'I didn't realize anyone had moved in.'

He came out, extending a box of liquor chocolates in my direction. 'I just moved yesterday. I was about to knock and give you guys some chocolate and say hello. Have a chocolate? I'm Dhruv, by the way.'

I took a chocolate, nodded at him and said, 'Arshi. That was my flatmate, Topsy.'

'It's just the two of you?'

'Yes.' I tilted up my chin to give him the look over. No, he didn't look like a potential rapist; perhaps just a little too curious. 'What do you do?'

In Delhi it's easy to figure out whether or not someone is potential friend material. There's usually a set of three questions, like a checklist, that come after 'What's your name?' The people you meet are then ranked according to where they live, what they do and which school or college they went to. Which is, I agree, superficial, but say I was at a party and talking to someone who was a software engineer and there was another guy who worked in films, the film guy would be a better choice for me to talk to, because of our media backgrounds, see? Or say the person lived in Gurgaon or Noida or some other place much too far for easy commuting. Well, of course, if the software engineer was an anomaly among software engineers and was cute and charming and smart then all rules went out of the window.

'I'm in HDFC,' he said. 'I work in their sales and marketing department.'

Good lord, a banker type. I never had much to say to them. Call it an inverse snobbery thing but I just can't see the point of people making too much money. I mean, I'm sure they exist for a reason, but I've never really understood how they can spend their lives swinging from one corporate job to another, with no other passion than for increasing their income. Granted that PR is not the most stellar or the most vibrant of all the jobs I could have picked, but I was justified because PR was not my passion, not what I really, really wanted to do, just a placeholder till I found something else. But with Chubby Dhruv, this was probably where he wanted to spend the rest of his life. That makes me so depressed, like one of those born-again believers. I want to shake people who are in corporate jobs and say, 'Fuck this, go look at other career options! Run!' I wondered if Dhruv would let me shake him up. In fact I wondered if I could shake Dhruv at all, standing stolidly at our doorstep, now (ew!) picking up the empty whisky bottle from the trash and fondling it. I must have given him a particularly disdainful look, because he asked 'What?' in an injured tone and then said, almost immediately, 'Can I meet your flatmate?'

'Sure, go ahead, ring the bell, she's probably out of the shower by now.' I rang it for him, and hung around, not wanting to leave just yet.

I heard irritated footsteps slap-slap-slapping inside, and our screen door opening violently. 'What?' snapped out Topsy, her eyebrows meeting in a thick furrow above her nose.

'I'm Dhruv,' said Dhruv, looking crestfallen at the prospect of having us as neighbours. 'I just moved in yesterday, I wanted to give you some chocolate.' He opened the box for her. Topsy shot a glance at me and gingerly took one.

'It was his whisky bottle,' I offered.

'Oh.'

Bravely, despite our iciness, Dhruv jumped into the conversation, 'Yeah, I had some friends over yesterday, just to, you know, inaugurate the flat, and they brought over a bottle. I thought I'd call you guys but it looked like you had people over as well.'

My sharp corners began to melt. Sweet guy. Harmless, really. I should have gone easier on him. 'We have people over a lot,' I told him. 'You should come by for a drink sometime.'

'Oh, I will!' His eyes lit up with such gratitude that I felt magnanimous and open-hearted. It's a good feeling to have. Topsy, too, I noticed, was relaxing her tight grip on her elbows and was actually leaning back against the doorpost, a sign that this guy had passed a certain test of comfort level.

'Really,' she said now, and then, looking at me sharply, asked in too polite a voice, 'Don't you have to go to *work*?'

I clearly had not been forgiven yet. Well, whatever. She was being a moody cow, and what with Kabir acting the way he was, all distant and Ice Prince-y, I didn't have the energy to humour her.

'Yes, I should be going,' I said, and to Dhruv, 'See you later.'

Actually I didn't see him later, not for a while after that first meeting, till the time the electricity went off one evening, and I was, for once, home before Topsy. Our flat was pleasant enough, not too cold after I lit some candles and shut the door to the balcony, but I got spooked at the idea of sitting there all alone and I was sure I heard footsteps start to echo from the other room. I decided to go for a movie by myself. I'm not so good with movies on my own, but I suddenly felt empowered, like I didn't really need any company. Calling Kabir would have been of no use because he would have sighed and said he was busy and that he'd call me back. Inevitably, he wouldn't call and I'd end up calling him the next day feeling more and more like a loser when I checked my 'dialled numbers' and saw his name on top of the list, or sometimes second on it when it was Topsy I had just spoken to. I had begun to hate the way my voice sounded chirpy if he picked up the phone and said, 'Hi,' which meant he was free and could talk to me, or changed to crestfallen if he said 'Hello' brusquely, which meant he was busy and would 'call me back'.

I exited the flat, making sure to blow out all the candles before I left. I'm really scared of fire. My mom didn't let me light matches at all when I was a kid, not even to light firecrackers, leaving me feeling like something of a wimp when my cousins who were much younger than me lit the fuses on bombs and rockets with so much style, tossing the evil little ladis away to set up a timpani of noise. I stayed far away from sparklers as well, holding them at arm's length when I was forced to. I didn't even like to fry stuff on the stove now because the oil spattered on my bare wrists. In my head being burnt is surely the worst way to die. I don't know how all those sati and jauhar people managed it, jumping willingly into a fire. Death by drowning comes a close second to that. I had watched a *Baywatch* episode where the girl and guy are making love in a pool, and when he swims underwater to kiss her she handcuffs him to the railing of the pool so he can't surface. It gave me nightmares for weeks, imagining the man's lungs filling with water, the scary feeling of the throat constricting, of not being able to breathe.

Outside, I heard noises in Dhruv's flat. The door opened and a girl stepped out, and Dhruv after her. I couldn't see them clearly in the semi-lit hallway.

'Arshi!' he said, sounding really pleased to see me. 'Pia, this is Arshi, my neighbour. Arshi, this is my sister, Pia.'

I smiled at both of them. Pia, who I could now tell was pretty young, about seventeen or eighteen, looked at me curiously, but gave me a sweet smile.

'Where are you going?' asked Dhruv.

'I thought I'd watch a movie. Topsy's not around and I got a little scared sitting in the house by myself.'

'Come in, then, we were just about to order dinner,' he said, jerking his head in invitation.

'Oh, I don't know,' I glanced shyly at the two of them. Suddenly, I changed my mind about not wanting company. I badly wanted people around me, to hear the sound of someone else's voice, not to be constantly thinking and *thinking* all the time.

'Come,' Pia said softly. 'Why do you want to go for a movie by yourself?'

'Okay, thanks,' I said, and followed them in.

Dhruv's place was completely unlike ours, at least from what I could tell by candlelight. He had zero furniture; just a mattress on which he slept and a stool where he had piled up quite a few books. The rest of his books were on the floor. He hovered around me earnestly, emptying the stool for me and dusting it with his hands, while Pia went to her spot on the mattress curling up there and watching me. She began to look through take-away menus by candlelight.

'What'll you have to drink, Arshi?' asked Dhruv, looking anxious. 'I have wine and some beer, Baileys and vodka. And a very nice coffee liqueur.' It dawned on me that he wanted to impress me, wanted me to like him as badly as I wanted other people to like me. It surprised me that like the people who knew I wanted to be liked by them I too was being slightly stand-offish, slightly amused by his eagerness, and was treating him like I would treat a friend's dog. It's such a vicious circle, the games people play.

'I'll have vodka,' I said, 'with whatever.'

'What should we order, bhaiyya?' asked Pia, making me jump, because I had more or less forgotten she was in the room. It was easy to think I was alone, because Dhruv was like a non-person, even in his own house. The drink he made me, with soda and lime juice and salt on the rim, was really terrific, and I lit a smoke and made myself comfortable.

We decided on pizza, the safest option—vegetarian, because it turned out the two of them were. I learnt that Pia was Dhruv's cousin, his mother's sister's daughter, which made the two of them practically siblings, because I believe you share a special relationship with your mother's sister's kids, much more than with your mother's brother's kids or your father's sister's kids. I don't know why that is, but it seems to be true of most people I know. She was in Class 11, in Amity International School, studying commerce with maths, and had been in the neighbourhood for maths tuitions when she dropped in.

'Dhruv-bhaiyya is like my real brother only,' said Pia, biting down on her bottom lip. 'He is the only one in the family who understands me. Before, my house was close to his parents' house, so I used to go over all the time, but I haven't seen him in really long now.' I was a little surprised at Dhruv being anyone's role model, but I still shared a conspiratorial glance with him, the kind two people of the same age will inevitably exchange if there's someone else in the room who's either far younger or far older than them.

'Chhoti is my buddy,' he said, leaning over and chummily

taking a drag of my cigarette. 'But now she has all these boyfriends and I keep telling her she's much too young for them. Isn't she, Arshi?' Now Pia and I exchanged a glance, the kind two women will inevitably share when a man says something that so gives away his gender. Honestly! I rolled my eyes, but I saw both of them were waiting for me to say something.

'I don't know,' I said. 'How old are you Pia, sixteen, seventeen?'

'Seventeen and a half,' she said, proudly. She was still in the 'and a half' stage. I'd forgotten how long it had been since I'd said something like that.

'Well, by that age I was dating people. It's perfectly normal,' I announced, loving the attention, feeling super-cool, kind of a Charlie's Angel meets Agony Aunt. I was hot and I was smart. I pouted sultrily into my glass.

'See, bhaiyya? Everyone does it. There's nothing wrong,' she said to Dhruv, who looked like he wanted to say something really rude to me but had just remembered he too wanted to look cool and that objecting to my statement would certainly not do it for him.

'Never mind him,' I told her gaily. 'He's just jealous because he doesn't have a girlfriend.'

Too late I realized it was probably the most tactless thing I could have said. Pia gave a shocked giggle, Dhruv looked traumatized, and when I gave a nervous laugh to diffuse the situation and said, 'Hello, it's a joke, it's a joke,' he laughed too, but forcedly, more like he was hiccuping. 'Heh-heh . . . Actually, you know, I've only ever liked one girl.'

'Neha-didi, no?' asked Pia, sitting at attention. Dhruv hadn't, in all likelihood, taken her into confidence about this.

He glanced sideways at me to see if I was listening. I was,

but didn't want to seem too eager. I was busy trying to figure out if this sharing of information would entail the crossing of a certain boundary. When one person shares a story it's almost like the other person has to, because it would be impolite to do otherwise. Sort of like in the olden days when one soldier dropping his weapons meant his opponent would have to do the same; it was considered bad form not to reciprocate the gesture. But I wasn't about to reveal anything to Dhruv. I didn't want to discuss my deal with Kabir, or with Cheeto, with this weird, eager-to-please fat boy.

'She was my neighbour, in Patel Nagar,' he said. 'We wanted to get married.'

'And?'

'Her family moved to Manchester. I think her dad wanted to start a restaurant business there, so they all moved.'

I could imagine what Neha was like. Slightly pear-shaped, her hair highlighted with blonde streaks, with a distant, godlike father who gave her stuffed animals for her birthday, and a mother whom she was never that close to but who knew all about her life, unlike her father; a newly rich family, full of ambitions and plans, for whom the UK was the perfect place to be since parts of the larger family had already settled there and were now ready and waiting to take them in despite their houses being too cramped to accommodate a bunch of disoriented relatives. Or was I being too cynical? Perhaps Neha was an artist, her father a man with visions of selling his mother's mango pickle to the hordes in England. Perhaps they had a serious marketing plan and strategy, and she now lived in a mansion with a stable and a Shetland pony and a library filled with books by P.G. Wodehouse.

'Are you in touch with her?' I asked Dhruv, who was sweating heavily and had, I noticed, downed his glass of beer.

'Yes, we mail each other all the time. She's lonely there, she wants to come back. Plus she lives in her cousin's house and it's very small for all of them.'

So I wasn't that far from the truth. 'How long has it been?'

'Nine years. This was when we were seventeen. Now her family is putting pressure on her to get married.' Sweat stains had formed in Dhruv's armpits and I tried hard not to look at them as he lifted his arm to wipe his face.

'It must be tough for you,' I said, trying to sound sympathetic.

'It is.'

Pia's cellphone rang making all of us jump. I saw her glance irritably down at the number, then smile widely. 'I'll be right back,' she told us, and picked up the phone as she stood up and walked out into the dark hallway. 'Hello! You're so mean, yaar, you haven't called me all day and I've been waiting and waiting and . . .' Clearly, even if Dhruv thought she was too young for a boyfriend, she had one.

Dhruv glanced glassily at me. His eyes were beginning to glaze over. 'Um . . . could I have another drink?' I asked nervously.

'Yes, sure,' he said, but made no move to get up. His face was turned away from me, and I raised my eyebrows behind his head trying to gather what was going on till he made this really weird sound and I realized to my horror that he was crying.

Not that I have an issue with men who cry. I think it's wonderful—well, not wonderful but refreshing anyway—to meet a man who is secure enough about himself to weep in front of someone. Just as long as they're not your crybaby variety who cry at everything—and believe me I've had my share of those. So I'm not sexist or anything, it's just that I'm not good with tears, even if it's someone I know and love, which Dhruv most certainly was not. I'm a good post-tears person: I dispense advice like a diva, I rub backs, I make jokes which get people laughing more often than not, but the actual hugging and rocking and comforting is just not my cup of tea.

I had once sort of dated a guy who cried in front of me the day after we made out for the first time, because he had been to see his grandmother and it made him sad to see she was getting so old. I was still on the make-out high you get from having been physically intimate with someone and seeing him almost naked. I still remembered the feel of his mouth against mine and the slight bite of his stubble pricking my palms as I cupped his face, so I thought his crying in front of me was a sign he was truly comfortable with me, that we would get married some day, or at least date for a really long time, and I cradled his head and rubbed his back and felt uncomfortably and thoroughly maternal. He responded to this mothering as all men do; I mean, hello, which woman hasn't looked down at some guy at her breast and wondered whether he really, truly thought spending an hour making weird noises, sucking away to glory, was supposed to make her hot and horny? Especially if you can only see the top of his head in a strange, disjointed way. Anyway, so he wept for a while against my T-shirt and when we made out afterwards he was a lot rougher than he had been the previous day, but I was still feeling sorry for him so I let it be. But then, three days later, he called me and started crying again, this time because he had had a fight with his father. I was less maternal this time but still a little oh-he's-going-through-a-bad-patch sympathetic, but when he bawled *again* at a nightclub because he saw me dancing with someone else I started to think that perhaps it was time I exited this particular relationship. It took me a while, though, because I was so afraid he'd start weeping in front of me and I wouldn't be able to handle it that I did the one thing I've always accused men of doing. I vanished. I stopped taking his calls, stopped responding to text messages, and that was that.

Now, watching Dhruv's shoulders jerk up and down, I set my glass on the floor and looked longingly at the door.

'I'm sorry,' he said, turning towards me, face wrinkled, catch in his voice. 'I just get so lonely and I have no one to talk to about her.'

'That's okay,' I said, giving him an awkward pat on the back. 'What are neighbours for anyway, no? We all have lonely days.'

'I find it hard to believe you could ever be lonely,' he said, looking up at me, wiping his cheeks.

'Oh no, dude, what are you saying? I get lonely a lot, we all do,' I smiled cheerily, a chin-up-old-boy-things-aren't-as-bad-as-they-seem-now-stop-crying-cause-you're-freaking-the-crap-out-of-me smile. I think it worked, because his mouth twisted into a watery semi-smile.

'Well, now that I'm next door, you don't have to get lonely any more,' he said shyly.

'Uh-huh, yes, absolutely.' If I was a character in a video game, my Mission Status would be shrieking RED ALERT! RED ALERT!

And then, without any warning, Dhruv sat up, lunged forward and made an awkward grab for my face, his lips pouted. I don't think I've ever moved so fast in my life. I was on my feet, stuffing my cigarettes into my bag. 'I should go.'

'You don't like me,' he said, his eyes filling up again.

'No, it's not that.' I looked around for my phone.

'Then you do like me?'

'It's more complicated than liking you or not liking you.' I was at the door.

'Listen, don't go, Chhoti will think it's damn weird. I won't do anything, I promise. Just stay till dinner comes.'

'I really should go,' I said as I put on my shoes. The bloody lights came on right then, making us both wince. I saw his moist face illuminated horribly, his wet mouth glimmering in the white tubelight, and I wanted to throw up.

'Are you scared of me? Really, Arshi, I'm saying I'm sorry, no? People make mistakes and I'm a decent guy, anyone will tell you that.' He was beginning to sound defensive and exasperated.

'Yeah, okay.' I gave him a terse smile.

'Listen, will you just trust me?' He reached out and grabbed my elbow.

'Let me go,' I heard my voice saying. I couldn't even feel my mouth forming the words but I loved how assertive I sounded.

Pia walked into the room right then and Dhruv dropped my arm like he had been burned. I watched as his expression changed to nonchalance and Pia's eyes widened. Should I say something? No, let her figure her cousin out on her own. I didn't want to get involved.

'Are you going without eating dinner?' asked Pia, looking back and forth between the two of us.

I nodded, said 'Bye' and squeezed past her into the hall. Luckily Topsy had returned and she let me into the flat. We made some Maggi and had a drink, and she listened to the story, gagging slightly as she heard it.

We made it a point to avoid Dhruv after that, and I think he did the same, because we never saw him again. We only knew whether he was home or not from the light shining through his window. Once, early in the morning, we came face to face, each letting our maids in, but he looked away first and I stumbled back into bed.

12. in which deeksha gets engaged and i meet an old crush

I HAVE AN OBSESSIVE personality. It's like my mind gets set in a loop and the same thoughts keep returning over and over and over again, like the skipping of a scratched CD. Usually when I am alone, driving or just idling, my thoughts come back to taunt me like an army of monster children screeching 'Ha-ha, you'll never get rid of us!' as they ride a merry-go-round in my head.

Lately, all my thoughts centred on Kabir. What did I see in him, I wondered. Sure, he was still super-hot. But after you've known a person for a while, after you've loved him, it ceases to matter what he looks like. If you squint your eyes his face becomes a shape, his nose a triangle, the ears sort of like cones, so you stop dissecting, stop saying 'Oh, he's so hot' because his face becomes *him*, not something you can define any more. Occasionally, when Kabir and I were out together and I saw other women checking him out, turning their heads slightly and, more often than not, turning to look at me to judge if I was good enough for this guy, whether we were in fact dating or 'just friends', and so on, I'd remember he was attractive and that this was perhaps why I was so drawn to him.

It's not like he was cruel to me. I mean, he was sweet and all. He asked about my day with a kiss and told me about his, bought me coffee if he saw me looking longingly into a coffee shop, watched movies with me. He made my body sing in a way no one had ever done before, and we hadn't even slept together yet. He totally got my strange ways, my love for pulp fiction and airport reads, for instance, or the way I liked to eat spicy food with lime juice sprinkled all over it, or how I liked to lie back with my head on his stomach and ask him for stories from his childhood. He told his stories with flair, always beginning them properly with all the background information: where he was living at the time, what everything looked like, what it felt like for him. His stories stayed with me, particularly the one about the time his mother was pregnant for the second time and suffered some complications. Kabir, then just about five, had been left to fend for himself with only an ayah at home, and constantly thought the worst, assuming his mother was going to die. He would plant himself by the window on top of the stairs which overlooked the main entrance, and stare for hours through the translucent glass to catch any movement of people entering through the front gate. When he moved out and had his own house, he told me, he'd never have glazed windows because they depressed him so much. His mother survived but gave birth to a stillborn daughter. When she came home a week later, he ran to her wanting to touch her, to reassure himself that she was *home*, that she was *alive*, but she disentangled herself from him and his father sharply reprimanded him: 'Don't disturb Mummy.' After that she shut herself in her room for a week. As he told me the story I could feel him leaving me, going back to being five and feeling rejected and so completely alone. It explained so much about him, that story. It explained the constant stream of rejections that I faced from him. He was always, always pushing me away, saying he didn't want to get involved with anyone, constantly telling me that I was brilliant, fantastic even, and it wasn't me, it was him.

Still, however much I tried to understand, it never ceased to bother me that he would not acknowledge to anyone that we were 'together'. 'Because you're not together,' Topsy told me severely. 'He's just using you. Get that into your head.' Why would Kabir use me? He wasn't like that, I told her. He was sweet, and honest, at least; he wouldn't do that to me. But I couldn't ignore the fact that if we went out with his friends or with mine, he would always keep an arm's distance. He would refuse to let me touch him. He wouldn't say anything, you understand, but sort of flinch if I stroked his arm or touched his face, which was normally what I did when we were alone, just to make sure he was around in my world, and to let him know that I was happy to be near him. The fact that he perhaps wasn't as into me as I was into him crossed my mind, but I pushed it away. How could he not be into me? We enjoyed each other's company and I gave him his space. What more could anyone want?

Cheeto had loved these very qualities about me, I often remembered. I found myself thinking of Cheeto more often, in a way I hadn't in a while, wistfully and not bitterly. And I plagued myself with the thoughts that had eaten into me in the weeks following our break-up. Maybe it was my fault that he'd cheated on me. Maybe I was incapable of keeping a relationship together. It was in my genes, lying dormant for several years, cropping up repeatedly every time I fell in love and breaking my heart about the same number of times. And the worst part of it all with Kabir was that he didn't fit into any of my neat little categorizations so I didn't really know what we were doing, whether we were dating, or whether we were just, well, as much as I hated the term, fuck-buddies.

'Dating someone is when you're not formally seeing them, but just about,' Esha explained to me. 'Like Akshay and I are dating, technically, because we regularly go out for dinner-and-movie-type outings.'

'But we do those things, you and I, and we're not dating,' I pointed out.

'Uff, it has to be between a *guy* and a *girl*,' she said, sounding pained at my ignorance. 'A guy and a girl who are *non*-platonic, before you say anything. There have to be *intentions*.'

'So, what if one of the two has a crush on the other and they go out for coffee and drinks? Is that dating?'

'No, it has to be reciprocated.'

'And what is "seeing someone" then?'

'That's when you acknowledge that your relationship is going somewhere in the long run. Like when someone is your boyfriend—then you're seeing each other.'

'I thought that was a "relationship".'

'It is, but you don't say "I'm having a relationship with so-and-so", you say "I'm seeing so-and-so".'

'Like an adjective.'

'Sure,' she yawned widely. We had been up till four the night before at Elevate, with her 'date' and my 'whatever-it-was'. Esha had come back to our place to sleep.

'So what would Kabir and I be?' I asked her.

'I think you guys are dating,' she announced.

'But he doesn't.'

'Then he's kidding himself. And you should dump him.'

'That's what I keep telling her,' said Topsy, walking into the room and plopping down on my mattress.

But I couldn't even think of dumping him, because I

couldn't shake off the feeling that we were perfect for each other and, eventually, would wind up together forever. I badly wanted Kabir to be The One in my life, but in order for that to happen, he would have to feel the same way about me and he didn't seem to be showing any signs of feeling anything like that. So one evening, after he had promised to come over and didn't, and I had downed close to half a bottle of Smirnoff on my own, I decided it was time to end it. Enough, Arshi, no more heartbreaks, I told myself.

The next morning, during a cigarette break in the office I called him and got straight to the point. 'We're not going anywhere, are we?' I said calmly. Shruti was taking a break too so I murmured into the phone as softly as I could.

'What?' he snapped. I felt a little scared, but repeated myself anyway.

'Arshi, I've told you, I don't know. I can't say.'

'Just pick a side, will you?'

'Okay, then: NO. We're not going anywhere as of now.'

I waited, feeling the tears begin to prickle behind my eyelids.

'Hello?' he said, sounding a little apologetic.

'I'm here.'

'Well, okay then. I'll talk to you later.'

'No,' I said, turning away so Shruti wouldn't see my chin wobble. 'Don't call me, I'll call you.'

'Okay.' He sounded so nonchalant that I wanted to kill him right then. Don't guys feel *anything?*

'Bye,' I said softly. Any moment now he could stop me and say he had made a terrible mistake.

'Bye.' He hung up.

My next call was to Topsy. 'Good for you,' she said. 'I know you feel miserable right now, but trust me it's a good thing it ended.'

'I know,' I said when I was done sniffling. 'Shall we get plastered tonight?'

'Aren't we supposed to go for Deeksha's engagement thing tonight?'

Fuck. I had completely forgotten. Now that Deeksha was in Delhi for a bit, I had assumed we would be spending a lot of time together, which was obviously a mistake. Her parents, though not thrilled by the fact that she and Jean-Luc had decided to get married, hadn't reacted as badly as Saurabh had. In fact, after the first *oh-my-god* was over, they pretty much threw themselves into the spirit of things. It was rather chic to have a foreign-returned daughter marrying an Adonis-like man, and Deeksha's parents dearly loved entertaining people, so they jumped at the chance to host the largest, poshest wedding their circle had seen. The date had been quickly fixed for early December, just over a month away now. I had offered to go shopping with the family, pick out clothes and material and sweets and card designs. But Deeksha had thanked me, nicely, and said it really wasn't necessary because she had some five female relatives tagging along for each trip. '*I'm* bored out of my skull,' she said, 'I wouldn't want to inflict that on you.'

Ever since Deeksha had returned, she had been running crazily between joining a consultancy firm for her internship, getting Jean-Luc settled into his internship with UNICEF, shopping for clothes and jewellery for the wedding, booking guest houses for the hordes of relatives who would inevitably descend, arranging outings with her family and Jean-Luc so that they would get to know each other and, lastly, the part that broke my heart, applying for a Canadian citizenship so she could live there as Jean-Luc's wife.

'Why can't he get an Indian citizenship and you guys stay here?' I asked her, sulking slightly.

'Because we're both going to work in Canada. My being a Canadian citizen makes it a lot simpler. I don't think I'm going to live in India again for a while.'

'But why? How can you give up everything you've grown up with? Things are just getting exciting in India. You *have* to stay, you can't go!'

Deeksha looked at me and slowly shook her head. She had just about managed to squeeze in forty-five minutes of free time between work and taking Jean-Luc to her grandparents', to meet me for coffee at the Green Park Barista. I had already smoked five cigarettes in spite of her protests and glares, while she daintily sipped her latte. 'I'm getting married, Arsh. That means I have to think of things like getting a house and a car and making investments for our future and eventually kids as well. Financially and practically, it just makes more sense for me to live in Canada. Besides'—her face brightened as she said this—'I love Canada. I love the fact that there aren't that many people and the skiing and the walks and everything. You'll love it too when you come and visit.'

I nodded distractedly and said, 'Kids? Really?'

She laughed. 'Well, not immediately, you know. But, yeah, sometime in the future. And they'll have to go to school and ballet classes and orthodontists and all the rest of it.'

'Oh Deeksha, aren't you scared?'

She was quiet for so long I thought she hadn't heard me, but I noticed her face processing my query. It's one of the things I love about Deeksha. She takes every question you ask her very seriously. I mean she really ponders over it and answers it in all seriousness, and she likes to get her facts straight before she makes a statement. There's no bullshit about her. Our teachers at school used to get really impatient with her in the beginning, but then they realized that if, for example, they asked her to name the chief products of Madhya Pradesh, she'd name *all* the chief products without a single omission. 'I'm terrified,' she said finally. 'What if things don't work out. I mean, it's cool when it's just Jean-Luc and me, but when I think of him as my husband and his parents as my in-laws and the whole wedding thing, I just want to call it off.'

I rubbed her shoulder. 'Don't be silly. You'll be fine. It'll be perfect. I mean, if your gut instinct says you should do this, then you totally should.'

She smiled. 'I hope so, Arsh, I really do.'

'Besides, you can always get a divorce,' I said, trying to lighten the situation.

'Gee, thanks!' she swatted at me with her hand and we were Arshi and Deeksha again, not one almost-engaged person with her best friend whom she was fast leaving behind.

The engagement party turned out to be very posh and *huge*. They had decided to have the party on their sprawling terrace. Liveried waiters flitted through the crowd serving drinks and a variety of kebabs. I spotted two fairly famous TV anchors, a gay theatre actor, an aging danseuse and the head of a political party, all tossing their heads back and laughing, and scarfing the delectable shammi kebabs as soon as they were brought around. A cluster of foreigners stood in one corner, who I assumed were Jean-Luc's family. Deeksha's mom soon dragged me over for an introduction. His parents looked slightly bemused at the opulence of the Punjabi wedding. No doubt they had come to India with the impression of it being a country of starving millions; to see such lavish display of wealth must have been a little daunting. His older sister, married and the mother of a cute toddler, was busy pacifying the cranky child, and his younger sister, who looked about fifteen, chewed disinterestedly on some gum.

Topsy and I made our way to the bar area where a gang of

young people had monopolized the seats. They were Deeksha's and my friends from school, all gorgeously dressed and looking very grown-up. Deeksha was the first of our lot to get married—well, there was one Sujata Bajpai who had an arranged marriage in the second year of college, but no one ever saw her again, so she didn't really count. I hadn't met any of them in ages, and it was comforting to see how easily we slipped back into being teenagers, laughing about old teachers, recalling ludicrous classroom incidents, excitedly catching up on gossip—and getting smashed out of our minds.

The boisterous rhythms of a *Dhoom machale* remix rent the pleasant evening air, a desperate bid by the DJ to get people on to the dance floor. I was about to take a bite of some scrumptious-looking hariyali chicken when I was hauled to my feet by none other than Gagan Sharma, a guy I used to find really hot in school. I managed to grind a little bit, tossing my hair back and smiling in a way I hoped was seductive. The music had segued into *SexyBack* and I sang along, 'Dirty babe, you see the shackles baby, I'm your slave,' as I swung my hips and shook my head from side to side. Gagan looked at me appreciatively. It wasn't as sexy as it sounds, though, because by this time, the heels I was wearing were beginning to hurt like crazy and I could feel the sari pleats coming loose. I excused myself from Gagan and tottered, still giggling, to the nearest table.

I watched Deeksha and Jean-Luc circulating among the crowd, very elegant, very adult, very together, greeting people, accepting their wishes, making conversation. It looked to me like they'd switched nationalities because Jean-Luc was wearing a black achkan (which made him look unbelievably hot), while Deeksha looked radiant in her shimmering apple-green cocktail dress with a Chinese collar that offset the diamonds around her throat and on her ears, wrists and fingers. My heart contracted as I watched them. Deeksha looked so unlike the girl I used to know, with her snorting laugh and plump cheeks and large eyes, who shed tears at the drop of a hat. It hit me quite suddenly, with great force, as though my head had been struck with a hammer, that this was what my life, our lives, had turned out to be. The Future, if you know what I mean, was Here: The point in our lives we had looked towards when we were younger, half laughing as we said that some day this will be us, because we didn't really believe we could be anything other than sixteen. We were so sure we'd never be 'grown-up', never be surprised by adulthood, that life wouldn't sneak up on us, tap us on the shoulder and make us jump.

I hadn't noticed all this while, but Gagan had been standing behind my chair (I've no idea for how long), watching me looking at them and smiling dreamily. 'Look good together, don't they?' he whispered into my ear, tickling my neck and giving me goose pimples.

'I can't believe she's getting married,' I said, turning back to look at him, wanting very badly for him to *get* what I was saying.

'I know, dude, fuck, she's so young.'

He hadn't understood and I knew that perhaps he never would. For me it was like I was watching the world from a swing when it was at its highest point, when my toes pointed upwards and everything that I had left behind seemed so small, so minute, that it made me feel giddy. At that moment I really wished Kabir were there, because he kind of understood these things about me. But Kabir was a fuck-wit, I told myself drunkenly, and I didn't want his shit any more.

'I like this song,' Gagan was saying, one hand drawing me up, the other at my waist, ready to pull me into jive mode, which I remembered he did really well. I've come to believe that if you're a naturally good dancer you'll almost certainly be good in bed. It follows logically. If you, say, do the salsa really well, and you know the moves and everything, then you know exactly what you have to do to keep up with or complement your partner. Guys who follow a set rhythm while dancing are usually a lost cause in that case, because they'll be equally predictable in bed. They'll start with your mouth, move to your neck, to your breasts, back to your neck a couple of times before their fingers fumble with the buttons on your jeans and you're expected to gasp a little to acknowledge their execution of a perfect sequence, almost like a thundering applause. But then, I'm really not in a position to judge anybody. You see, I'm a terrible dancer. I start off fine but end up standing in one place, wiggling my hips a little and bobbing my head from side to side. Go figure.

I danced with Gagan for a bit to the sixties' rock the DJ was playing. Jean-Luc's parents hit the floor as well—Deeksha's mom with Jean-Luc's dad and Deeksha's dad with his mom in this we're-all-going-to-be-family-soon moment. Gagan swirled me around a couple of times to *Wake me up before you go-go*, a song I absolutely adore, and I was pleasantly conscious of his hand resting on my waist, above the sari. He was really good at leading me, putting just the right pressure on my back as he held my hand, so I twirled and twisted quite elegantly, all the while concentrating on keeping my sari together and watching my feet so I didn't step on him by accident. Then he dipped me so low that my hair touched the floor and everyone clapped. I saw Topsy look up from where she was talking to a group of people, and Deeksha, who was among them, gave me a big smile and a discreet thumbs-up. Gagan had me on my feet again immediately, trying to get me to dance to the next song, but I was out of breath and sweaty, so I went to find a table to maybe sit down for a while. Gagan was soon accosted by three girls, old acquaintances from school, who wanted a piece of him and I was quite happy to part ways for a bit.

I got myself a drink, the headiness of the earlier instalments having worn off with the strenuous dancing, and found Deeksha, sitting down at last, eating kebabs and sipping wine. An old man had got hold of her and was animatedly telling her something she was evidently not paying attention to, because she kept looking around the terrace in between polite nods. Devyani appeared, looking flushed and pretty, and threw her arms around me as two of her friends who were with her sat down at the table.

'God, where have you been?' she asked. 'Oh yeah, all that dancing . . .' she grinned mischievously.

'You've been so busy too,' I said archly, nodding at the boy sitting across from us.

'Oh, he's just a friend,' she said, blushing.

'Ri-ight. From the way he's looking at you, it's obvious.'

'Who's the boy *you* were with?' she countered.

'*That*,' I said imperiously, 'is none other than Gagan Sharma.'

'No way! He actually came?' said Deeksha looking up.

'Not only did he come, he's spent the whole evening flirting with me, thank you very much.'

'Really? Have you told him how you had the hots for him since school?'

'Ssshh! Not so loudly, he might hear you!' I said giggling, as the object of our discussion sauntered up to us.

'What's so funny?' Gagan enquired, as Deeksha, Devyani and I cracked up.

'Nothing,' I managed and looked sharply at Deeksha, who pulled herself together, tucked in her lower lip demurely and glanced up at Gagan through her eyelashes. He had been by far the cutest boy in school for three years and we had all taken turns to have a crush on him.

'Aren't you going to say congratulations, Gagan?' she asked in a put-on husky voice that set me off again. But Gagan seemed to find nothing amiss and looked at her admiringly.

'Yeah, man, I was going to say congrats all this while, but you've been so busy socializing. Good party, though. And so, you're getting married?'

'So it would appear,' said Deeksha, waving her hand around to indicate the crowd.

'I know, obvious question, sorry.' He shook his head adorably. 'When do I get to meet the lucky guy?'

'You can meet him right now,' she said, craning her neck to see where Jean-Luc was. 'Devi, sweetie, go find Jean-Luc and tell him to come here.'

As Devyani trotted off, the old man who had hung around listening to our conversation broke in and informed Gagan and me that he had known Deeksha since she was a baby. 'I knew her when she was only thiiis big!' he said, moving his hands a couple of inches across. 'But I always knew she would turn out to be beautiful.'

'Manu-uncle, you flatter me,' said Deeksha, fluttering her fingers at her throat. Her gestures truly amazed me that evening and I watched her perform this new one with my mouth half open.

'No, no, no flattery,' he said gallantly. 'Tell me, young man, have you ever seen any young girl look so beautiful?'

Gagan, may he go to a heaven with harems, looked at me for one blessed moment before he shook his head and said, 'No, sir. I think Deeksha is lovely.'

'And how do you two know Deeksha?' he enquired of me.

'We were in school together,' I told him and he nodded, coughing violently, in the way only old men can cough, with a great clearing of throat and spit everywhere. I flinched and Gagan scrunched up his face for a second, but Deeksha, in her new calm socialite avatar, just gazed at him serenely till he was done and then judiciously asked whether he wanted any water.

'No, beta, I'm fine. What to do, when you get to my age everything gives up on you,' he said, looking at us sadly.

Jean-Luc had appeared by then and Deeksha and I turned to him with exclamations of delight, then introduced him to Gagan. Manu-uncle hovered for a while before he was hailed by another group of old men and shuffled off nodding his head at all of us to say goodbye.

'Are you enjoying the party, Arshi?' asked Jean-Luc.

'Oh yes, it's a killer. And you guys are being so good, talking to everyone and all.'

'We don't have a choice,' said Deeksha, pulling a face. 'I wanted a quiet dinner at home, just family and close friends, but my parents said that wouldn't be fair.'

'Fair to whom?' I asked.

'That's precisely what I asked! And they were like it won't be fair to the other people, who weren't close friends or family but who would still like to see me married in style. So then I said they can see me married in style, but surely they don't need to see me engaged in style. They said I didn't understand. Personally, I think they're doing it for their own sake, because neither Jean-Luc nor I give a tiny rat's ass about who wants to see our wedding.'

'My parents seem to be having fun,' offered Jean-Luc, picking at a seekh kebab.

'That's probably the point. They want to show your parents a good time. Any excuse to throw a party, I think. This is just mom's way of having a quickie before the wedding. She can't wait another two months.'

'Less,' I said. 'December is like a month and a half away.'

'Where's Kabir?' asked Jean-Luc looking around. I made violent shushing and slashing motions, which thoroughly confused him, but by that time the damage was done and Gagan, who had stretched himself out in a chair, suddenly looked alert and glanced at me.

'Who's Kabir?' he asked casually.

'Oh, just some chutiya Arshi used to date,' said Deeksha flippantly. 'The love of her life sometime back.'

I wanted to kill her. 'Um . . . not really the love of my life, but yes, we were sort of dating.'

'How can you be sort of dating?' asked Gagan.

'Thank you!' said Deeksha, pointing at him and then at me. 'That's just what I've been asking her, but you know Arshi, she sees so many different people that it's hard for me to keep track!'

Great. Now it sounded like I was a slut.

'Really?' Gagan raised an eyebrow at me. I love people who can raise a single eyebrow. I can't, although when I was much younger I used to practise in front of the mirror, cellotaping one eyebrow down and then raising them both, until I got a terrible rash from the cellotape glue and had to apply a smelly yellow ointment on it for a week.

'What Deeksha means is, um, I don't really date a lot of people, but, um . . .' I floundered around trying to think of the best way to end that sentence. I don't really date a lot of people, but I sleep with them? No. I don't really date a lot of people, but I slip poison into their drinks so that they can't date anyone else? Nope. I don't really date a lot of people, but I do have a fair amount of social engagements? Ah, that was a good one. I opened my mouth to say it, but Jean-Luc got there before me:

'Someone as wonderful and smart and pretty as Arshi has to do a lot of looking around before she finds the right guy.' I wanted to kiss him, but held myself back and settled for smiling at him adoringly.

'That I can believe,' said Gagan, miraculously unraising his eyebrow and slipping his arm around my waist. 'Can I call you sometime?' he asked, looking at me as though there was no one else in the room. 'Perhaps we could go for coffee?' I looked around to see whether Deeksha had caught this, but the three of them had drifted off. I spotted them across the room talking to Topsy who had just emerged from somewhere inside the house.

'I love coffee,' I said, showing an imaginary Kabir the finger.

'Great, just give me your number.' Gagan pulled out his very cool flip-phone and entered the digits as I spoke them. Then he kissed me on my cheek, saying he had to leave and that he would call me the next day to fix up where we would meet. I watched him go and, still smiling, turned around to catch Deeksha's eye. It was not a happy eye. She must have just come up from behind us.

'What?' I asked sulkily.

'I do hope you know what you're doing.'

'Tchah. Of course I know what I'm doing. I'm not a child.'

'You're not over Kabir yet.'

'So?' I said, looking at her fiercely. 'So what good has being into Kabir been so far? Is it going anywhere? No. Is he ever going to date me seriously? No. So the point of sitting around and pining away for him is *what* exactly?'

'You might *hurt* this guy?' Deeksha could look pretty severe when she wanted to.

'Oh, please. He just wants to get into my pants. That's what they all want.'

'I can't have this conversation with you any more, Arshi. You're just so, so thick sometimes, it makes me mad.'

'Well, sor-rree for breathing!'

We sat glumly for a while, staring at our empty wine glasses. Then I turned to her.

'I'm sorry, Dee. It's your special day, I know. But as far as I know the best way to get over someone is to be with someone else. It worked with Cheeto, didn't it? I mean, I forgot all about him once I met Kabir.'

She reached out and stroked my arm. 'I'm sorry for snapping at you, babe. But I worry about you. I just don't want your life to follow a pattern you can't get out of.'

'I'm smarter than you give me credit for,' I told her.

Just then, Jean-Luc the Lovely appeared with more wine in fresh glasses. Devyani and Topsy had also gathered at the table and together we toasted Deeksha and Jean-Luc and made fun of everyone who'd been at the party till it was time for Topsy and me to go home.

13. in which michael hosts a birthday party

WHEN I WAS YOUNGER, I used to draw social maps. This was much before the Internet or email, or sites like Orkut or Facebook where you just need to check a list to find out who knows whom. I would draw a little circle and write 'A' in it, for me, and then draw other circles around it with my friends' initials in them and connect my circle to theirs and theirs to each other's to see how many degrees of familiarity there existed between us. If someone I knew was equally close to someone else I knew, I drew a line connecting the two of them. If I knew someone only through someone else, I was connected to the person only via the other circle; there was no direct line. Sort of like the maps you see at malls, or at stations, with big signs indicating your possible destinations, the purpose of your visit, and a separate circle with an arrow pointing to where you should be, captioned in big, red, taunting letters: YOU ARE HERE.

Sometimes I wish my life had a sign like that, just so I could see where I was placed in the larger scheme of things. You see, I always know where I am but I'd always rather be somewhere else. If I had the sign I'd say, Look, I'm here, exactly where I need to be. But then, this is life, and life is weird. I wish sometimes there was some kind of sign to indicate that a particular moment in my life was indeed a significant moment. Like in the movies, where the music builds up to a resounding crescendo or takes on a new strain at a defining moment. But there's nothing, no music, no sign saying you've reached, no big 'Congratulations, You've Made It' with coloured balloons and noisy whistles and confetti. Because that would make it too easy.

It was at Michael's birthday party that I met Cheeto again, for the first time in six months. He came with his new girlfriend. It was a drizzly, chilly day, the kind of day that lifts my mood, plants tunes of old Hindi songs in my head, makes me want to drive around the city even if every road is jammed with traffic.

It was unusual for Michael to have a birthday party in the first place. It's true I had known him for only two birthdays now, but I was quite sure he wasn't a birthday party kind of person. The year before this, he had celebrated his birthday with a small dinner party at his house and it turned out to be the most boring affair I had ever been to. He had called two of his friends from school who were as dull as plaster. We had opened a bottle of wine and eaten a lot and then generally sat around, studying the pictures on the wall while one of his friends cracked vague jokes about what Michael had been like in school. Michael spent the evening squirming and blushing severely, and I spent my time glancing less and less discreetly at my watch to see when I could go home.

But this year Michael had new friends from work and Chhaya's friends were now more or less his friends as well. I guess he wanted to show them off to each other, which warranted a fairly big bash at a cheap joint near his house called Dragonz Resto-Bar. Dragonz was, by far, the shadiest place I'd ever been to. I had been there a couple of times with Michael, who loved it. I doubt they ever changed their tablecloths, which were so encrusted with beer and gravy that if you rested your elbows on them you had to have a bath later. There was all of one light in the centre of the hall-like space. It emanated a dim red glow that hid the booths in the corner, which people chose, I imagine, for secret romances—though what kind of 'romance' you could have in a place like that was beyond me. Shady is as shady does, I say.

Surprisingly Michael had found the place to be after his heart. He was a regular; the waiters knew him by name and brought us our thirty-rupee pegs without us having to order for them. That was the sole advantage of the place. It was bloody cheap, and I suspect the staff was drinking the alcohol on the sly because they let the customers do as they pleased. One time, Michael brought in a mixed-music CD and they let us play it even though some of the couples in the corners glowered. Over his many visits there, Michael had nagged them to fix the dusty old pool table that lay in a corner, and they did, bringing in much more business. In gratitude they'd always chase away other people who were playing if Michael entered.

It hadn't occurred to me, though it should have, that, thanks to Michael's exclusive relationship with this joint, Dragonz would no longer be that shady if the whole damn place was booked for an exclusive do. Michael's the kind of person who never does things by halves. When I entered I was glad to find that the tables had been stripped of their stained tablecloths and pushed against the walls in neat lines to create space for a dance floor. There was a real DJ, someone Michael had hired at his own expense (with a slight discount, he informed me triumphantly, because the guy was also trying to land a job at Dragonz), and the waiters had shed their usual sleepy-eyed, slack-jawed look and were bustling about most efficiently. A man in a blue suit stood at the door, extending his hand to me and introducing himself as 'Vinod Dhar, Manager. If you have any suggestions or complaints, come to me.' It looked like this was the hippest thing to have happened to Dragonz since it had opened.

I turned up promptly and politely at ten, since the invitation had been for nine, and was surprised to see that I was early, the only invitee to have arrived. Michael was busy bossing the DJ around, while Chhaya was anxiously checking on the waiters who were setting up the food and gently instructing them from time to time. They didn't see me come in, and I hung back a little to watch them, marvelling again at how perfect they were for each other. There are some couples who *fit*; you never wonder how they got together because it seems as though there was never a time that they weren't together. Michael and Chhaya were like that. I stood around at the door, not wanting to intrude on their private moment before Michael became who he was in front of everyone else, sort of trying-too-hard-and-trying-not-to-look-like-he-was-trying-too-hard, and watched as he gave Chhaya a light squeeze as she murmured something to him. He asked the DJ to do a sound check and he and Chhaya danced to the foot-stomping beats completely without inhibition. They stopped dancing as soon as they spotted me.

'Happy birthday!' I said, coming forward to hug Michael awkwardly. We had never been great at hugs, Michael and I. I handed him the John Mayer CD I had bought for him. I wasn't sure he liked John Mayer, but I knew Michael enough to know that if I recommended something to him, he would willingly listen to it.

'You look great,' he said, setting the gift down on a table, as Chhaya walked up behind him and nodded in agreement. It struck me what a very clear-hearted person she was, how she herself had no 'social face' at all and in turn unquestioningly accepted other people's artifices as just a charming part of their personalities. The way Michael sort of stiffened around me, if I were her I'd totally hate me for being a source of discomfort for my boyfriend. But Chhaya seemed to have made it simpler, for herself and for us. In her head, unlike mine, Michael could love me and love her and the world wouldn't stop turning.

'Hello Arshi,' she said warmly, giving me a hug. 'You're our very first guest!'

'I noticed,' I said, looking around. 'What time is everyone else getting here?'

I knew immediately that it was the wrong question to have asked, because Michael's forehead furrowed and he glanced at his cellphone. 'I don't know,' he said, sounding worried. 'Some of them called to say they're on their way, and I've given directions and all, so they should have been here by now.'

'They'll come, jaanu. It's Saturday night, they'll come late only,' said Chhaya, rubbing his back. 'Calm down now. Why don't you make Arshi a drink?'

'Yes, yes,' he said, distractedly. 'Arshi, what'll you have? Vodka-Sprite?'

'Yes, please. I like what you've done to the place, by the way. It doesn't look shady at all.'

'No?' he beamed at me. 'I've been working hard, yaar, for two days straight, to get this place in good shape.'

'I wanted balloons,' said Chhaya, sticking out her lower lip.

'Balloons *would* have looked nice,' I laughed. Michael rolled his eyes theatrically to show he'd got the chick-bonding thing we were doing.

By the time the bartender had made me my drink and given Michael his beer and Chhaya her fresh-lime soda, people had started to trickle in and I saw Michael's face lifting with each arrival. Actually, there were a lot more people than I had expected to see. I loved Michael, but part of that love was also tolerance. I knew I couldn't hang out with him for sustained periods of time, but I had come to accept that as part of our friendship. I just found it weird that other people loved him too. His new-found popularity made him appear somewhat cooler in my eyes.

For a while, I didn't see anyone I knew. Chhaya hovered near me, for comfort and to give comfort, I suspect, because she tossed me a worried look whenever Michael beckoned to her to join him. After a while I said, 'Go, go,' and waved her away, reassuring her with nods that I'd be fine.

'Go talk to someone,' she whispered before going. 'Do you want me to introduce you around?'

'In a bit,' I said. 'I'm fine for right now.'

I *was* fine. I quite enjoyed this stage at a party, when you don't know anyone so you stand mysteriously by the wall and smile into your drink, occasionally making deliberate eye contact with people and making it seem like you're laughing to yourself. Later, depending on my mood and if boredom snuck up on me, I'd strike up a conversation with someone, or attach myself to Michael and let him introduce me to people. I took another sip of my drink and just as I turned and half smiled at the group of people standing near me, I saw Cheeto walking in.

It had been a while since I had last seen him—six months, like I said. I knew I looked different, thinner than when we had been dating, my hair had been *styled* as opposed to just being plain cut and now hung in a feathery mass around my shoulders, my eyes partly covered by the perky bangs which I casually flicked out of the way now and then. I was wearing a top that belonged to Topsy, a contraption of silk and string in vivid

violet shot through with gold thread, that hung perfectly on me
and looked like a trendy tube top instead of the corset it was
supposed to be. I had worn my jeans very low and had strung
a beaded belt into the loops, which I touched every now and
then for comfort. I was clutching it like a rosary now. I had shed
the long jacket I had been wearing so my midriff was now well
exposed, and I had just finished my period so my stomach was
gloriously flat. I ran my fingers over it when I spotted Cheeto,
just to make sure the jeans had not ridden up and covered it.

I was pleased to see that he looked much plumper than
when we were going out. Not that he was *fat* now, but he had
been the skinnier of the two of us, with a lean stomach. I
remembered now, shivering, how I had liked to kiss it, butterfly-
style, with just the merest hint of my lips and eyelashes, the tip
of my tongue following the quivers as his muscles contracted
under the smooth skin. It's always like this when you meet the
people you've been sexually intimate with, I think: an instant
porn movie inside your head.

I saw Michael walk up to him to say hello and I wanted to
grab Michael by the ear and yell my lungs out at him for not
warning me about this. Why was my loathsome ex-boyfriend
invited to the birthday party of one of my closest friends? And
then, like in a movie, I saw a hand grab Cheeto's arm in slow
motion, demanding his attention, and when he looked around
to acknowledge the person I recognized the smile that creased
his face, the smile I once thought had been created just for me.
I stepped back a little against the wall to see her better, the one
who made him cheat on me. I had met her once at a work get-
together of Cheeto's to which I had tagged along and she had
been sugary-sweet to me, but only when Cheeto was around,
flipping her hair at him to see whether he noticed.

Manjari, that was her name. A fairly ordinary-looking girl

from where I stood, with longish hair that was held back with a scarf, wearing a T-shirt over a sweatshirt and a denim skirt and boots, like some sixteen-year-old. I mean, who wore those clothes any more? She had a round face—'pleasant' if you like them fat, I thought sourly—large, black eyes and a snub nose embellished with a shiny silver stud. She was whispering something to Cheeto, laughing and poking his stomach, and when he grabbed her in a headlock and knuckled her hair, she kicked and squealed, generally drawing attention from every corner of the room. We had been quieter, Cheeto and I; in fact, I had been bloody quieter, because he had always wanted to be in the spotlight. A journalist, he called himself. Well, if he had been a really good journalist he'd want to efface himself and sit back and watch other people, tell their stories through their eyes, or at least objectively. But his stories as I remembered them, full of big words and catchphrases, read like he was showing off, like the telling and the teller were so much more important than the story itself. At one time I had thought they were wonderful, really impressive, but had gradually come to realize how me-me-me they all were. Oh yes, after a point I stopped moral-policing myself and just let the snark loose in my brain.

I watched Cheeto and his girlfriend wend their way through the crowd, greeting people they knew, sometimes parting company with Michael when he stopped to talk to someone. Chhaya had joined them too and was waving to a waiter to get them a drink. Trust the bastard, I seethed to myself, trust him to come for my friend's birthday party with his new girlfriend and act like he owns the place. Who does he think he is?

Michael was bringing them closer now, introducing them to a bunch of people standing next to the bar and Cheeto glanced around and spotted me. Before I could pretend I wasn't looking their way he gave me a crooked half smile, the kind you give someone when you're in on something together, like acknowledging a secret alliance, sure as hell not the kind of smile you give your ex-girlfriend. I raised my chin and my hand, bending the tips of my fingers into a wave, and smiled too—sardonically, in a woman-of-the-world kind of way, I hoped, as opposed to looking slightly asinine and loser-like on my own in a corner. I made sure of course that it didn't look like a beckoning wave, just an oh-hello-I-see-you gesture.

'I was just telling Manjari how little places like this have so much charm, which we lose out on by choosing five-star elitist establishments to party in,' I heard Cheeto's imperious voice float above the music. *Oh please!* One of the things about Cheeto that used to irritate me even when we were dating was his habit of going only to expensive places. He could afford to not because he was making a lot of money in his profession, but because he knew this or that PR person who handled events at that particular place. I didn't personally handle any restaurant accounts for my firm, but Cheeto had buttered up one of my colleagues who did and had her number on his phone. I remember how embarrassed I was one day when this colleague and I were eating lunch and her phone rang and she announced that my boyfriend was calling. I gestured to her and took the call. I don't think there was a speck of hesitation in his voice as he asked me if the two of us and a couple of our friends could get into Elevate free. Wordlessly, I handed the phone to my colleague. Eventually she fixed something up, telling me good-naturedly, 'Now Arshi, you owe me one.' Every once in a while, I'd suggest to him that we could go somewhere cheaper, somewhere we didn't need 'contacts', where there were all-night happy hours or something, but he never seemed to want to. He had no objections to eating at cheap places, mind you. Often, after clubbing, we'd cruise down the AIIMS stretch looking for egg parathas or eat kathi rolls at an all-night kebab joint because it was considered cool, but drinking at cheap places was just cheap. I think I had told myself at that point that I loved him and there are some things you have to overlook about your lover, or you'll just drive yourself mad.

I wondered now whether he still loved me. He had never said he didn't, just that he had met someone else who was 'better for him'. It was funny how even now, after all these months, just the sight of him could make me so bitter. Quickly, as I saw him approaching, I composed myself, counting to three on each drag of my cigarette. I hadn't thought about him in a while, not since Kabir had entered my life, but seeing him now made me feel like I had when we first broke up, depressed and feeling a desperate need to never get out of my pyjamas again.

He bent down, smiling affectionately, and kissed me hard on each cheek. 'It's been so long since I've seen you,' he said softly. 'You look good.'

'Thanks,' I said, smiling back genially. You could've got sunburn from the two of us, the way we were piling the 'warmth' on.

'I want you to meet Manjari,' he said, and as my eyes involuntarily grew wider, he hastily added, 'only if you think you can handle it.'

The arrogance in his voice made my blood boil. 'Of course I can handle it,' I said tersely. 'Why would you think I couldn't?'

'Oh, I don't know, just your expression. Manjari, this is Arshi; Arshi, Manjari.'

When Cheeto and I were together I'd loved the way he could read all my expressions, the way he slid effortlessly under my skin and nestled against my organs, near my lungs, napping on my heart, entwining himself around my kidneys and my spine. I felt closest to him when I knew he knew exactly what I was thinking and what to say to me, startling me like he'd grabbed me by my ankles and tripped me so I fell backwards and into him. Now it just made me feel annoyed, and super-vulnerable, with no protection to shield me from his taunts and the way he could laser right into my mind. If I tripped now, I had no one to catch me.

Manjari turned, almost in slow motion, flipping her hair around and sliding her arm casually around Cheeto's waist. 'Hi,' she said, her mouth curving in a smug smile even though it looked like she was trying to stop it. 'It's nice to finally meet you.' But she evidently didn't mean it, because the next instant she was tugging at Cheeto's sleeve and whispering something into his ear.

'In a minute, Manjari,' he snapped, which made it my turn to smile smugly. But in that moment of perfect, suspended bitchiness, I also felt slightly ashamed. I suddenly found myself thinking of the first boy ever to have professed his love for me, when we were ten and *almost* aware that we were different sexes. His name was Tarun, he wore spectacles and was the only one in Class 5 who wrote with a pen, a Parker pen at that. We used to have handwriting tests then, and Tarun and I had been paired together. Unlike my handwriting, and that of the majority of our class, still dribbly at the sides, Tarun's was small, neat and well formed. I asked him how he got his letters to look so good and he said his father tied all his fingers except the thumb and forefinger together so that he'd learn how to curve his hand around a pen. I tried it, too, when I got home, but the string kept unwinding and my hand got cramped and tired after a bit so I gave up. We wound up being in the Science Club together as well—the only two people from our class, which was quite a big deal, because the Science Club usually took only seniors. Every Friday after school we'd walk to the chemistry lab and spend the next hour doing experiments with litmus paper and iodine. We were considered really cool then and all our peers thought we rocked.

Tarun's parents moved soon after Class 5, and on our last walk together to the chemistry lab he told me quite matter-of-factly that I was the nicest girl he knew besides his sister and that he loved me. I took this bold declaration in my stride as impassively as it had been made to me, even told my mother about it, which was a mistake, because she instantly blabbed to all her friends and they sighed over it and made dumb remarks about how quickly kids grow up and other similar things. Anyway, about a year after his family relocated, our class teacher came in one day and gravely announced that we should all 'keep one minute of silence for our former classmate and friend Tarun who expired two days ago'. That was the word she used, 'expired', like he was a product or something. I was quite shaken for a day or two, then faked being sadder than I was, like kids do, for the attention I got from my mother and my teachers. Three months after we'd heard of Tarun's death, I remember I was laughing at something and one of the girls in my class turned to me and said quite seriously, 'How can you laugh when Tarun has passed away?' I didn't laugh in school for a while after that, not in front of my classmates at least. I learnt later that his death had been an accident. He had been riding his cycle and a car had crashed into him, reversing too fast or some such silly thing that could have been so easily avoided. I hadn't thought of Tarun in forever, and I didn't know why I was thinking of him then, except that he was a boy who had loved me and hadn't been afraid to tell me he did because it was so simply a declaration that didn't need one back. He had thought I was nice, 'the nicest girl' he knew, and I was being so un-nice just then that I wanted to cry.

Cheeto cleared his throat and I looked up. 'I'm sorry, my mind was wandering,' I told him.

'I know, I noticed. What's the matter, babe, stressed at work?'

No one had called me babe in such a long time.

Okay, okay, stop feeling sorry for yourself.

Oh my god, Arshi, tell me you are not going to cry. Oh boy, here they come; at least turn away so he doesn't see you.

'Arsh? Are you okay?' Cheeto looked at me, his face full of concern as the tears that had been welling up in my eyes finally made their way down my cheeks.

'I'm sorry,' I said, sniffing madly. 'I've just, um, got a lot on my mind.'

'Is everything all right?' asked Chhaya, coming up. 'Arshi! Why are you crying?'

'I'm not crying,' I replied sharply. 'Just, like, give me a minute and I'll be fine.'

'Is she drunk?' Cheeto asked Chhaya. 'She gets emotional when she's drunk.'

'I am NOT drunk. Cheeto, shut up.'

'Do you guys know each other?' asked a genuinely confused Chhaya. I didn't blame her. The vibes in the air were going haywire.

'Um, yeah, Arshi and I used to date,' said Cheeto, his eyes turned to his feet.

'*Used to* being the operative term here,' I said, finally dry-eyed though still sniffling.

'Used to what?' asked Manjari who had vanished and had now suddenly reappeared. I looked at Cheeto. I was beginning to enjoy this. He had wanted the spotlight, after all. I let him have it.

'Arshi and I *used to* date,' he said sighing.

'Oh . . . that,' said Manjari.

'Yes, oh *that*,' I said, flatly, and then I couldn't stop myself. 'It ended because he cheated on me.'

Cheeto inhaled sharply, 'Arshi!', like a warning.

'What?' I asked, innocently. 'Chhaya wanted to know.'

Chhaya was beginning to back away.

Manjari looked at me and raised an eyebrow, 'Some things are in the past for most people.'

Good god, what was with the attitude?

'Oh, it's in the past for me as well. Very much in the past. It was, actually, your boyfriend who brought it up.'

'That's enough, Arshi. We're going.' Cheeto turned on his heel, took hold of Manjari's elbow and walked away. It was *the* dramatic exit of the decade. Really, I didn't think people did that outside movies.

I spotted Michael lingering nearby, chatting to some people. Without excusing myself I grabbed his arm and dragged him into a corner.

'What? What?'

'How could you invite him, Michael?' I hissed, feeling my nose beginning to itch again. 'How could you invite *him?*'

'I wanted to warn you,' he said, looking sheepish, 'but I never thought he'd actually show up. I bumped into him at a disc and he said oh we should meet up and I said ya I'm having a birthday party next week, you should come.'

'*You should come?* What is wrong with you?'

'I was drunk, man, and I was just making conversation.' Michael blinked his eyes slowly. 'Honestly, with the whole Kabir thing, I thought you were over Cheeto, I would never have called him if I knew you'd be so upset.'

I sighed. It was true. How was Michael to know that just being around Cheeto was a supreme mind-fuck for me? 'It's okay,' I said sourly.

The rest of the party was pretty uneventful. Cheeto and Manjari left me severely alone all evening and I only bumped into Cheeto again purely by accident, when we were both waiting for the loo to be free. He lit a cigarette and pretended to ignore me. I stood around for a bit and said softly, to my shoes, 'I'm sorry.'

'You should be! That was really unlike you!'

'I don't know what got into me, okay?' My voice was beginning to squeak.

'Please don't hate me, Arsh.'

My eyes widened. On a scale of one to ten of Least Expected Responses I'd say this was a twelve. 'I don't hate you.'

He gave me his half smile again and hit me lightly on the shoulder. 'So we're cool?'

'Yeah,' I said, shrugging, 'we're cool.'

Whatever *that* meant.

14. in which i do something totally reckless

GAGAN DID CALL, AS he'd promised, but almost two weeks after the engagement party, by which time I'd forgotten I'd ever given him my number. I was busy with a new client, and Shruti was being a complete bitch that day—very prima donna, barking orders at people and refusing to acknowledge me because I had made a mistake in a presentation we were to give to some top guys at TGIF. It was, basically, one of those days, and I couldn't wait for it to be over so I could go home and crash.

But home wasn't much fun either. Topsy's dark mood had escalated. Her parents were due for a visit the next day and she and Fardeen spent most of the time he was over fighting. I could hear them screaming at each other through the wall we shared. Okay, not at each other, but Topsy screaming at him. And it always ended with her crying violently. I had even walked in on her sobbing in the loo in the middle of the night, crying really, really hard, her throat muscles contracting violently and animal sounds coming out of her mouth.

'Oh Topsy,' I said, lowering the toilet seat and sitting on it so I could put my arms around her. She didn't even acknowledge my presence, didn't say a word to me; she just kept crying and crying. Finally she stood up, washed her face and went to her room, shutting the door behind her. Yes, Topsy was being really peculiar those days.

Anyway, so around six in the evening, when the awful day finally got over and I was hanging around wondering whether I should meet a couple of friends for a drink before I went home just so I didn't have to go home immediately, my phone beeped and informed me I'd got a text from Gagan.

I love people who use punctuation in their text messages, commas and capital letters and parentheses. And paragraphs. I'd once carried on a mighty Internet romance with a boy from Australia, whom I met on ICQ, just because he put brackets in his emails. Punctuation seduces me the way little else can. But Gagan was cute, which made up for the fact that his text read: hi, r u free 4 dinner 2day? Dude, there's a dictionary on your phone. Use it. But it still set off little butterflies of possibility in my stomach. Anything could happen. So what if his verbal skills weren't fantastic? This was Gagan, the cutest boy in school, someone I had lusted after for three years, even playing that game with our names—FLAMES, it was called. We would write out our name and the name of the boy in question in full, cross out the letters that were common to both, do a little counting and figure out what we were to our dream-guys and what they were to us: Friend, Lover, Affectionate, someone we'd Marry, Enemy or Sweetheart. Okay, so the game didn't offer much distinction by way of relationships, but as I recall Gagan and I always wound up with L, the big letter, the one everyone wanted. Lovers. It was perfect for us twelve-year-olds, though I suspect twelve-year-olds nowadays have their own version to keep them occupied and dreaming.

I texted back in the affirmative and he said he'd meet me at

Big Chill in Khan Market at eight. I had been battling a pasta craving for over a week so I happily agreed. Then I felt guilty for abandoning Topsy and called her to ask whether she wanted to join us, hoping of course that she'd say no.

'No,' she said, sadly into the phone, 'you go. I'm going to get some sleep. I haven't been sleeping well at all these days.'

'You sure you'll be okay?'

'Yeah, don't worry. I'll be fine.' Right, so guilty conscience about flatmate being left alone was taken care of.

I went to the bathroom to tidy up, brushing my hair vigorously in an attempt to make it look human and not formerly the possession of a Cocker Spaniel. (That's one thing I will say for my firm: We have fabulous bathrooms, with divinely scented soaps, lotion dispensers, and a hand-dryer and a potty shower in each stall—although I've been warned not to use a potty shower in a public loo, with good cause I'm sure.) The hair attempt didn't seem to work. I felt fat and I noticed a new pimple developing right on my cheekbone, but I was happy—I was going out for dinner with someone who seemed to want to see me. I was grateful to him for asking me out, because I had forgotten what it was like to be treated with courtesy and grace. It wasn't a very healthy state of mind, but it was the only state of mind I had at the moment so I suppose I had to live with it.

Shruti pounced on me as I emerged. 'You're still here, Arshi? Good, just look over this press release.'

'I, uh, can't. I have to leave.'

'It's five-forty-five,' she looked from her wristwatch to me. 'You came into work at one. I don't think a couple of extra minutes will kill you.'

'I came into work at one because I was at a press conference from nine in the morning.'

She laughed unpleasantly. 'It's not like you're overworked, Arshi. How much work do you really do? I mean, you spend all day online, surfing junk on the Net. We might have to rethink your job description.'

I felt anger collecting at the base of my spine and familiar twists of frustration in my stomach. The problem is that while I have a short temper I also have a very hard time expressing anger. Most of my rage turns inwards. I can't speak when I'm angry, if I try it comes out meek and shaky and makes me even more annoyed with myself. When I'm really angry I cry, which people interpret as weakness, which irritates me all the more.

I knew of someone, a friend of a friend, who had the same problem. Apparently, he spent his entire life getting really angry and not expressing it, so everyone just walked all over him and became super-aggressive when they were around him. One night, after a party in a farmhouse in the outskirts of Delhi, his friends were teasing him about something or the other, calling him a loser and what not, and he drove his car straight into a pile of concrete slabs. I mean, he literally took a sharp left turn off the road, floored his accelerator and drove into the concrete blocks at the side of the road at some 120 kmph. One person in the car survived the crash, and she had to have her legs amputated because the car crumpled with immense force into the backseat, where she was. Which was how everyone else knew the story. She said he'd clutched the steering wheel so hard she'd got scared and told the others to lay off. But they said, 'Oh dude, he won't mind.' It made the headlines for weeks after that, with everyone trying to figure out more about the Suicide Driver, which is what the media named him. They gave the girl just one story on the inside page, preferring to go with the popular conception that the guy had been part of some evil cult and had been planning the 'mass murder' for weeks because he had offered to drive everyone there and back. Anyway, since then I've never underestimated the power of passive aggressiveness.

What I would have absolutely loved to do at that moment was to drive a car with Shruti in it straight into a large, solid rock and jump out of the car myself just before the crash so she'd die a horrible, painful death and leave me alone forever. But, as always, I swallowed my anger and looked through the press release, correcting at least fifty spelling mistakes the intern who had written it had made. God, you'd think they'd teach them how to spell in a mass comm course. Or at least how to operate the spell-check function on MS Word. But Anubha the intern was sweet and charming and plumply pleasant and totally non-threatening in any way to anybody, so I guess she couldn't be a super-speller on top of all that. Anubha and I had had lunch together that day. She'd brought a delicious salad with little bits of avocado and fresh crunchy cucumber in an amazing vinegar dressing, because she was on a diet. Only, I had eaten most of it and given her my sandwich in return. Hey, it was a nice sandwich. A Subway sandwich, which I'd picked up after my press conference in the morning. I'd got a chocolate-chip cookie too, but had eaten it on my own. Subway makes the best chocolate-chip cookies. Well, Subway first and my mom's friend Frieda second. Frieda's Australian, though she's lived here for the past ten years, working at Mother Teresa's orphanage and helping out with other NGOs that work with kids, which is how she knows my mom. Sometimes, when she comes over to the Farmhouse, she brings warm cookies, fresh out of her oven, all uneven and jagged, with bits of chocolate in them that have baked to hardness on the outside but are molten when you bite into them. Although normally I prefer a good cheesecake over anything chocolatey, I eat Frieda's cookies by the handful, reaching for the second one even as I'm manoeuvring the first around my mouth.

I ran a quick spell-check over the final, edited copy of the press release, took a printout and went to give it to Shruti, who was wrapping her shawl around her, obviously ready to leave the office. 'Leave them on my desk,' she said, 'and Arshi? I don't want to see you slacking off so much tomorrow.'

I clenched my fists by my side. And then, like magic—actually not really like magic at all, because magic implies fun, happy stuff, and this moment, I can safely say, was the scariest in my entire life—as though puppet strings were pulling at my mouth, I announced, 'You won't have to deal with me tomorrow, because I quit.'

Shruti's reaction to that, now that was magic. It was fun, happy stuff, watching her jaw drop, her eyes narrow and her shawl, about to make the circuit from her right shoulder to her left, fall straight down on the floor.

'Really, Arshi,' she said, with that little laugh that some people give that is even more annoying than the three sounds that annoy me the most: (a) a guy honking over and over again in jam-packed traffic; (b) really cranky babies shrieking for attention; and (c) the sound of someone clicking a ballpoint pen over and over again. In fact, I think it may have been the laugh that made my mind up for me, because no less than seven different voices in my head were screaming *Arshi, noooooooooo!*

'You'll find my resignation on your desk tomorrow morning,' I said firmly.

'Now, Arshi, I think you're being a little rash.' Shawl picked up, placed on the table. Bag firmly set on a chair. She wasn't going anywhere for a while.

'Do you? Because I don't, not really. I'm not happy in this

job, I'm not growing at all, I'm not being challenged, oh, I could go on and on.' I watched her astonished, ugly face twist around and then, I don't know, I just wanted it to end. Sure, it had been a bad relationship, but break-ups were ugly enough anyway without the nastiness accompanying them. I was done with sucking my triumph out of this situation.

'Look,' she said, 'Let's talk about this. I never knew you felt this way. Maybe we can move you to a different team? Are you bored of working with the media? We can move you to client servicing. Just don't take a decision in a hurry.'

'I don't think that will help, really,' I said, smiling sadly now. 'I need a change. Sorry.'

Shruti sniffed, twisting her mouth a little more. I looked at the floor and at her toenails, bright red, showing through black sandals. She always wore black, all black. Sometimes, for a change, she'd wear all white. But she had no oranges or greens in her wardrobe. She wasn't an orange or green kind of person, which is, come to think of it, a little sad.

'You realize you have to serve a one-month notice?' she said snottily.

That surprised me. Our company policy normally puts people on probation for two years before they become fully qualified employees and thereby obligated to serve a month's notice after they quit. I had been here just a little under two years—December would be when my confirmation came up—which meant I could still walk out of there at a day's notice. 'I'm not confirmed yet,' I said.

'Well, if you don't serve one month's notice, I'll make sure no one in PR ever hires you again.'

If that was going to be her attitude, I saw no reason to waste good old-fashioned guilt on her. 'Yeah, sorry, I don't ever want to work in PR again.' I almost followed that up with a 'So there!' but restrained myself. I sashayed to my desk and stood awkwardly near it. I wanted her to leave so I could write my damn resignation now that I was all fired up about it, but she just stayed and stayed. I could feel her eyes boring into my back.

'You're not indispensable, you know,' she barked from where she was standing, 'and this is not professional behaviour! Just . . . just make sure you give all your client information and media sheets to Anubha.' And, finally, she left.

I admit this wasn't as easy as it sounds, but I felt so completely liberated. How should I describe it? If you stand in a doorway for a while, and push really hard on either side of you with your hands, using your entire strength for about five minutes, then step outside, your arms sort of raise themselves on their own, free of the commands from your brain. That's how I felt. Like a skydiver. Like jumping off a really high diving board.

As I sat down at my computer, I noticed my knees trembling a little bit. It felt like they were going to give way beneath me. What in the name of fuck was I going to do for money? And rent? What was I going to tell my mom? And Topsy? Maybe I should change my mind, I thought, maybe I should call up Shruti and say, 'Sorry, I was PMS-ing. Please forget what I said.' No, I couldn't do that. I wouldn't do that. I'd get another job, with a newspaper or something, it wasn't that tough. I met journalists every day who were way dumber than our least intelligent interns and they were still employed and drew pretty decent salaries. Yes, that wouldn't be so bad.

I typed out the resignation letter like an automated machine, my mind blank, pressed 'Print', mind still blank, and picked up my cellphone, wondering whom to call first to break the news. I'd struck both my mom and Topsy out of the list because they'd just lecture me and snatch away what little joy I was getting out of it. Esha wouldn't get it, having never worked in her life. Michael was out of town. Deeksha was too busy. Gagan, no, I didn't know him all that well. Oh who was I kidding? The one person I really, really wanted to call was Kabir. From the moment I had announced my decision to Shruti, the one thought circling in my head had been: What would Kabir say when I told him? But I'd steeled myself. I wasn't going to call. This time I wasn't going to be the one to make the first move, not after he had told me we were going *nowhere* and I had been so brusque and businesslike.

You know, I don't really believe in god (and that's the reason I'm using the small 'g'). I haven't believed in god since I was six, I think, when a boy I was in school with coolly told me that if god did exist, well, where was the proof? It was that simple, really, like learning that Santa Claus and the Tooth Fairy are actually your parents, not because you've ever caught them at it, but just because, like this boy had said, where was the proof that those fantastic people existed? I'm a seeing-is-believing kind of person, which sort of worked with my parents, who didn't want to get into the whole Church vs Temple thing, so they drifted off into their own non-belief and never put any effort into my religious upbringing.

The only reason I might have believed in god till I was six was because, well, it's hard to live in India and not be religious. I had a friend who told me, in all seriousness, that if you prayed really hard to Krishna, round the clock, took his name a hundred and eight times in the morning and a hundred and eight times at night, anything you asked for would be yours. The girl who told me this gave up on it after a while, because she had been praying really hard for a baby brother but she got a sister instead. 'You must have done something wrong,' I told her. 'No, even if I had, my mummy and my nani were also praying for me to have a baby brother, and *they* couldn't have done anything wrong, no?' she said piously. A fact I had to concede to, because even if we didn't believe in anything else, we had no doubts about the perfection and infallibility of our parents. But non-believer or not, in god or the powers that be or whatever, something was on my side that evening, because as I sat with my phone in my hand it rang, and I knew by the ringtone that it was Kabir. I had a special ringtone for him, *Light my fire* by the Doors, the happy, skippy guitar part in the beginning that seemed at the time I set it to represent everything I felt about and around him. I accepted the call trying not to sound happy and surprised and thankful that he had called, but of course I failed miserably.

'Hello, little one,' he said in response to my tremulous 'Hi'. 'How've you been? I haven't heard from you in a while . . . I was missing the sound of your voice.'

'Really?' I breathed into the phone. 'I've missed you too!'

'How's everything in the world of Arshi?' He sounded buoyant and upbeat and at that moment I wanted so badly to kiss him, feel the warmth of his palms circling my face, fingers drifting to the base of my neck, his soft lips on my mouth and forehead. Why had I thought I could give him up so easily?

'Um . . . good, actually. Or at least I think so. I just quit my job.'

'Wow, really? Good for you. You were wasted at that place, absolutely wasted. I always thought so.'

'I'm glad someone else thought the way I did. But now I'm shit scared. I totally don't have a back-up plan.'

'Who does?'

There was a bit of a pause here and I thought, oh no I've lost him because between the old Kabir and Arshi there were never any silences; in fact, we'd be interrupting each other trying to get our sentences in.

'So, what are your big celebratory plans for tonight?' he asked.

'I'm actually having dinner with a friend but I can blow that off if you want to meet up,' I said eagerly, hating poor Gagan at this moment for daring to be in the picture.

'No, no, you carry on. I'm meeting with some old school friends anyway. I just wanted to say hi. Give me a call sometime.'

'Yeah, okay.'

'Bye Arsh,' he said, and hung up, not waiting for me to say 'bye', or to ask 'why aren't you meeting me', or 'which friends', or 'if you say you miss me then why don't you sound like it'. Still, I felt good that he'd called because it meant I could call him again, every day, like I used to. Perhaps, now that I was free and all, one of these days we could even hook up again.

Having regained some confidence after my conversation with Kabir, I broke the news to my mother and Topsy, both of whom reacted in startlingly (though expectedly) similar ways, asking me why I couldn't have held on till my GRE applications were done, and what I was planning to do for money, and, really, Arshi, do you not have any clue? My mom, after her lecture, told me she'd give me some cash but that I should think about moving back home if I didn't have another job soon, and there really wasn't any point getting another job because if my admissions came through I'd have to leave soon enough anyway. Topsy was short and distant with me and I could tell she was preparing to go into a major sulk.

Later at Big Chill I slid into the chair across from Gagan, who had been waiting for me, and announced happily, 'I quit my job today!'

'And you're happy?' he asked hesitantly, waiting for my emotion before he decided on a response.

'Yes, I think so. I feel strangely free. I haven't been

unemployed in a while. Of course, my mother and my flatmate think I'm nuts.'

'I think every now and then it's important to do what you want and screw everyone else,' he said, sweetly serious. I nodded. He really was cute, even in that awful pink pin-striped shirt he was wearing. And he was saying the right things.

We had a fabulous time that evening. After dinner, we drove to India Gate and bought ice cream and walked among the families who were beginning to emerge for late evenings outdoors with the first hint of winter. We looked up at Delhi's polluted skies and talked about people we knew from school and how they had changed. Okay, so the conversation was a little stilted, but I loved the way the dimples in his cheeks danced when he smiled and the way, every once in a while, he squinted his eyes and looked thoughtful. Being hot makes up for so many things in a man.

15. in which topsy's parents come to visit

LIKE I'VE TOLD YOU earlier, I have sincerely come to believe that relationships are all about power—who has it and who lets the other person have what they deny themselves. It follows, I guess, that they have the potential of becoming hotbeds of abuse.

First, there's your obvious physically abusive relationship. Example, Sarupa—a colleague I was quite chummy with when I'd just started working and was not quite so wary of or so bored with my colleagues—and her boyfriend, Vimahat. He was married, Vimahat, to someone else, and Sarupa and he had been having a clandestine affair for about five years. He promised her, almost every week, that he'd leave his wife, but didn't, and if she reminded him about it he'd hit her. Hard. With the back of his hand, or his knuckles, or pinch her with his toes, or burn her with cigarettes. And he had a drinking problem, on top of everything else. I stumbled on her predicament because I happened to notice the distinctive red-brown circle of a cigarette burn, which I can identify only too well, on her upper arm once. I knew something was fishy because I was pretty sure she didn't smoke. Gentle probing was all that was required for her to tell me everything, in an outburst, because she was so thankful to have someone to finally unburden to. Frankly, it was weird, because when she showed me the bruises she seemed almost proud of her injuries, as though they made her feel she was with a 'real man'. They were carefully hidden: right above her heart was a thumbprint, where someone had obviously pressed very hard into the soft flesh; a blue ring of fingerprints embedded on her upper arm; and she raised her skirt to show me deep scratches on her inner thighs, which meant she couldn't keep her legs together, or wear jeans, something that mortified her but seemed oddly symbolic to me because, if she could, then she wouldn't be in this mess in the first place, right? Anyway, I guess that story had a sort of happy ending, because Vimahat did eventually leave his wife and marry Sarupa, but only after she threatened at first to leave him and subsequently to commit suicide. I'm not sure which one worked, but Sarupa got her man. For better or for worse. It's not just Sarupa. I know other people like her who are proud of their battle-scars, proud to be constantly wounded and bleeding. And they'll never admit it's a problem, because that would make them look stupid. And no one likes to look stupid.

Then there's the emotionally abusive relationship. Case in point, my parents. There are people you come across who you think should never have been thrown together, no matter what, not even in last-man-or-woman-on-earth situations, because of the pain and heartbreak they will eventually and inevitably cause each other. That's how my parents were.

My dad was one of those avant-garde geniuses who predicted virtual technology and the information revolution way back when old DOS machines were the maximum India had experienced and were considered pretty snazzy. My mother thought his ideas were ridiculous and that he was building castles in the air, and they fought incessantly about it. Towards the end of their marriage, especially, I would hear whispered accusations late at night, about my father applying for a work visa in the States, about my mother wanting to go back to work, and sometimes about other people, the names hurled across the room. To give them credit, they waited till they thought I was asleep before starting to argue, but they'd forget to keep their voices low and I would cringe as their loud, throbbing voices beat against my bedroom wall. Dad was always critical and sharp, his voice snapping, bouncing off my mom and catapulting straight towards me; my mother punished him by withdrawing completely, and letting out occasional flashes of anger. My stomach still curls up in knots when I think about it and I have to remind myself that it's okay, it's more than a decade later, and everyone concerned is now happy and 'normal' in their own way. Even me. My dad's sweet to Barbara, though, and I don't think she knows how to withdraw herself really. Everything about Barbara is very out there—a very American thing in my personal experience.

I had actually been thinking a lot about my father, and about Ma and Barbara, because in response to an email I sent him about how I had quit my job and was planning to take my GRE and come to the States to study for a bit, he sent me an incredibly long letter. (I can't even call it an email because it began with 'Dear Arshi' and was signed 'Love, Dad' and went on for at least four MS Word pages. My dad likes to type his letters in Word and send them as attachments. It's strange, and many people don't open his emails because they think they're viruses, but he absolutely refuses to type straight into the Compose page of his mail service provider.) It was all about Barbara and him and the two mongrels they had adopted from the animal shelter and named Pakora and Poe. (*We each got to name one*, my dad had written. *I chose Poe, because he is one of my favourite poets. Barbara wanted to call hers after her favourite Indian snack that your grandmother sometimes makes when she's here.*) Come to think of it, they were both so strange that they were probably made for each other.

We used to have a dog, too, the only pet I've ever had, actually. We got her—Tasha, she was called—around the time I was two and I was about ten or eleven when we had to put her down because she had cancer. She was only about eight or nine, a pretty young age for a dog to die. Knowing about Tasha is important if someone's trying to get to know me, because having a dog when you're about two means that you and the dog pretty much grow up together. Tasha was of no particular breed. She was supposed to be an Alsatian, which was a very popular breed at that time but she really didn't look at all like an Alsatian when she grew up. (It's funny how different breeds have different popularity periods. As I grew up, the Alsatian and Spaniel phase passed and it was all about Pomeranians and Apsos for a while. Then it was the Labrador and the Retriever, and now people prefer fancy breeds like Pugs or Terriers and even Dalmatians.) Tasha was large and shaggy, with a blunt nose and a tail that curled over her back, something only mongrel tails do. I loved her tail, I loved the quirk in it. I loved its softness and the way she'd curl it catlike round my feet and if I patted or caressed her I could feel her bottom quiver and the tip of her tail tickle my toes.

Tasha was important to me, and will always be, because my parents bought her when they were still wildly in love with each other, and lived with each other and with what they had created together, i.e., me. It's hard for me now to even imagine a time like that, but there are pictures to prove it. Me holding on to

Tasha's fur with all my might, trying to stand up (I walked very late; my parents were beginning to think I'd go to college dragging myself on my butt), with my mom's face in the background, one hand stretched towards me, her face tilted towards the photographer, my dad, and her mouth stretched in a very wide smile, the kind which stays behind on your face long after you're done with being happy. Tasha died around the same time my parents began to talk about getting their divorce, so I suppose it's all very symbolic in some way. She was our happy years, mine as well as theirs, because you're never the same when your parents aren't together, no matter how old you are.

Dad was the dog person in the house. I love dogs too, but I could never get one after Tasha because my mother wasn't at all into the toilet-training and the picking-up-after, and we never had a full-time servant. I don't think Barbara's a dog person either, but my dad's good with the training and the walking and the feeding and so on. I wasn't very sure how I felt about his getting new dogs; we'd talked about Tasha so much, for so many years. It had been my mom's main argument when I whined too much about getting another dog: 'There will never be another dog like Tasha.' 'But there could be,' I'd say, and she'd clinch it with, 'She was a part of our family and you can never replace family members.' The new dogs wouldn't be the same, I knew, nothing would be the same, exactly, and sometimes I couldn't help wishing I could just rewind and relive the times I liked in my life, the good stuff, over and over again.

In his letter my dad sounded totally thrilled with my idea of going to the US to study, but then I had known he would. He'd been pestering me about it ever since I finished school. Perhaps I should have, because he wasn't married to Barbara then. In fact, he hadn't even met her, and his secretary (the one before

Barbara) was a sweet old woman who knitted sweaters for him and kept a check on whether he was keeping warm. He regularly mailed me long letters about his life in the US, like he was making sure I was part of his new life in some way. I had a sneaking suspicion, though, that the other reason he was so gung-ho about me going there was that he's always felt a little guilty about marrying a second time. Very few Indian parents do that; they tend to either stay in unhappy marriages forever, or split up and basically live a life of virtue. My dad's new lifestyle had led to quite a few jokes back home when my parents' common friends got to know, and he's never come back to visit. Not once.

Barbara was very happy and excited when I told her of your plans, he wrote. *She thinks it will be a good time for the two of you to bond a little. You have never really spent any time with her, but it is important to me that the two most important girls in my life love and cherish one another. You know, Barbara loves you. She's always wanted a daughter, but sometimes she feels hurt that you do not make enough of an effort. I know it is hard for you, Arshi, but it wouldn't hurt to try. You're not a little girl any longer.*

Point taken, Dad, I muttered. Barbara and I have an odd relationship. I have to keep reminding myself that since she's my stepmother, perhaps I should be making an effort to get to know her a bit. I try not to think about it too much, though, because given that she's married my father, they are, in all likelihood, having sex. Gross. I'm sexually active myself and I've reached an age when the thought of your parents doing stuff in the bedroom should no longer be repulsive, but for me it still is, vehemently so. That, and her wannabe Indianness—the yoga, the clothes, the aarti, the sometimes forced enthusiasm for spicy food—it all *grated* a little. The last time I visited them I could see she was tired and cranky from having to be on her best, most cheerful behaviour for me, the slightly sullen, grown-up daughter of the man she had married. She snapped at me once, I remember, and it undid all the good stuff she had done till then, like driving me around to whichever place I wanted to see, looking up reference material about Delhi before I arrived so she could ask me informed questions and sustain a conversation, and even staying away from TV serials she was addicted to so I could use the computer in the room in peace. But all that didn't matter any more. She had married my father and she was pretty young compared to him, thirty-something, and now she had been short with me—reason enough for me to not like her very much. Fair enough, I thought, marvelling at the levels of tolerance Ma and Dadi possessed. They were more used to being grown-up, I guess, whereas I have to keep reminding myself that I'm now officially in my mid-twenties and I can no longer say 'What's with these grown-ups, man?', because, dude, *I'm* the grown-up now. Wow.

I was sitting at home, reading the letter, thinking of old times, and listening for the sounds of Topsy's parents' arrival. Usually they drove down, but their driver was on holiday and they'd decided to take the train instead. I had offered to go with her to the railway station, but she said it would probably be better if she met them alone first.

Topsy and I had finally had our first real conversation in a while. She had been sitting with her blanket pulled up to her chin, hair loose, looking thoughtful. 'I think this visit is basically to get me to meet some eligible men,' she said, glancing at me. 'It's such a pain. I have to keep turning them down and I'm running out of excuses.'

'You're still kinda young to be thinking about marriage, no?' I offered, flicking channels.

'Mmm . . . I suppose, but I've tried that before and they

said, "Don't worry, beta, we'll have a long engagement, as long as you like",' she did the nasal, whiny tone she put on when she was imitating her parents' voices.

'Try saying you're looking for a job then.'

'That might work, but then they'll say "You can work after you get married also, we'll find you a modern family". No, I think it's just better to go with them, see the guy, point out how he's fat or old or a cripple or something, and then say okay, ta-ta, go back to Meerut.'

I laughed, 'Cripple?'

'Oh, yeah, you'll never believe this. One time, a family came over to our house in Meerut. I must have been in Class 12 or something. And they were like, oh your daughter would be so perfect for our son, she's so beautiful.' Topsy was laughing so hard at this point, she choked and I had to thump her on the back. 'Thanks. Anyway, so they were going on about their son, how nice he is, how sweet, with no bad habits, and my parents were nodding and smiling, and they suddenly said, we'll get him. They go outside to the car, where he's been sitting *all this time*, and bring out this massive guy. I'm not kidding, he must have been about 300 kilos. And he's smiling vaguely and limping and I'm like horror-struck, and it turns out not only does he have a crippled left leg, he's also a little off in the head!'

My jaw dropped. 'Noooo, you're kidding!'

Topsy had that happy, triumphant expression she got when she was telling a good story. 'Uh-uh, I swear he was. His parents even admitted it after some time. His mom had measles when she was pregnant with him and that caused some complications. Basically, they wanted me to clean up the gene pool a little, have smart, good-looking babies, with their surname attached. And they thought they were doing me a favour!' She shook her head. 'He was their only son, and they had a large family business which he would inherit but I would run.'

'Ew, imagine sleeping with him,' I said, shuddering.

'Don't even go there.' She made a face. 'Anyway, *that* is what my parents are capable of doing.'

'Oh, come on, this wasn't their fault,' I protested.

'No,' she said darkly, 'but it could have been.'

Now I could hear footsteps clattering up the stairs even before the bell rang. They were a noisy bunch, Topsy's family, and they travelled in packs. This time it was her parents, her dad's sister and her husband, and their kids, Ananya and Mahesh, or Chhutki and Monty as the family called them. I could hear Topsy's bua, who happens to be one of her all-time favourite people, laughing her honking laugh as I went to open the door. Instantly, I was engulfed in sweatery hugs, the strong smell of mothballs assaulting my nostrils. 'Arshi, you've become so thin,' said Topsy's mother, disapprovingly. 'Timala, also, she's so thin. The two of you are killing yourselves here. Just pack up and come to Meerut, we'll fatten you both up.'

'Arrey, bhabhi, this is the style for young people these days,' said Topsy's bua, grinning at me as she dumped several plastic packets on Topsy's bed. 'Is it not so, Arshi? Even my Chhutki is trying to lose weight all the time. The other day she even asked me for waist-hugger jeans.'

'Hip-hugger, mummy,' said Chhutki, blushing deeply. She hero-worshipped Topsy and her cool Delhi life—and me, as a result of reflected glory. I smiled sympathetically at her.

Topsy emerged from the kitchen bearing a tray I had never seen before, with several glasses of water on it, and began offering them around.

'Anyone for tea?' she asked sweetly, in her pink salwar-kameez. 'Papa? Chai?'

'Yes, please,' her father said, patting her on the head. 'I

think tea is a good idea for everyone. Good to see you looking so homely, Timala. Living alone has almost made a housewife out of you.'

I snorted, but Topsy shot me a dagger-laden look so I converted it into a cough.

'Yes,' said her mother. 'Now is a good time for you to get married also, then. The time is right, beta.'

Topsy rolled her eyes. 'Ma, I've *said* no, I don't want to get married for some time. I want to think about my career also.'

'What is there to think?' said Phupha-ji, her bua's husband, a large, silent man. 'It's only marriage, an alliance between families. Of course, we will find you someone who thinks the same way as we do.'

Her father nodded, waving his hand expansively, 'We'll find you a first-class boy, someone who lives in Delhi, or maybe even with a green card. Hanh?' He looked at her slyly. 'You like to travel, no, beta? What better way to do it than with your husband? It will be so exciting!'

Topsy did her coy act, faking a smile and turning her eyes to her feet, but I could tell from the set of her shoulders that she was preparing for a big fight. 'Arshi, will you help me with the tea, please? Papa, what time do you have to check into the guest house?'

'Soon, I think,' he said, looking at his watch. 'We'll just have our tea and go, then we'll go out for dinner tonight. Arshi, you are most welcome to join us.'

I glanced at Topsy, who nodded briefly at me. Right. Moral support.

'I'd love to join you, uncle,' I said.

Dinner wasn't that bad actually—from my point of view, anyway. For Topsy, it was torture. We went to Bukhara, part of the set routine her family followed when they were in Delhi.

The first night it was dinner at Bukhara; the second day would be spent shopping at Lajpat Nagar, followed by chaat at Haldiram's, then dinner at Chopsticks. The rest of the plan included a movie, a trip to the malls in Gurgaon, a day of shopping at Connaught Place and a day of visiting ancient relatives in Old Delhi. During the dinner, I had a rapid under-the-table texting session with Gagan, the upshot of which was that he was coming over after we got home, with a bottle of wine. (It made me feel very posh and cosmopolitan, seeing as people were bringing *wine* over for me to drink, even if it was the cheapest in the market.) I would probably kiss Gagan that evening, but I didn't feel particularly excited about it, just strangely indifferent.

'Timala,' Topsy's mother began, dipping her naan into the murgh malai. 'We have actually spoken to some boys' families here in Delhi, so we thought, since we are here for two weeks this time, you should meet them.'

I saw Topsy's nostrils flaring, but she simply said, 'Yes, ma.'

'I don't want to hear any choo-choo about how this one is too fat and that one is too thin this time, you hear?' rumbled her father from the other side of the table. 'These are good, decent boys. Your mother and I have done checks on their family background; they will gel very well with us.'

Topsy's bua stroked her hand sympathetically. 'Your parents love you, beta. They only want what is best for you.'

'I *said* okay, didn't I?' Topsy retorted.

We resumed eating dinner in semi-silence. The only person who seemed oblivious to the awkwardness around the table was Monty, chugging at his third glass of Coke and playing games on his father's cellphone. Chhutki looked wide-eyed and fascinated with the whole conversation. Topsy's bua tried to change the subject with exclamations about some new 'suit' she wanted embroidered, and how some woman back home had got the same work done on her chunni and had told her about a shop in Lajpat Nagar where you could get great crêpe material and they should definitely go there tomorrow.

'Delhi means I have to spend more money,' said Silent Phupha-ji, clicking his tongue.

'And what about all the things you buy?' snapped Topsy's bua, turning to her brother to complain. 'He bought *two* new cellphones last month. And one fancy-fancy computer. So much money, and he grudges me even a little to spend on clothes.'

'Computers are good for children,' said Topsy's father sagely.

'Good? Good?' Topsy's bua piped up. 'My son'—Monty finally looked up from his game, slightly interested in this reference to himself—'never goes one minute without turning on the computer. Chat-shat, download-vownload, all that, not concentrating on his studies at all. And when he's not doing computer, his sister is. When I call them to eat meals they say, one minute mummy, one minute mummy, till the food has gone ice-cold.'

Topsy laughed a little, and the atmosphere lightened. Her bua looked pleased, but her kids began defending themselves noisily.

Soon the cheque was on the table, and paid for, and Topsy got up. 'Arshi and I have to run, now,' she said, nodding at me to rise. 'We've called the plumber in the morning.'

'Arrey, beta, stay with us tonight,' said her mother, puzzled.

'No, no, you all sleep comfortably. I'll meet you tomorrow.' She was practically walking backwards now. 'Okay, come on, Arshi, okay, bye!'

As soon as we got into the car, she sighed, shook out her hair and switched on her cellphone.

'Hi baby,' I heard her murmur into it. 'No, not too bad. Can you come over?'

Fardeen must have said yes, because she lit a cigarette with evident satisfaction and leaned back, her eyes closed. I thought of her and Fardeen, him rubbing her back, both of them curling up together to go to sleep, and I wondered how they did it.

'Topsy?' I ventured.

'Hmmm?'

'Don't you and Fardeen ever get, um, carried away when you're making out?'

She opened her eyes and looked at me. 'All the time. But, you know, he's so wonderful. Even when I want to take it further, he's like, are you sure? I don't want to rush you. And then my head clears and I know it's not the right time.'

'Are you *ever* going to have sex with him?'

'I don't think so,' she said. But I could see the thought of having sex with Fardeen and what it would mean and how it would feel cross her face. She shivered, just a little bit, rapidly rubbing her upper arms with her palms.

When we got home, she changed into track pants and a tank top and threw a shawl over her shoulders. I stayed in my salwar-kameez. I liked how I looked in it, demure but adult, firm but graceful. I walk differently in a salwar-kameez. Perhaps it's because I wear jeans so much, but in traditional Indian clothes I sway a bit when I walk, my footsteps fall closer to each other, almost like my feet have been bound. In a salwar-kameez I feel capable of doing domestic things, like pickling a mango, perhaps, or putting the right tadka in a dal. In my regular clothes, jeans and a T-shirt, I look far too young, far too 'Western' in the sense in which conservative people say it here, spitting it out like it's a bad word. Once, when Topsy and I were looking for a place to stay, the broker told us discreetly that our clothes were much too 'phoren'. Could we please not dress like that when we met the landlord? We glanced at each other in amazement. 'Phoren'? Us? Topsy was in a vest, I was in a fitted T-shirt, but a T-shirt nonetheless, and we thought we looked okay. I mean, we wouldn't win any contests for traditional Indian womanhood, but we weren't branded with the scarlet letter or anything, the way he made it sound. We didn't go back to that broker.

The doorbell rang and both of us shouted 'I'll get it', but Topsy got to the door first. It was my date, though, not hers. Gagan gave her a kiss hello, even though they hadn't been introduced yet, no one having got around to it at Deeksha's engagement party. He handed me the bottle of wine—white, which I normally don't drink—and made his way straight into our kitchen. Topsy raised her eyebrows at me, I shrugged, and we both followed him, watching, our mouths half open as he pulled out glasses, located the corkscrew from on top of the fridge and proceeded to uncork the bottle, pour the wine out efficiently and hand us our glasses.

'What?' he asked, smiling at our shocked expressions. 'I'm good in kitchens. I have kitchen sense.'

'Like ESP?' Topsy offered, taking a large sip.

'Exactly. Except in my case it's KSP.' He chuckled, glancing at me for approval. 'Get it? Kitchen Sensory Perception.'

'I get it,' I said, laughing through my nose, like an extra-strong exhalation. He was slightly goofy, but in a good way, the kind that made you 'quirky' not 'odd'.

The doorbell rang again and Topsy did a quick about-turn, rushing for the door.

'Her boyfriend,' I explained.

'Oh, she has a boyfriend?'

'Yeah.' His eyes looked wistful and I felt a sudden stab of jealousy. 'Too bad for you.'

'I don't care, dude. I'm here to see you.' Gagan stretched out his hand, palm first, to push the hair back from my forehead. Such a small gesture, not even a finger-twining hand-hold or a kiss, but it made me feel cherished. Oh this guy was smooth all right.

We handed Fardeen a glass of wine, too, but Topsy beckoned to him as subtly as she could and the two of them vanished into her room.

'I guess we won't be seeing them for the rest of the evening?' asked Gagan.

'Uh-uh. They've gone now. I won't see them till tomorrow morning.'

'It must be hard for you,' he said softly.

'Why?'

'Because you must get lonely and surely this,' he waved at Topsy's shut door, 'doesn't help.'

I blinked at him. It's hard for me not to categorize people, which is actually kind of ironic because I get so pissed off when people do it to me. Anyway, in my mind right now Gagan was a himbo, the slightly brainless guy with no insights whatsoever on anything. With the guys I'd had as lovers so far, I'd always wanted to unravel them a little bit, listen to stories about their past. But it was a little hard to believe that before he met me Gagan even had a past. He just seemed so bland, so wholesome, so no-skeletons-in-the-closet-type that, hey, where would the stories come from?

'Arshi?' he said, setting his glass down and looking at me.

'Yeah?'

'Can I, um, kiss you?'

I began to giggle in his face. I couldn't help it. I guess it was a combination of nervousness and trying to postpone the moment, but how could I explain that to him? I stopped, though, when

I saw an expression of deep hurt beginning to spread over his face. Clearly, this had never happened to him before.

'Can I kiss you?' I repeated, to lighten the moment. 'Dude, how old are you? Like fifteen?'

'I thought it was polite to ask,' he said coldly.

'Aww, don't be mad.' I inched closer, placing my hand on his shoulder. 'You just took me by surprise.'

I didn't want him to kiss me, I'm quite sure of that, but I didn't want him not to kiss me either. I guess I wished that the moment was already over, that the kiss had finished and now it was time for us to say goodnight and not get into awkward post-kiss conversations. He stood stiffly for some time, not saying anything, and I began to despair that this wasn't going to go anywhere, ever. I sat back down, a little sheepishly. Suddenly, I was tired and sleepy. I could feel the weight on my eyes and the first yawns trying to escape my throat. I did a couple of the closed-lip yawn things, where your nostrils flare and your eyes water, but I don't think he noticed.

We had finished half the bottle of wine when, very gentleman-like, he picked up my hand and pressed it to his lips. I wondered whether my fingers smelt of smoke or mutton burra, whether the nail polish I had on was chipped, whether he could feel the stubble of hair on my knuckles, and whether all this was totally turning him off. I sighed a little, which he interpreted as a sign to continue and tentatively leaned towards me. Reflexively, I did too, closing my eyes. The first peck of his kiss was like a light brush before his tongue slipped through my clenched teeth and I heard his breaths coming fast and hoarse through his nose as his fingers went up, behind my head, to entangle themselves in my hair. I concentrated on returning the kiss, not caring very much any more, but my hands stayed mobile on his upper arms.

You can usually tell how much someone is into a kiss by

how much they move their hands. When I'm really having fun, my hands cup the person's face, or slide across their back, or lock around their neck. Right now, Gagan's hands were doing all these things, even sliding up underneath my shirt, struggling a bit with my bra (a moment where we both paused, our mouths still attached, for him to get it), unhooking the bra and letting his fingers drum and scratch on my skin. But the only part of me that moved was my mouth. When we were done with making out, I said goodnight very properly, as did he, kissing me on the cheek and looking meaningfully into my eyes, as if this was the night we'd be looking back on ten years from now, marvelling at how young we were and how we didn't have the slightest clue that we'd soon fall in love and have babies together. I felt somewhat stupid for not getting the significance of the moment, but I blamed it on being tired after a very long day. I'll feel better tomorrow, even see butterflies and pink clouds and a rainbow, I promised myself.

16. in which esha gives us a real fright

BEING AN ONLY CHILD, I had read in an article somewhere, is not easy. Well, duh, I thought at the time. Being a *child* is not easy, period. Either you're the oldest kid, which results in the whole sibling rivalry thing, or you're the middle kid, in which case you don't really know where you belong, or you're the youngest, which either means people can walk all over you for the rest of your life or the exact opposite. Big bloody deal.

I'd come across the article in one of those fancy foreign magazines—you know, the ones that have glossy perfume ads with an actual scratch-and-sniff tester area, and publish articles titled 'The Night I Bonked a Backstreet Boy' and 'Dealing with PMS the Easy Way' accompanied by huge photographs of pretty people and bylines of writers who refer more to themselves than to anyone they're quoting. So this story had some very attractive 'onlys', as the writer called them, one with a red beret posing outside a Manhattan cafe, another in a bikini reading a book on a beach, and a young man playing the piano, with a cigarette dangling sexily from the side of his mouth. Probably the only thing I had in common with those beautiful people was the fact that we had no sisters or brothers, but oh how I wished I had been born to be photographed beret- or bikini-clad, cigarette between my fingers, drinking cappuccino that left a white froth on my upper lip—a sexy white froth, may I add, not the kind that makes people look at you and look away and uncomfortably rub their own upper lips in the hope that you get the hint and wipe it off.

Anyway, according to the writer, behind their sprawling houses, lavish lifestyles and Porsche convertibles, lay a sad truth. Each of these people, used to being told by their parents from early infancy how wonderful they were, needed the same kind of bond to develop with their friends. If it didn't, they spent their whole life desperately forming obsessive emotional attachments, which would ultimately be detrimental to their social development. That was a nasty thing to say. I wondered how Sandra, seventeen, sunning herself on her father's private beach in California, felt when she read that. If it were me, I'd be mighty pissed off, especially since the writer had added somewhere in that paragraph that she had three younger sisters. Well, so what the fuck was she talking about?

On the other hand, I must admit there's a grain of truth to it all. I've always loved my friends far more than they loved me, but I thought that perhaps that was just the way I was, that it was my role on this planet, as it were, to be more loving than loved. My friends like me a whole lot, most of them anyway, but I don't think they love me in quite the same way as I do them. A slight from them is like betrayal for me. I remember weeping my eyes out when a friend in school didn't invite me for a sleepover. She called three other girls, as I recall, girls whom I knew, used to meet at birthday parties, sometimes go for a movie with, or maybe for a walk to the nearby park to buy ice cream. And when one of us bumped into another at boring adult functions—we all lived in fair proximity to each other, so neighbourhood wedding invites usually included all our parents—we would feel relieved that we didn't have to go through the evening alone, that one of our own was there. We even had a secret *club*, for god's sake, with a password and a little box with a lock in which we kept all our treasures, things we found or picked up, sometimes things we stole. Like the time two of the girls shoplifted a clear nail polish from a nearby store and another one stole a pretty scarlet scrunchie from one of her classmates. I was too chicken to do the actual stealing, but all of us used the nail polish and took turns wearing the scrunchie at the 'meetings'. So, see, it was okay to be heartbroken when she didn't invite me. I hated her after that, hated her with a vengeance. She meekly tried to explain that her mother had said she couldn't invite more than three people, and I shrugged and said it was okay even though my chin was trembling and I could feel the corners of my mouth turn downward no matter how hard I tried to control it. The secret club pretty much stopped after that. One of the girls went out of town and the other three, including the chick who hadn't invited me, started hanging out exclusively with each other. So, yeah, that was the end of that. I proceeded to make a voodoo doll of her out of chart paper—a really ugly caricature with warts and hair that stuck out—and stick pins into it, and I felt much better.

You'd think I would have become wiser over the years, right? Actually, my 'detrimental social development' continued in college as well. On the third or fourth day after we joined, I danced up to a girl I thought was good-looking, smart and funny, and asked her where the tutorial rooms were and where the canteen was, fully prepared to follow that up with the story of how everything was very confusing and how I was getting lost . . . and did she want to join me for a cup of coffee in the canteen? It was really bad coffee, I would say, inserting a clever eye-roll, but it was better than nothing. And she would be my new best friend. Only, she looked at me and said, 'Uh, the maps are over there,' and walked off without even a backward glance with a bunch of other girls who had suddenly appeared and surrounded her. I felt so insignificant then. Flushed and moist-eyed, I ignored all the other people in the corridor who might have overheard the conversation and walked very firmly towards the maps, drawn with glitter pen on lavender-coloured paper by the seniors, and studied them over and over again, not really registering anything. And this, when she wasn't even close to being my friend.

Touch wood, ever since I've entered the twenties I've been okay. I've made good friends, and they seem to like the image I'm choosing to project, not probing if I don't offer information. But their love is sort of reserved, very understated and mature, which is a strange way to love, if you ask me. I mean, why do we save our best, most childish, most impetuous love for our lovers? It's a fabulous way to be, passion-filled and spontaneous, exuberant, sometimes unreasonable, and I'm sure our friends deserve it way more than our lovers. I'd like to stamp my feet at my friends, sulk or cheer and dance for them, or even, you know, touch them more, not sexually but generally, like kids constantly touch, kiss, rub knees and cheeks and noses, compare belly-buttons, poke skin. Adults should do more of that with their friends, without being given weird looks, like when you're on a girl's night out and one of your friends has made you laugh so hard you snort a little, it should be okay to kiss her hard for that and throw your arm around her shoulder or clap really loudly. It might even help us get over our huge you're-invading-my-personal-space issues.

Among my friends, though, there were some whom I was

actually a little surprised I was friends with at all. Esha, for instance. She was so unlike me, with such warped priorities, that half of the time I couldn't even have a real conversation with her, the kind I could have with Deeksha or Topsy. When we met up without the guys, we usually went for drinks or dinner, basically some sort of food-centric thing, so we'd have something else to do, and once we were done eating or drinking we rapidly parted ways. I was more surprised, I think, by how much of an effort she put into our friendship. She would always be the one calling or texting, making a plan, which I would then simply agree to. And she bought me little presents, handing them to me nonchalantly, with a casual 'Oh, I got you something' while she rummaged in her bag to pull out whatever it was. A couple of times it was earrings, once a funky key chain I had admired at Benetton, a purple scarf, a little china puppy, that sort of thing. I would keep asking 'Why do you keep bringing me presents?' and saying 'Thank you!' but she sort of just waved it away.

I was even a little mean to her, to tell you the truth. I didn't think she was very intelligent, for one; sweet, yes, but she seemed to have the IQ of a slightly ditzy kitten. I teased her about not having read much—actually, not having read anything. She was quite proud of it too, and declared 'Oh, I've never read a book' out loud to everyone. Sometimes I pressed the silent button on my phone when she called, didn't reply to texts for a couple of days when I didn't feel like meeting her, even snapped if she came over while I was watching TV. I'm not proud of the fact that I did all this, but some people just bring out the bully in you. Usually it's people who like you more than you like them, which would probably explain my terrible track record when it came to feeling used, but there's a certain kick in the power you hold over other people and you would have to be somewhat like Mother Teresa not to use that power every now and then.

It's not that I wasn't fond of her. Honestly, it's very hard not to be fond of someone like Esha, who sort of needs you to do stuff, like make basic decisions for them and tell them they're good people and listen to them talking about their lives. It's like having a puppy; only puppies are small and furry and cute and lick you when you cuddle them, and Esha, well, Esha didn't inspire cuddling. Wait, I'm being uncharitable. There were some things I really, really liked about her: (a) her voice, which was this funny mixture of nasal and husky (that sounds ridiculous, I know, but it was quite a trademark). Sometimes I just liked to listen to her talking, to the rumbles of her 'r's and the way she said 'aye' for 'I', and 'buh-hut' for 'but', and 'did-ant' and 'should-ant' for 'didn't' and 'shouldn't'; (b) her knowledge of cosmetics, garnered mainly from reading all the available women's magazines from cover to cover. Actually, this should have a sub-point about her collection of magazines, which I really admired. I used to love sitting for hours on the pot in her loo with the latest *Cosmo* or *Elle*. Which leads me to the third point, (c): the way she just let me be. I'd be in her loo for hours, and when I would emerge, she wouldn't say anything about it, just continue to buff her nails, or talk on the phone, or even nap; and (d) the imitations she could do of anyone—mainly all of us—usually snarky ones, taking off on the stuff we did unconsciously, like rubbing our eyes or licking our lips or chewing on our hair. She'd have Topsy and me, and sometimes Fardeen and Akshay, in splits, and all the while that we couldn't help laughing our guts out we'd secretly be thinking 'What *else* has she noticed about us that she'll make fun of at any moment?' So you see, I wasn't all mean to her either.

Esha filled another really important role in my life. She was my clubbing friend. I had clubbing *acquaintances*, but that's never the same thing as a clubbing *friend*—one kind of friend everyone should have: someone who likes the same party places you do, who is up for adventure at any time, who knows all your emergency contact numbers and, most importantly, who's okay with leaving a place whenever you say you have to go, even if she, or he, is having a really good time. We went to Elevate quite often, Shalom sometimes, Aura, too, and she would always be bouncing to the music and getting more drinks, and, if Akshay was around she'd be even more bubbly and into the evening than she normally was.

Esha and Akshay had a strange relationship. They were dating, as in, neither of them was seeing anyone else, but she was a lot more into him than he was into her. Like Kabir and I, I guess. But unlike us (me, actually), she didn't seem to care. Well, maybe that was just the image she was trying to project but she did a pretty good job of it. I marvelled at her, especially when Akshay cancelled at the last minute for something she had been looking forward to or kissed her roughly when he was all sweaty from playing football and she would either sigh and say 'Okay, next time', or squeal and swat at him. Akshay was okay otherwise; he was fun to be around, and he always smelt good, which made me feel posh and added a celebratory touch to the evening every time we went out.

Esha, Akshay and I went to Elevate one night. She'd come by to pick me up from my place and we'd got dropped to Akshay's house in her car. From there Akshay would be driving us to Elevate. Akshay had a wonderful house, a two-storeyed bungalow, where his parents occupied the ground floor and the entire top floor was his. It was completely independent, too, with a guest bedroom and a kitchen, and a fully stocked bar and fridge. His bar was great, with Cuban rum and Absolut, but I loved his fridge more. Sometimes I'd just open it and hang around, weighing my options between foreign cheese with French names, varieties of cold cuts, Hershey's chocolate syrup, Gatorade. It had nothing like bhindi or lauki or cucumbers, or leftover rice, or anything ordinary. I also liked the way his house smelt, of manly colognes and hair products and dry-cleaned clothes. His loo looked like it had never been used for gross bodily functions, like loosies or anything, but just to get cleaned up. Only, in the way guy's loos usually are, it wasn't very neat. Rolled-up towels and fancy Calvin Klein boxers would be strewn all over the floor, a capless, oozing tube of toothpaste would be lying next to the basin, that sort of thing.

We got to Akshay's place while he was still getting ready, so he was in his jeans when he greeted us. He looked slightly paunchy, but smelt wonderful, as usual, and his slightly long hair was wet and all over his face. Esha took a long look at him and I could tell by the way her nostrils contracted slightly that she was inhaling his scent and looking forward to later that night when they just might hook up. It surprised me sometimes that Kabir and Akshay were such good friends. On the face of it they seemed to be pretty similar, both from the same posh boarding school, both with very wealthy parents, but, unlike Kabir, Akshay milked his circumstances for what they were worth. He enjoyed being wealthy, which I suppose is fair. Who wouldn't? He took pleasure in his creature comforts, his designer clothes, air conditioners, fancy car and cellphone, his job at his father's consultancy firm, which would ensure that he enjoyed the same kind of lifestyle all through his life. He didn't quite get people like me, and the way we lived. The one time he had come over, I noticed him crinkle his nose at the acrid smell of leftover potatoes being warmed up in the kitchen and gingerly settling down on the rug, looking very uncomfortable indeed.

Kabir, on the other hand, genuinely enjoyed spending time at our place and was quite open about envying Topsy and me the choice of being able to live on our own. He liked slumming it, taking an auto if his car wasn't working, sitting at dhabas and eating anda-bhurji with hot rotis and pickle. Esha, too, was more like us than she was like Akshay. Her parents weren't wealthy, but you wouldn't have been able to tell by looking at her. She lived way beyond her 4000-a-month pocket money—she was the only person I knew not doing anything, no college, no job, nothing—but she wasn't in Akshay's league, and he knew it.

'Dude, you're still getting ready?' I asked accusatorily.

'Oho, come on, Arshi, man, you know we only have to get there by like midnight, yaar,' Akshay patted me roughly on the head and I ducked away to smooth my hair down again in front of the mirror.

'It's only ten, Arshi,' said Esha, sitting daintily at the edge of the bed. Someone had once told me that the best way to see if a guy wants to hook up with you is to watch where he sits when he enters your room. If he sits on the bed, you know it's an open invitation for you to sit next to him and eventually lie down, perhaps with his hand on your stomach. If he sits on a chair, on the other hand, your plans are in danger and you might as well settle for being his best friend, because he clearly doesn't want any contact. On the other hand, he could just be old-fashioned. Men are confusing, and women are no less, I'm sure, but Esha's craving for Akshay was quite in evidence this evening.

'I've asked Vir to get us on the guest list anyway, so chill,' Akshay said loudly from inside the loo. In a few minutes he emerged in a white, slightly crinkled, very fitted shirt that was the rage at the time, and which used to really annoy my mother, like my low-waist jeans did. 'Why can't that boy iron his shirt?' she'd hiss to me when we went out and saw men dressed in those shirts, or 'Really, Arshi, pull up your jeans. You might as well go out in your panties, you know,' she'd say to me tugging at the loops of my jeans.

'Drink, Arsh? Baby?' he asked, stopping to give Esha the same rough caress he'd given me.

'Yes, please,' I said. 'I'd like a vodka-Red Bull.' I could've asked for a crème de menthe and he would have produced it from his fancy industrial fridge. Rich people fascinate me.

'Coming right up,' said Akshay, and then turned to Esha again. 'Oye, fatty. Is it snowing in Delhi tonight?'

I laughed, thinking he was referring to her slightly dazed expression as she rummaged through her bag, but she perked up her head and smiled broadly at him. 'Yup,' she said, and I watched the back and forth between them, intrigued and confused.

'You met with Deep then?' asked Akshay, raising his eyebrows and quirking his mouth.

'Ya, he was *damn* sweet. You were right.'

'Um . . . Akshay? My drink?' I said from my corner, feeling left out of this absurd conversation.

'Oh. Sure. Sorry.' He disappeared into the kitchen and Esha went back to her rummaging, finally emerging with a pack of cigarettes.

'Since when do you smoke?' I looked at her quizzically.

She grinned and opened the pack, offering it to me. It was empty, except for a paper-wrapped cube inside.

'Hash?' I asked.

'That's for losers,' said Akshay, coming back in and handing me a tall glass. 'This is good shit, Arshi.'

He took the pack from Esha and as he unwrapped the paper

covering I noticed that the stuff wasn't a dark brown slab, it was white powder.

'*Chemicals?*' I squeaked. I didn't want to seem like a coward or a spoil-sport or rain on anyone's parade, but this was just not okay as far as I was concerned. Other people could drug themselves silly and I didn't give a rat's ass, but these were people I was going to spend the next couple of hours with, and Akshay was supposed to drop us home afterwards. 'I want to leave right now,' I said, firmly.

Esha wasn't saying anything, just giggling like an idiot. Akshay knelt to my level and put his hand on mine as I was packing up my phone and cigarettes.

'Don't overreact,' he said.

'Over*react?* You think I'm overreacting? This stuff, it kills your brain cells. Do what you like to yourselves, but I'm not getting into a car with you on this shit.'

'And you think alcohol is not a drug?'

'Well, at least it's legal. There's a reason.'

'I'll be fine,' Akshay smiled at me. 'It'll just get me into a party mood. Come on, Arsh, you've seen me coked up so many times before.'

'I have?'

'See, and you haven't even realized it. Everyone should do stuff, but in moderation. I'm not an addict.'

'Famous last words,' I sniffed, but stopped preparing to leave.

Esha was nervously playing with the packet. 'Hurry up, no, Akshay,' she said, as if our conversation hadn't even happened. I very much doubted she had ever done this before, but I decided not to say anything. This is none of my business, I thought, looking the other way, gulping my drink. *None of my business.*

Akshay pulled out a CD from his CD tray, Coldplay I think it was, and very carefully, his hands shaking just a little, poured out about a quarter of the powder on it. Then he folded up the rest with the same deliberate, careful motions and put the packet back in the cigarette pack on the bedside table. He reached into his jeans, pulled out a fat, brown wallet and checked the side panels till he found a credit card, which he used to slice the powder on the CD into four thin, even rows. He was frowning slightly, and I leaned forward, very curious despite my heart thumping violently against my chest.

Getting more and more nervous by the second, I attempted humour. 'So do the lines work with any old credit card, or is it better if you cut them with a platinum one?'

Akshay ignored me but reached for his wallet again, this time going through the notes till he found a 500-rupee note. 'You have a thousand?' he asked Esha, who started, and looked in her purse, but shook her head. She didn't have one.

'Does it make a difference?' she asked anxiously.

'No, it's just that the thousand is longer, so it's easier for a first time.' He rolled up the note he had into a cone and placed it at the end of one of the rows and beckoned to Esha. 'Come on,' he said.

Esha shot a defiant look at me, like I was her mother or something, but I looked away. Then she went and knelt by the bed, one hand reaching tremblingly for the note, her face towards Akshay. 'What do I do?'

'Close one nostril, like this. No, cover it fully. Yeah. Now make sure the end of the note is in your other nostril fully, so the stuff won't spill. Now inhale. Do it slowly, so you don't get the entire line at once.'

But Esha had already snorted hard and almost all of the white powder had disappeared up the note and into her nose.

She dropped the note and rubbed her nose violently, almost upturning the CD. Akshay made a grab for it. 'Be careful,' he snapped.

'But it burns,' she wailed.

'Obviously. It's the first time you're inhaling this stuff. It's going to burn.' He reorganized the rest of the lines carefully, so they were separate again, and with closed eyes and a sharp, decisive pull finished an entire line. He stayed as he was for a moment, his eyes closed, one hand still cupping his nose, head tilted back. Esha and I watched him, our mouths slightly open. Esha had begun to blink rapidly, I noticed.

Between them, that evening, they managed to finish the four lines. 'Managed' is actually not the correct word to use here. They inhaled the lines with great gusto. Esha grew more wide-eyed with each of her snorts, which she moderated consequently so only a bit went up her nose at a time, and Akshay's head began bobbing up and down to the trance music playing softly in the background, and he finished almost my entire packet of cigarettes. Meanwhile, I downed two more vodka-Red Bulls, figuring I deserved them. When they were done with the snorting, Akshay wet his finger and ran it over the CD surface, picking up the minute crumbs that were left, and then rubbed his fingers over his gums and sucked at his fingertips. 'I also want,' said Esha, wavering in a corner. Akshay laughed and leaned towards her. She swallowed his finger right up to the knuckle, her eyes on him. I turned away, draining the last drops of my vodka, slightly nauseated by Esha's awful behaviour and this carnal display, but suddenly wishing I had someone's finger to suck on too.

We carried some more alcohol in the car. Akshay drove fast, but not rashly, and Esha stuck her head out of the window, despite me screeching 'It's *co*-old, shut the window.' I don't think I existed for her any more. Her emotions had swelled and enveloped the car and formed a bubble around her and Akshay, and I was the blurry speck in the background. I had never seen her like this. On the Noida expressway, she unbuckled her seatbelt and sat on the ledge of the car window so her torso was outside. I was afraid for her, but Akshay laughed and only slowed down before we reached the toll booths, at which point she slipped back in and glowed at him. Her eyes sparkled and shone; in fact, despite the fact that she was obviously very high, she looked beautiful to me. All her movements had become very rapid, even the way she licked her lips so they gleamed.

Some psy DJ was playing at Elevate that night and once we got in both Akshay and Esha behaved like they'd been given fresh shots of adrenalin. Akshay said loud hellos to a bunch of people who seemed to be wearing a uniform of ribbed black sweaters and dark blue jeans even as Esha dragged both of us on to the dance floor. Thanks to the vodka-Red Bulls I had guzzled, I was almost able to keep up with the both of them, jumping up and down in time to the music, while I stood in my spot, shaking my head rapidly from side to side, letting the music splash around inside me. I was quite drunk and I quickly grew tired. Pretty soon I stumbled off the dance floor and found a place to sit down on the steps leading up to the next level, in between couples who were making out.

I must have looked pretty out of it, because there were men, unattached, presumably, who took turns to plant themselves next to me and smile and say 'Would you like a dance?' to which I'd shake my head and wordlessly point at Akshay and Esha, whom I had carefully kept within sight. Akshay glanced over at me once or twice, checking to see where I was, but then I looked away for some time and when I turned back to the floor, they were gone. I wasn't immediately worried; I knew they'd return. But in a while my butt began to hurt from sitting on the floor and when I looked around Elevate looked a lot less full. I checked my watch and saw it was four a.m., so I decided to go find them.

I wandered around the club for a bit looking for them. I just wanted to get home and crawl into bed and not have to open my eyes ever again. Elevate is really, really large, and very crowded, so it probably wasn't a good idea, but I was drunk and tired as hell and wasn't thinking too straight. Besides, by this time most people were either too buzzed or too horny to even notice me. I think I remember pushing my way between a couple locked heavily at the lips, their hips gyrating against each other, but apart from a momentary lapse in their movements they didn't seem to register my presence. Finally, I spotted what looked like Akshay over at the far corner, near the bar, poring over his phone. I scampered up to him and slurred out something about it being high time we went home.

He looked at me and sort of smiled with one corner of his mouth and said, 'Esha's not picking up.'

'Hello-oh? You guys *left* me? Where were you? Why isn't Esha with you?' I was going to kill her, I really and truly was.

Akshay waved his arm in the air. 'We were here only. By the stairs. And then she said she had to go take a leak. It's been a while . . . She hasn't passed out in there or something, you think?'

I realized that they'd probably been making out while I was sitting around and worrying. It got me all the more annoyed with Esha. She was my clubbing friend, for god's sake. You didn't just do that—abandon your girlfriends for sex. I mean, you even ask your friend to come with you to the loo, so that they don't have to be alone. It's okay for guys, because they have this code that says you don't get in the way of your buddy and his prospective hook-up. It's 'hos before bros' for them, even if they deny it; the girls' equivalent is 'sisters before misters'. So there it is.

'She probably just can't hear her phone,' I said, sourly. 'Maybe she's puking or something. I'll go check. Which loo?'

Akshay pointed me towards the nearest one and I stomped off, getting more and more sober as I got madder. I was never going to go out with her again. Never. First the *drugs*, and then *abandoning* me in the middle of Elevate and, who knows, they might have even taken off without me!

I entered the bathroom and looked around. No Esha by the mirror. I rattled a couple of shut doors, but irritated voices yelled back they were just getting out and could I have some patience, yaar? The door to the last cubicle, however, swung open and I saw Esha huddled by the pot, her head lolling halfway into it, her bag and phone lying scattered by her side.

'Are you okay?' I asked brusquely. I wasn't planning on being sympathetic. 'We have to go.'

There was no response and I squatted next to her and called her name, this time more gently, as I put my hand on her back. Wow, she was pretty out of it. Well, nothing bed and a glass of cold water wouldn't cure. Maybe half a lemon. I'm a great believer in lemon halves—they've saved me from many almost-puking situations.

'Come on, babe, get up, let's go wash your face,' I tugged at her head gently, and her body passively gave way, falling heavily on my arm.

'Esha? Esh? Wake up!' I removed her elbow from my stomach and managed to get her head upright. Her eyes were spookily half shut and her mouth hung open. Trails of a white spittle-like stuff had dried on her face, leading downwards from the corners of her mouth. Some of it was in her hair. It was gross and, suddenly, very scary. I had no idea what was going on, but somewhere in my head the words 'drug overdose' began to echo in the voice of the guy who does the movie trailers—you know, the whole '*This* summer at a theatre near you, *four* young people, one dog, etc.' I had read about the symptoms, thanks to a recent media blitz about cocaine, some rich, politician dude had OD'd on . . . No, wait, that was heroin. But surely the symptoms had to be the same? Then I remembered reading a Sweet Valley High, about this chick called Regina Morrow, who was deaf, I think, and she did coke and died of heart failure. It was a terrible book for a thirteen-year-old to have read, but now it made me fumble for Esha's wrist and check for a pulse. Wait. Akshay had seen enough of this stuff. He'd know what to do. I reached for Esha's phone. I remember noticing that the floor of the loo was wet and that my jeans were soaked, and I really wanted to get up and sit somewhere, well, less wet. By this time, the loo attendant had come towards our cubicle and was watching with round, inquisitive eyes. I wanted her to go away, I willed it with all my might, but she wouldn't move. A couple of skinny creatures in halter tops and streaked hair had also gathered at the door to gape.

Esha's phone was ringing again by the time I reached out for it, shifting her body weight on my lap so that her head would be away from the floor. It was Akshay, saved heartbreakingly as 'Baby Cell', one of the cutesy things Esha would do. She had one of those phones with which you can take someone's picture and then save it with their number so when they call their face flashes on the screen. The picture she had taken of Akshay on her little phone camera was of him, shirtless, hair rumpled, holding up a bottle of Coke and evidently telling her not to take a snap, even though he was smiling. I accepted the call and heard his terse voice say, 'Where the fuck are you?'

'Akshay, it's me, it's Arshi.'

'Oh.' I heard the music in the background become a little louder; someone had probably opened the door to the club to get out. 'Did you find her?'

'Yeah, but she's passed out in the loo, and I can't get her awake. Can you come and help?'

'In the chicks' loo?' Akshay's sense of propriety never seemed to leave him; I bet even if there was an earthquake, and the only safe place to be was the 'chicks' loo', he'd probably rather die than enter it.

'Akshay,' I said, annoyed. 'I can't pick her up on my own, this is an *emergency*.'

'Okay, um, let me come to the door.' He clicked his phone shut and I was left pissed off and terrified and exhausted. Oh, why had I agreed to come out with them at all? I gazed at Esha's phone, wondering who else I could call to come to my aid, when one of the gawping girls in the audience said, 'Let me help you carry her outside.' I looked up gratefully, and suddenly there were three or four women giving me a hand, two grasping Esha's feet and the others propping her up so they could support her torso. They were probably seeing a part of their own life in this. Esha could just as well have been any of them, any of us. It was strange, bonding over something like this with random people in a crowded loo smelling of vomit and sweat and sickly floral freshener. I was getting quite overwhelmed with the thought that there were still good people in the world; Esha wasn't just my problem any more, so many strangers had felt the need and reached out to help. An inspiring life lesson, sure, but the timing was terrible, because my headache was developing into a full-fledged starburst-and-tadpoles-behind-my-eyelids migraine. Life lessons are like that, I think. There's no Chicken Soup-y moment when you sit back and say 'Wow, I'm learning something here! This is a potentially symbolic moment!' Maybe it does happen to the lucky few, but I always seem to have a headache when I'm about to be intellectually and emotionally enriched.

Akshay reached us just as we brought Esha out of the loo, the attendant holding the door open for us, another girl rushing in with toilet paper soaked in water to dab on her face. I felt important and busy, like the chief surgeon, barking out terse orders (only I said please, because at the end of the day it wasn't really their problem), dabbing water on her face and slapping her cheeks gently, though not as gently as I could have. Someone made a couple vacate a sofa nearby. Akshay had made his way through the crowd by now and suddenly I wasn't the chief surgeon any more, perhaps the chief nurse, but no longer surgeon because Akshay completely stole my thunder. He didn't seem to be into the audience-bonding thing either, because he didn't say anything at all, just shook Esha's shoulders a couple of times and then picked up his phone and walked off.

'Did she drink too much?' asked one girl, the braces on her teeth flashing in the light. 'I had a cousin who passed out because she drank too much.'

'I don't *think* she drank too much,' I replied. 'I mean, at least not more than she usually does. But then, I was sitting there,' I pointed to my place against the wall, 'and these two were dancing.'

'Is that her boyfriend?' asked a plump girl, whose low-cut knit top exposed lots of cleavage. I had seen her staring appreciatively at Akshay.

'Yeah,' I said, thinking how happy Esha would be if she heard that and thankful that Akshay wasn't around to give the whole we're-not-*technically*-dating spiel. Akshay returned from wherever he had been just then and I stalked up to him determined to be included in what was going on.

'What's the scene?' I asked, attempting to get my eyes to focus. 'What are we going to do? Shall I get the bouncer?'

'No, we don't want him calling the cops,' he said, looking at Esha. This was the most sustained attention she had got from him, ever, and suddenly I wished she had been okay enough to enjoy it.

'What are we going to do?' I asked again, and we both heard my voice crack a bit. Akshay put one comforting hand solidly on my back and rubbed it. 'I called Kabir.' My heart bounced a little at the mention of the name, and instantly I felt terrible for thinking that way when something terrible had happened to my friend and I didn't know what it was. 'He's coming to the hospital to help me out, so the cops don't get involved.'

'Cops?'

'Yeah.' His eyes refused to meet mine, and the rubbing on my back turned to patting, the kind of patting you do right before you stop contact. 'It could be the coke.'

This time I stared so intently at his face that he had to look at me; there was no way out. 'Nothing happened to *me*, did it?' he snapped. 'And it was her own damn idea and her own damn maal. She scored it on her own, though I don't think there was anything wrong with the stuff, because I know the dealer. I think she overdid it.'

Pound *pound* pound. The men with hammers inside my head had really got it going now. I took a deep breath, closed my eyes, and rolled my head this way and that. Then I looked at Akshay again, 'Are you going to tell her parents?'

'We might have to. I think the doctors will. Let's see, Kabir knows these guys, he's been going there forever, so they probably won't call the cops. But if she doesn't call home her parents will freak.'

'If they haven't called already,' I said, pulling out Esha's phone from my back pocket. 'Okay, no missed calls so far.'

'Chalo, let's get her to the car,' Akshay said, walking back to the sofa.

'How?'

'I'll manage. You get her stuff.'

I gathered Esha's things, checking her handbag for the things she usually carried in it. Wallet, check. Cellphone, with me. Keys, right there. Cigarette packet with cocaine in it, also right there. I pulled it out and held it under Akshay's nose, 'You might want to get rid of this before you take her to the hospital.'

'Oh fuck! Good thing you reminded me. Can you take it back with you to your place?'

'What if they search me?'

'Um, we're dropping you off before we go to the hospital. It's easier if you don't get involved.'

'Get involved! But I should be there! She's my friend!'

Akshay looked tired and exasperated. 'Trust me. The more girls there are, the harder it is. Ask Kabir, if you don't believe me.'

There wasn't very much to say after that, and even though I was a little hurt, I was also slightly relieved at not having to be a part of this adventure. It was five-fifteen now, my mouth was dry and tasted awful, the pain in my head was now slowly spreading to the rest of my limbs. Perhaps they were right. What would I do there? Akshay and Kabir would be authoritative, make snap decisions, amuse each other while they waited, know what to say to her parents. I wished they needed me, but they so clearly didn't.

I leaned over to give Akshay a tight hug when he dropped me off. 'Promise you'll call me the minute you know something,' I said, and when he nodded, I squeezed his shoulder. 'Don't worry.'

'You don't worry either,' he said, giving me a lopsided smile.

I trudged up the stairs to our flat, hearing the first sounds of morning, even though the sun was only barely making its presence felt. It was cold and the air smelt of woodsmoke and earth wet with dew. I drew my inadequate stole around me as I turned the key in the lock. Topsy's door was shut and I crawled into my bed, not bothering to change, just unbuttoning my jeans and unhooking my bra. Later in the morning I vaguely heard Gita-didi come in and sweep my room, and Topsy ask me something, but I slept soundly till my phone rang at about two in the afternoon.

It was Akshay. The good news was that it wasn't a coke overdose, but alcohol poisoning. They had pumped her stomach, and Esha was alive. The bad news was she wasn't conscious.

17. in which much is accomplished

ESHA MANAGED TO PULL through, finally. She was completely out of it for close to three days. I visited her at the hospital almost every day, sat next to her parents—her disapproving mother and her stern, cold father, their distress at the situation showing in the lines on their faces. Every now and then, Esha's mother would lift some water to her daughter's mouth—her lips looked so parched that it hurt me to look at them—and sometimes Esha would moan slightly, making all of us eagerly lean forward, but then she would just go back to taking deep breaths, her eyes still shut.

As Akshay had predicted, he and Kabir took all the blame for that night. Akshay kept Kabir as uninvolved as he could, but when the cops found out that the two of them had checked Esha in, they were locked up overnight for questioning. Akshay hadn't been to see Esha even once, or even called to find out what was happening. I guessed he had got into major shit with his parents but I still somehow wished that my comatose friend could sense who was rallying around her and who wasn't. And it was a sort of betrayal, right? I mean, if I had OD'd myself into hospital, I'd sure as hell want the guy I liked a whole lot to be there or just to care. It's just good manners.

I knew that as soon as Esha woke up—I was still sticking to saying 'as soon as' and not 'if' because in my mind there was no question she was going to come around; she had to, death was too grown-up a phenomenon to happen to one of us—her parents would clap her straight into rehab. It wasn't fair, because it's not like Esha drank that much or even did drugs regularly. The doctors had even said the problem had probably arisen because her body could tolerate less intoxicants than other people because of her ridiculously low weight. She looked so thin lying there, her mouth half open as she took ragged breaths, her nostrils flaring slightly, her arms resting on the sheet over her tummy that was gently rising and falling. On Day Two I brought along something to read and sat by the window near her bed drinking the vile hospital coffee and listening to the murmurs of her extended family who had gathered there. There was no one of her age and I guessed her friends and cousins had not been told because her parents were keeping it sort of hush-hush. In India, you can't get away with 'My daughter's in hospital' because every single person you say it to will want an explanation and all the details of what happened and what was going to happen. When I broke my toe earlier that year I was sick of people asking me what had happened, and I tried to keep it as short as possible, especially if someone I didn't know at all asked me about it, which happened a lot too.

When I entered the room on Day Three, Esha's mother was standing at the window, crying quietly. 'Aunty, has something happened?' I asked, alarmed, and looked quickly at the bed, but Esha was still breathing, the tips of her eyelashes flickering slightly. Her mother shook her head, burying her twisted mouth into her dupatta. Then, almost against her will, she said, 'It's been three days! Will my child never wake up? I thought we had raised her right . . . what have we done to deserve this?' I tried to comfort her as well as I could, but I was still a little scared of her cold mouth and eyes. 'Don't worry, aunty, Esha will be fine. The doctors say she'll pull through.' She nodded, but only out of politeness, and it got so quiet after that that I just had to leave the room.

'Can I get you some tea or coffee, aunty? I'm going to the canteen.'

'Yes, thank you beta, some tea would be good.' She crossed the room and sat on the chair next to Esha's bed, stroking her hand, settling the blanket around her, moving her hair away from her forehead.

The beverages took an unusually long time because the queue around the machine was enormous, and by the time I managed to get the tea boy's attention, pay him and carry the cups carefully back to the room, Esha was awake and the room was a racket of sobs and exclamations. Damn, I had waited for so long and the cow had to go wake up at the one time I wasn't in the room. I put the cups down and waited by the table, nervously sipping my coffee, not wanting to intrude into their family space. Finally, the crowd around her bed dispersed to allow the doctor to check her pulse and give her a shot and then it was only her mother next to her, stroking Esha's forehead, and me. 'Beta, can I get you anything?' her mother asked tenderly. Esha moistened her lips and murmured something and her mother smiled and said, 'All right. I'm going home for some time, I'll be back later.' Then, as she left, she turned to me, 'Arshi, can you stay for a while?' 'Sure,' I said, and went to sit by Esha's bed.

For the longest time after her mother left, there was silence. I knew Esha was looking at me, but for some reason I avoided looking at her. It was too embarrassing for me to have witnessed what I did, like when you know intimate details of someone's life, which left to themselves they would never want to share with you. We hadn't been close for long enough for it not to matter. The events at Elevate came swimming back into my memory and I wanted to erase them completely. For some reason, I felt embarrassed for Esha. I didn't want her to be lying there knowing that I knew. 'Akshay . . .' Esha managed finally, 'did he come?'

'No, babe.' I took her hand in mine, starting a little at how cold it was. Her fingernails felt like ice against my palm. 'Are you cold?' I asked, pulling the blankets around her chin so she was completely covered. She shook her head, but I could see her shoulders quivering. I lifted up her hands, cupped them between mine and blew at them to warm them up. This was something Cheeto had taught me. The sudden memory, so unbidden, caught me completely by surprise. I remembered the slant of his forehead, his eyelashes pointing downwards, the feel of his large, rough palms . . .

'Will you call him?' asked Esha.

I looked at her doubtfully. 'Are you sure you're up for this?'

She nodded, coughing a little. 'Please call him. I want to talk to him. And tell him I'm sorry.'

'Oh, all right, hang on, let me get my phone.' Dialling Akshay's number, I willed him not to pick up so I wouldn't have to have this conversation. But Akshay always had his phone on him, and when he saw my number he probably guessed it was about Esha and answered. He sounded slightly out of breath.

'Hey,' I said. 'How are you?'

There was a deep sigh at the other end. 'I'm okay. My dad paid off some of the dudes at the hospital, so, you know, I'm not going to get into too much trouble.'

'Oh good,' I said. Esha had reached out to take the phone from me, so I turned my back to her. 'So you're not in too much trouble?'

'Well, I'm fucked at home. But otherwise, no. What's up?'

'I'm in the hospital,' I said. 'Esha's just woken up . . . she wants to talk to you.'

'Oh. Um . . . okay, I guess . . .'

I handed Esha the phone and she sat up a little so she could talk. Her voice sounded awful—like when you haven't spoken in a while because you have a sore throat and it sounds like there's a frog stuck in it. She was all sweet and loving to him and it annoyed me that she seemed to have no pride whatsoever, chasing a boy who clearly didn't give a damn. I felt really, really irritated with her at that moment and I wanted to go home, get out, do anything with normal people, rather than sit around in that hospital any longer. Plus, I really wanted a smoke.

'I'm going to get a cigarette,' I told her, and she nodded and waved me away.

Outside, I walked past waiting families, some in the little coffee shop in the lobby, some huddled in groups, distributing folded chapatis and tea, looking tired and burnt out, and I just wanted to go home to Topsy, to listen to her bitch about her parents (who were still around) and moan about wanting to see Fardeen, and for her to fix us both a drink, mojitos, perhaps, which she made very well, or one of her sparkly drinks with one part Sprite, one part soda, lots of lemon juice and filled to the brim with ice cubes and vodka.

I loitered in the corridor for a bit even after I was done with my smoke and finally went back in to retrieve my phone and to see if Esha's mom was there yet so I could leave. She had just come in, and was spreading another quilt over Esha's legs.

'I'll be going home the day after tomorrow,' Esha told me

as I picked up my phone from her bed. 'Call me, huh?' I gave her a tight-lipped smile and nodded, but I didn't look at her. 'Arsh?' she said, and her voice sounded jagged. I tried a real smile this time, and patted her knee. 'Take it easy, okay?' I said. 'You've had a rough time.' She began to sniffle, and I was really glad her mom was in the room so I didn't have to hear about her conversation with Akshay. I felt mean and small, but I needed to leave, be elsewhere, maybe go see Gagan. I needed some attention.

Gagan wasn't free, and when I called Topsy she said glumly, 'We're going to meet some boy. I don't know why they call them boys, considering this one we're going to see is at least thirty.'

'Thirty is not that old,' I said, cheerfully.

'Um, yeah it is! And he's probably pot-bellied and wears a tie and stuff.'

'Ties can be sexy. Besides, these thirty-year-old men are majorly into working out these days, the whole metrosexual deal.'

'This is someone who's looking for an arranged marriage,' she said. 'I very much doubt he's metrosexual. Anyway. You're free tonight?'

'More or less.'

'Chalo, we'll get very drunk and I'll tell you all about the horrible boy and my horrible parents and how I hate the fact that Fardeen isn't here.'

'Excellent. I love having a conversation agenda.'

'Okay, ta-ta, they're baa-ack.'

'Good luck!'

So no Topsy, no Gagan. No point calling Deeksha, because she'd probably be up to her eyes preparing for D-Day. The sangeet was just a week away, and she had all the last-minute shopping to do and a million relatives to smile demurely at. It reminded me that, in fact, I too had to pick up a salwar-kameez I had given for alteration. And since the boutique was pretty close to Jor Bagh, there was no *harm* in me calling Kabir, just to see if he was free and all. No pressure, just a breezy hi. So I did. He said he was free, and I drove up to his intimidating house, where his maid let me in saying, 'We haven't seen you in some time.' I nodded and made my way upstairs to his room, where he sat working on his computer, looking positively scrumptious in a black sweater and blue jeans.

'Arsh,' he said, standing up when I entered. 'I haven't seen you in forever.'

This was all wrong, surely, this feeling that this was so right. He was bending slightly to kiss my cheek and I wrapped my arms around him, feeling the tautness of his back through his sweater. We stood like that for a bit, my cheek against his shoulder, my fingers entwined in the wool, till he had to pull away, his mouth rising at one corner, amused to see me so obviously desperate. I let out a ragged sigh and stood there for a second, or perhaps more, trying to make my own mouth turn upwards. I did finally, and he touched my face very lightly and said, 'Coffee?'

'Yes, please.'

We were back on familiar territory now. I could breathe and he could order the coffee. I dumped my bag on his bed and kicked off my sneakers and sat there, cross-legged and comfortable, and lit a cigarette. 'Do you want one?' I asked.

'No thanks, I've quit.'

'Really?' Once, I would have known whether he was quitting smoking, once I would have even helped him. It must have been hard. And now, if he kissed me—not that he *would*, but *if* he did—he would taste ash in my mouth. 'Like licking an ashtray,' a non-smoking boy had told me once when I kissed him, moving away a little and making me feel like a pariah.

Kabir was still looking at me a little oddly, and I suddenly felt totally self-conscious, like I had nicotine stains on my teeth and my fingers. I was sure I still smelt of the hospital anyway.

'What else?' I asked brightly, and he said, 'You don't have to talk all the time you know.'

'Well, you're not saying anything.'

'I don't have to.'

'Really now?' That's all I could come up with. I cursed myself. I should never have come to his house. I was so definitely not over him.

He sat down on the bed, next to me, and turned my face to his. My eyes were already closed when he kissed me. When he stopped I opened my eyes and saw him looking amused again.

'What now?' I asked peevishly.

'You're so sweet,' he said, kissing me again.

Sweet? *Sweet?* That's the best he could come up with? Sweet, as most people know, is a death-knell for anyone who hopes to be seen romantically, sweet means you're always the messee and never the messer, sweet means you'll never break any hearts. Sweet is a half-assed, terrible thing to be, like when you're *fond* of someone.

But sweet people surely didn't have their sweaters peeled off quite like that and their shirts unbuttoned, and their bras unhooked with an expert two-fingered movement, the sign of someone who's been doing it for a while. It's rather endearing when men can't undo your bra, it's a way of you being in control, being in charge of the unfathomable Woman Undergarment, and laughing at them a little bit when you reach behind to unhook it yourself. But then, it's not quite as sexy as when someone does it for you, so you know you're not in control and perhaps you never have been.

Kabir and I had never been in the sex phase, if you know what I mean. But now it seemed as though our bodies were other people's bodies, completely focussed and in sync. There were two slightly awkward moments—one when the maid knocked on the door with the coffee and Kabir yelled through the door for her to leave it outside, and another when he moved away from me and to his cupboard, from where he produced a condom, like magic, and I didn't know whether to feel insulted that he had one, or really happy that it didn't have to stop. And then there was some more foreplay, to make up for the pause in action. This was sex with someone who *knew* what he was doing but wasn't mechanical about it. This was the kind of sex where you're helpless and writhing and don't care about anyone or anything, including the volume and nature of the sounds that automatically leave your throat and the way your lips might twist into a half smile half grimace in the moment when pure, mind-numbing pleasure courses through your body. Yes, we were finally there, and marvellously, I was finally there, for the first time ever. Not even with Cheeto had I felt like this and Kabir knew, and I saw him watching me and waiting and I loved him for it. When he came, he moaned into the side of my neck and I felt pleased that it was me, *me*, who had reduced him to moaning and I felt protective and full of love and like the first woman in the world discovering sex for the first time.

When we were done, he rolled off and I lay there, spreadeagled for a bit. I could smell his cologne on my hands. Lazily, he reached for the quilt and wrapped it around us, pulling me closer so my head was resting on his chest. I didn't want to be anywhere else, ever. After a while, I sat up against the pillows, smoking a cigarette, and he stroked my arm, pausing every now and then to kiss my shoulder. I restrained every part of me that wanted to ask 'Now what?' Instead I let the silence lie comfortably between the two of us, with Damien Rice singing the melancholy *Blower's Daughter* in the background, like a present, my last present to him.

Life goes easy on me, most of the time.

Finally, he was the one to break the silence. 'What's your plan for the rest of the week?'

'I think I'm going over to Deeksha's tomorrow, for some last-dinner-as-single-woman thing she's planned.'

'How fancy,' he said, taking a drag from my cigarette. 'A hen party.'

'They're called bachelorette parties these days, actually,' I told him. 'Way cooler than the "hen" and sometimes they even get strippers.'

'I'd strip for a room full of women if they paid me for it.'

'Well, you're not invited. Besides this is a classy affair— dinner and Margaritas and lots of bitching about men.'

'Something I'm *sure* you're an expert on.'

'Hey, I call them like I see them.'

This wasn't good, this repartee. It made me feel too comfortable around Kabir, like I was in danger of falling into the trap again.

'Your coffee must be stone-cold by now,' he said, and I saw his chest rise and fall in a sigh and somehow I knew it wasn't a happy sigh. So I began to hunt for my clothes, without looking at him. I knew what had just happened didn't mean what I'd wanted it to mean. I knew he was no more in love with me now than he had ever been. But somehow it was okay. I felt much more okay than I had in ages, okay with the fact that Kabir and I would never be together in the way that I so wanted us to be. I drank my coffee rapidly, evaded small talk and got out of there. I think somewhere in the back of my head I was still waiting to break down and crumble and obsess about the whole thing, but, really, I felt quite good.

I had got four missed calls from Topsy during the afternoon, but when I called her back she didn't pick up. I let it ring several times, and then, still singing in my head, pulled over inside the gate of our building and practically danced—as much as my sore thigh muscles would allow me—up the stairs. I was dying to see her, to tell her everything, to talk and talk and talk, and see her roll her eyes, then maybe smile a little bit at my enthusiasm and applaud me for my detachment. The door was wide open when I reached home and our living room was filled with suitcases and stuffed plastic packets.

'Topsy? Topsy! What's going on?' I called as I entered, stopping at my room to dump my bag and my keys.

'Have you checked for the tickets?' said a voice from outside and I saw Topsy's mother frantically searching through her bag. She didn't look happy.

'Hello, aunty,' I said. 'Is something the matter?'

She didn't even look up at me, but asked someone in the other room—Topsy's room—whether they had the tickets. I walked in to look for her, but she wasn't there either. The bathroom door was locked.

I knocked on it. 'Topsy? Babe? What's going on?'

The door opened, just a little bit, and I peered in to see her sitting on the edge of the toilet seat, holding reams of crumpled toilet paper, her eyes and nose leaking, the tip of her nose red, the sides of her pink mouth turned downwards.

'Hey,' I said, pulling myself up on to the sink counter. 'What's happened?'

She turned soulless eyes to me. 'Fardeen,' she managed.

'They found out?'

She nodded, using the back of her hand to wipe her face. Why fall in love at all if it made you feel like that, I thought. There was no point, surely, to all the happiness and good times, when in an instant it could all be gone. Taken away from you. Making you look like Topsy did right now—a limp puppet with no will of her own. I put my hand on her shoulder, squeezing it. It was the only comfort I could offer.

'They want me to go back to Meerut,' she said, finally, sighing brokenly. 'The guy I met today, his aunt had seen me with Fardeen a couple of times. And they said that no one would marry me. And my parents cried, Arsh, I've seen my mom cry a hundred million times, but my dad . . . it was just so terrible.'

'Shhh,' I said, stroking her hair. 'It'll get better, babe.'

'Nooooooooo,' she said, fiercely, shaking her head away from me. 'It won't get better! It'll get worse! They want me to go back to Meerut! To be a housewife! I can't do that, dude, I can't. I need to be here I need to be with Fardeen I need him to be with me I need to be in my house here in Delhi or somewhere else if they take me back to Meerut I will die.' She said all this in one continuous scream, her chest heaving, her nostrils flared, and the next moment she had got up and left. I heard a distant door banging, I heard her voice rise, edgy and full of sharp corners, and I sat on her abandoned seat and hoped she wouldn't say things that couldn't be unsaid.

I waited for quite some time in the bathroom until, about an hour later, she emerged from her room, in track pants this time and an old sweatshirt, her hair loose around her face. She looked so beautiful, even though her movements were flustered and her eyes were too bright. 'I'm going out,' she said, hoarsely. 'I'll be back later. My parents are leaving soon.'

It somehow didn't seem to be the right time to bring up Kabir and what had just happened. I sighed. It could wait, I supposed.

18. in which there is an ending, (almost) hindi-movie style

IT WAS AN ODD sort of month, that month before Deeksha's wedding. The skies were suddenly overcast, it rained cats and dogs, every day, only fading into a light, cold drizzle in the afternoons. There was mud everywhere, and wherever there wasn't mud there were glistening roads and rippling puddles. And the background score—because, of course, there has to be a background score—was depressing classical music, the kind that never makes it to lifts or 'hold' tones. Perhaps this was the way it was supposed to end, my life in Delhi. I had never wanted to leave before. Even the thought crossing my mind made me feel oddly guilty and clandestine. Like I was cheating on a lover, or lying to my best friend. I had told my mother, in an effort to get her to stop nagging me, that I'd take the GRE the following year, and now, strangely, I was looking forward to it, even studying like I cared. And I *wanted* to leave, to do something more, see new places, meet new people.

I had ended things with Gagan about an hour after I slept with Kabir. I couldn't do it any more; he was funny and cute, and eminently available—and that was the problem. I couldn't see why he wanted to be with me and, even then, I rapidly got bored by how happy he sounded when I called him or when we met, how content he was to just go home with a goodnight kiss. It was beginning to dawn on me that I was just about as commitment-phobic as anyone else, that I cleverly masked my phobia by only dating men who were emotionally unavailable, which tricked me into thinking that what I really wanted was to be in a relationship. What did I really want? I didn't know any more. I knew Kabir still made my stomach flutter when I thought about him, about the forward thrust of his brown shoulders, my legs entwined around them, my head off the bed, back arched, as I watched him, my fingers digging into his forearms. But was that really enough? Had it ever been?

'I need to leave,' I had told Topsy, the week before everything blew up and her parents were still around, as we were sorting out the washed laundry into piles, hers and mine. 'I need to get out of here. I feel stifled, like, is this all my life has? I mean, I can even see myself ten years down the line. I don't want to see myself ten years down the line!'

Topsy sighed and wiped her forehead with the back of her hand. 'I want to leave too. I can't handle my parents being here any more. Why are they here still? Why aren't they going home? Do you know how long it's been since I kissed Fardeen?'

'Do you know how long it's been since I've *kissed*, period?' I said, rolling my eyes at her, 'At least, you have someone. Not like me, chronically single, like I have AIDS or something.'

'Tchah,' she said, swatting at my arm. 'What a terrible thing to say. You just haven't met the right guy.'

'I don't know, dude. I mean, I don't want to settle down or anything, but suppose there isn't a right guy? Suppose Kabir is my right guy but I'm not his right girl? I mean, these things should come with instruction books. Look at me now, Tops, I had an excellent education, blah blah blah, and now I'm almost twenty-six with no career, no real boyfriend and friends who are getting *married*. Jesus.'

Topsy finished rolling up her panties, and stacking her bras neatly, one cup nestling in the other, before she patiently said, 'There's nothing you can do about the friends part. As for your job, you quit, so now find something else to do. You're studying for the GRE, no? And love comes when you're not looking for it. Besides, if you keep rewinding and rewinding, you'll never make new memories.'

Just like Topsy, I'd thought, to see the bright, happy side so clearly. We didn't know then, Topsy and I, just how many new memories we'd make or how much our lives would change in a few short days.

The day of Deeksha's sangeet had been dark and overcast but I had been too excited about it all week to let a bit of gloom get in the way. Topsy was supposed to come with me for the sangeet, but she slunk around the house most of the day, even when I bounced off to the salon, and in the evening, while I was dressing, she came into the room and said, 'Listen, I'm not feeling very well. Will you apologize to Deeksha for me?'

'Sure,' I said, a little irritated, not really feeling like listening to her excuses, which would probably be half-assed anyway. She just wanted to brood and maybe wait for Fardeen to drop by so she could let out her frustration a bit, I knew.

Devyani met me at the entrance of their house, holding a silver plate with flowers on it and sweetly instructing her little cousins to stop playing with the candles and start handing out the roses they were holding. 'Welcome,' she said, in a way I knew she had rehearsed, voice low, eyes sparkling, mouth straining not to say something familiar and friendly to me, because that would spoil her image.

Normally, sangeets are only for women, but Deeksha had insisted that her parents combine the sangeet and the 'young people's party' that was scheduled for the next day because 'I can't handle any more functions.' For the earlier half of the evening the women would sit with Deeksha on the terrace getting their palms decorated with mehndi and listening to the loud Punjabi folk singer belt her way through gruesome songs about mothers-in-law. Deeksha's to-be mother-in-law, Jean-Luc's mild mother, had been sitting with one or another member of the family having the ceremonies translated and explained while she shot every movement on a camcorder. I wondered how accurate a translation she would be given that evening of the folk singer's songs. Later, when the singing was done and the henna dry, we'd eat dinner with the men—who were planning on having a bachelor party-style drinking session in the lawn—and then head somewhere, either Elevate or Laidbackwaters: 'Just a normal, fun place,' Deeksha had told me on the phone, 'something non-wedding-y.'

I could understand her need for non-wedding stuff. We'd gone through five events for her wedding already—an engagement, another engagement, a small dinner party for the bride's relatives, another one for the groom's, and now the sangeet, which would be followed by the wedding three days later and a reception immediately after. Hell, I was a little weddinged-out myself, to tell you the truth.

I joined the crowd on the terrace, and watched Deeksha as she peered at her gorgeously mosaiced palms. 'I don't like it,' she said to her mother. 'I wanted something less . . . you know, dhinchak.'

'It's fine Deeksha. It's what everyone wears at their weddings,' said her mother, sounding tired.

'Hi, aunty,' I said, walking up to them and smiling at the expression of relief on both their faces.

'Is this too dhinchak?' asked Deeksha, shoving her hands in my face.

'Not at all,' I said. 'You look very pretty. Oh, and hello, by the way.'

'Hiiii,' she sighed. 'I'm sorry I'm so distracted and we haven't spent any time together, and then we'll be off on our honeymoon and then I won't see you again.' I noticed her eyes begin to brim with tears. Poor Dee. She was probably so exhausted.

'Don't cry, babe,' I said. 'It'll be fine. You're tired and nervous. It happens. And I'll come to Canada and spend time with you there. Besides, I'm applying to colleges soon so we'll at least be on the same continent.'

It started to rain then, just as it had been threatening to all day. Water poured down around us, the candles that had been arranged all around the terrace got extinguished and the women ran into the house squealing and clutching their finery. I waited next to Deeksha under a low parapet, so both of us were safe from the rain, and suddenly I remembered being sixteen.

I was spending the night at her house studying with her for a maths exam that was three days away and it had begun to rain madly. It was around ten when we heard the first clap of thunder and she'd looked at me and said '*Fuck* this exam' and we'd held hands and run up to the terrace where we spun around and giggled loudly, not caring that Deeksha's parents had come upstairs and were commanding us to get back to studying. Instead, we dragged them into the rain, and Devyani too, when she came to watch, her mouth open. Finally, wet-haired and bedraggled, we went downstairs, to be rubbed thoroughly with towels and given dry clothes and hot tea.

'Do you remember the night it rained and we danced on this terrace?' asked Deeksha just then.

'I was just thinking of that.'

'Arsh?'

'Yes?' I turned and looked at her and she had the same expression on her face she had had that night and I knew what was going to happen.

'I suppose it would be terrible of me to spoil this mehndi,' she said speculatively.

'Deeksha!' I shrieked. 'You *can't*. Your make-up, your outfit, everything will be *ruined*.'

'Oh Arshi . . .' She stood up now and, cupping her hands beneath her chin to protect her henna as best as she could, she stepped into the pelting rain. 'Sometimes I wonder why we had to grow up at all.'

Of course, I joined her, thinking how very much this was like a movie. The sappy part in the middle with the music rising in a clamour and two girls, mindless of their expensive clothes, dancing in the rain, trying to preserve a little bit of what they once had. This was *my* Deeksha, the Deeksha I was soon going to lose to Canada and Jean-Luc and matrimony. I was so happy in that moment, even though I could feel my carefully styled hair (which I'd paid a bomb for) completely rat-tail itself and stick to my face. And yet I was sad, because this was going to end and it didn't really feel *real*, you know? We both knew this was just something we were doing because the moment demanded it, not because of an impulse, not because of the need to feel the rain on our faces, because, well, it seemed like something we would have done at sixteen and we weren't ready to let those sixteen-year-olds go just as yet.

Deeksha's mother came charging up the stairs and began to yell at both of us, and the rain stopped as suddenly as it had started. I looked at Deeksha, mascara running in streams down her face, foundation all patchy and hands a mess of henna.

'Oh dear,' I said. 'You look a mess.'

'I'm changing into jeans,' she told me.

Ignoring her mother's hysterical screams, we went down and changed into normal clothes. I watched her as she blow-dried her hair and put on her lipstick and eyeliner again and then looked at me in the mirror.

'We're never going to be different, right, Arsh?'

'How do you mean?' I asked.

'This,' she waved at the air between the two of us. 'Let's always have this.'

That set me off completely. I started to cry and Deeksha got weepy too, but soon we were laughing at ourselves as we cried. Devyani came in with a glass of wine for each of us and almost collapsed with shock to see us out of the wedding finery. Later, as we danced at Laidbackwaters, and I was happily on my fifth drink, I knew that sometimes everything had to change in order for it to be the same. We need to move, to grow, and if we're lucky and the people we love are moving and growing too, at some point in the future we'll find ourselves right back at the start.

Elsewhere in the city, Topsy was losing her virginity. She told me about it later. Of how she had gone over to Fardeen's flat and had been crying as she had constantly been the last two days, wondering what to do about her parents, when the thunderstorm had caused the electricity to go out. Fardeen had lit some candles and made her some tea and she watched him as he looked at her worried, lying across his bed. She loved him, she knew that, but in that moment she knew how *much* she loved him, how the choice she was making would not be easy, but if she chose to leave she would hate herself for it. So she let him kiss her and, as he did, she stretched out her hand to the crotch of his jeans. And when their clothes came off, as they often had while they were making out, she hadn't stopped while the two of them lay, boxers to panties. Instead she'd wiggled out of her underwear and reached to remove his.

'Are you sure?' he'd asked, like he had many times before.

This time she bit her lip and nodded, smiling so he would see *exactly* how sure she was.

'What if it ends?' I asked her later. 'What if it doesn't last?'

'This is not about Fardeen,' she said. 'It's about me. I can't live like two people any more. I like who I am now, and if I were to go back to Meerut I would be a hypocrite.'

'What about your parents?'

She smiled, but with difficulty, I could see that. 'They said I've brought shame on the whole family and they can't hold their heads up in Meerut any more, and if I decide to stay on in Delhi I can be sure of not getting any financial support from them.' Her sigh was ragged and pained. I knew how much Topsy's family meant to her; she was perhaps the most family-oriented person I knew. I rubbed her back as she talked. 'But I told them the same thing; this is not about Fardeen, or anyone else. I like my life in Delhi; I don't want to give it up.'

She got herself a job a few days later, which she would start immediately after she graduated. It was with a production house, which meant she would get to travel all over India, something she was very much looking forward to. The starting pay wasn't great, but she had been promised a raise in six months. And though her parents still refused to take her calls or reply to her emails, she was working on her brother to make a case for her before them.

I was at Deeksha's wedding, two days later, when Kabir called me. I saw his number flashing on my phone and felt oddly irritated. I was helping Devyani arrange the marigold garlands around the platform on which Deeksha and Jean-Luc would sit for the ceremony and I really didn't want to take any calls.

But this is Kabir, said the voice inside me. *You've always wanted to speak to him.*

I still liked him. I'd just slept with him. And the idea of a relationship where he was my boyfriend and I his girlfriend still made me feel . . .

Perhaps not as excited as it once had?

I couldn't be over him, surely? Not like this, not this fast, when I had actually made an effort over so many months?

I moved to a corner, gesturing to Devyani that I would be back, and took the call.

'Hey,' I said.

'Lovely Arshi,' his voice was smiling. 'What are you up to?'

'Decorating for Deeksha's wedding.'

'Oh that's right, it's tonight, right? I was actually just calling to see if you were free and wanted to hang out.'

Once I would have said 'What time?' and 'Can you wait till the ceremony is over?' and I would have been restless the entire evening, barely stopping to say goodbye to Deeksha, reasoning to myself that with so many people there she wouldn't really notice whether I was gone or not. And I would have felt butterflies romping around in my stomach as I pulled into Kabir's driveway, sick with dread that the evening might not go as well as I wanted it to.

On the phone I said, 'I'm afraid I can't tonight, Kabir.'

Once I would have followed that up with 'Tomorrow? Day after? Whenever you're free next?' This time I waited.

'Oh, that sucks,' he said. 'Well, have fun. I'll catch you later.'

I put the phone away and went back to where Devyani was trying to untangle the strings of brilliant orange and yellow flowers. My heart was beating a little faster, but more than anything else I was filled with an overwhelming sense of relief. Kabir was never the villain, I realized. He was never the mind-fucker. Some of us are sadomasochistic; some of us thrive on having our minds messed with, our hearts constantly in a churn of adrenalin. As long as our fix is met, of people who will play basketball with our hearts and minds, we somehow feel justified in being the victims. Well, I was done with being the victim. The credits had rolled, and I was now going to live the rest of my life.

acknowledgements

I get by with a little help from my friends.

This book is for many people.

Puja and Shakti, who I wish were here to see it.

Diya and Poulomi at Penguin India for the immense patience they had and the grace with which they overlooked missed deadlines telling me to 'take my time', perhaps not realizing I'd take it so literally.

Samit, who makes better decisions for me than I do.

The Biatches: Isheeta, Nayantara, Neha and Prerna.

My surrogate soul sisters: Nayantara, Mihira and Samira. They never doubted that I'd be the next Plath.

Meghna and Dhati, flatmates extraordinaire.

And people who defy categorization but must be thanked anyway—Sarnath, Samrat, Jeet and Neha. All of whom read it and told me I was awesome.